Quarry

Quarry

Crime Stories
by
New England Writers

Edited by

Kate Flora

Ruth McCarty

Susan Oleksiw

LEVEL BEST BOOKS
PRIDES CROSSING, MASSACHUSETTS 01965

Level Best Books
P.O. Box 161
Prides Crossing, Massachusetts 01965
www.levelbestbooks.com

text composition/design by Susan Oleksiw
Printed in the USA

ISBN 978-0-9700984-7-4

Library of Congress Catalog Card Data available.
First Edition
10 9 8 7 6 5 4 3 2 1

Quarry

Contents

Introduction

A trend in current writing is short, pithy statements that are meant to summarize a mass of information or a complicated situation-we love PowerPoint presentations, short emails, and now tweets. We think we can reduce understanding to a single declarative sentence-or even a sentence fragment. But instead of falling to that temptation, offering here a definition of the short story as we see it today, we offer Irwin Shaw's views on short fiction: "The form of the short story is so free as to escape restriction to any theory. Theories just don't hold up."

The variety of crime fiction written today is proof of Shaw's position. After seven years and, with the publication of *Quarry*, seven crime story collections into our own exploration and celebration of short crime fiction, we are delighted that there is no one formula, no one set of rules, that governs the rich variety of stories submitted each year for our consideration. Our writers follow rules, break rules, bend rules, and make up their own rules as they explore the many ways criminals are formed and caught and crimes committed.

In 2003, our first collection, *Undertow*, was intended to be a one-time event. We little imagined, as we sat on a gray winter day and selected eleven stories for the collection, how exciting it would be to sit on the editorial and publishing side of the desk, the thrill of accomplishment the first time we held our "new baby," our first book. We did not imagine the sense of honor we would feel in being the first publisher for so many of the region's talented writers, nor how proud we would be of the trust by established writers who submitted their work.

In the introduction to our first collection, we described how we set out to take a snapshot of the region's mystery writers: what they're imagining, who they're wondering about, and what stories they want to tell. We also wrote about our own goals in undertaking this publishing project--our love of New England, crime fiction, writing, and literature in general.

To that, we must add our love of authors and the richness of their imaginations and the language they use to tell their stories. Our authors have received national recognition for their work. Stories from our collections have won numerous Derringer awards, and been nominated for Edgar, Agatha and Macavity awards. A story we returned to be reworked won the prestigious Robert L. Fish Award for best crime story by a first-time writer.

As our reputation has grown, so have the number and quality of our submissions. Reviewing this year's submissions, we faced both the best and worst situation editors can face-a collection of so many high-quality stories that we could have done two collections-and the consequent necessity to reject dozens of stories we wished we could publish. It was a painful process; it was also a most fulfilling one. We believe that this is a truly special collection, one filled with stories and characters that will do what good short stories should do-leave you with a small sigh of satisfaction as you lift your eyes from the page, or images and characters that linger in your imagination long after you've put the book down.

We hope you will smile, as we did, at the proud and bemused father-and thief-whose daughter shares his work ethic and is following in his footsteps. Admire the "voice" of the downeast lobstermen who decide to work their own version of a Nigerian scam. Feel the terrible pain of an honest woman who faces the scorn of her hardscrabble community when she reveals an accounting fraud.

You will see the world through the eyes of a heartbreakingly damaged homeless woman trying to save a child, or the resentful child not quite understanding what his father's new girlfriend's sad daughter is telling him. An airline voucher leads some travelers to a terrifying motel, where one man's act of kindness may mean his last night on earth. Boston's elegant Back Bay is the setting for a battle of wits between a writer and a con man, and a golf game on the site of a former quarry stirs up memories and old resentments among those who know what lies beneath the fill. *Quarry* is New England, with ice storms, ice out, superettes, and gun shows.

Welcome to the New England writer's mind.

Kate Flora
Ruth McCarty
Susan Oleksiw

Death Is the New Sleep

Hollis Seamon

Ice-out in New Hampshire happens, usually, end of March. Sometimes not until early April. Either way, it's a big deal. I mean, up here, we love it when winter's skin cracks open and sets the lakes free. We wait for it. Everyone feels better when stuff starts flowing. Streams rush, waterfalls gush and the blood in our veins runs faster.

If the blood is moving at all, that is. The guy whose body came down the falls at the Old Mill in Meredith, that sunny spring day, well, let's just say that his heart had stopped pumping a while back and whatever blood he'd had was washed clean away. So maybe ice-out had set him free, too, but he didn't know a thing about it. And I wish I didn't either. He ruined a good roast beef sandwich and the first nice day in months.

Before you can understand the whole story of the body in the falls and everything that happened after, you have to get a grip on the geography around here. And, I guess, my little place in it. I'm Sophie Sheridan and last summer I inherited my grandmother's cottage on Lake Waukewan. That's where I live, with my two dogs and a cat that comes and goes. Now, Waukewan is not the Big Lake. The Big Lake is Winnipesaukee and everyone knows about that one. Waukewan is the little lake on the other side of the village of Meredith, to the west and uphill.

1

Waukewan is a glacial lake, small but very deep and very cold. Used to have great bass fishing. Still okay, if you know the spots. And it sits on higher ground than Meredith. When you walk the half-paved, half-dirt road from the village to the east shore of Waukewan, you know you're going up. Your legs start to ache. At least mine do.

Not surprising, really; I'm in shit shape. Even if I do walk everywhere. Not by choice. By order of the Belknap County courts. A bit of trouble with my driving record. And a lot of trouble with my old friends Jack Daniels and Sam Adams. But I don't want to talk about that. Point is, I walk down to the village to work—minimum wage in the hardware store and lucky to have it, because the manager was sweet on my grandma, back in the day—and then I haul my groceries and newspaper back up the hill to the cottage, every damn day. I won't even bother to talk about what that's like in winter. You get the picture. So, yeah, I was waiting for spring like some folks wait for the Messiah. Anyway, first really warm day, on my lunch break, I splurged on a fancy roast beef/red onion/fresh spinach/Russian dressing/croissant sandwich and a mug of tea at the Old Mill, which is an upscale tourist trap with a hotel, eateries, shops, and so on. A place I usually avoid, where I can't hardly afford to breathe the air. But it's quiet in late March, more like a local place.

Anyway, it was so nice that day I even took my food outside, where some optimistic restaurant employee had stuck a little metal table and chair out in the sunshine.

Now, you'd think that the water in the Old Mill falls was all tamed for the tourists, the way it comes down between carefully arranged boulders set right beside the hotel and little shopping mall. I mean, it seems so tidy, the way the water flows down in three well-engineered parts. First, the water falls about twenty yards straight down from the man-made canal that runs out of Waukewan. Second, it swirls round and round in a deep rock pool, all golden amber like it's been colored by the pennies the tourists drop from the footbridge; and third, it scampers on off down another, much smaller, falls and goes into a rock-lined canal, emptying finally into the Big Lake, right next to the village park and bandstand. All pleasant and well-mannered and fun to look at/listen to, on summer days when people walk around in their bathing suits and lick their Ben and Jerry's. Nothing like a water feature to set off the hanging baskets of petunias on a hot July afternoon.

But, in March, just after ice-out, that water's not so domesticated, let me tell you. I mean, it comes crashing down the rocks, all green-white and spitting dirty foam. It's huge. It's full of debris and incredibly loud. So, if a girl is sitting at a little metal table nearby, her croissant gets splashed and her sweatshirt misted with spray. But, hell, it's spring, so she doesn't care about a little bit of dampness. Nah, that's fine. But when the body comes, that's a whole nother thing altogether. That's a nasty shock.

So, I'm sitting there, chewing and enjoying, when I hear, I don't know exactly, a strange chink in the roar of the falls. It's a kind of soft thumping, something bumping around in the middle of water's rush. And, you know what? Before I even look, I know. I just know that whatever is thunking around in there is not a log. Or a tire. It's something made of flesh and bone.

The body comes tumbling down the falls like a bunch of peeled sticks, white and shiny. Arms out, legs akimbo. Face hidden in the froth. The body races head-first down the rocks, shuddering and twisting as it comes. I stand up. I've got my hand over my mouth and I can feel the scream pushing against my fingers, but it's not out yet. The body lands, twirling and spinning, in the deep pool of water at my feet. Can't help it—I look at it. The arms and legs are skeletal, bits of cloth—or something—clinging here and there to the bone. The body spins face down, until a new rush of water flips it over. Face up. No eyes. Only staring sockets. Hair like a grotesque halo around the skull. Some kind of chain around its neck bones. A big old grinning jaw, flapping open and shut, clackety, clackety, clack. Just like some joke skull at Halloween. My fingers fall away from my mouth and the scream gets out. It's even louder than the falls and people come running.

□ □ □

Long story short: I got the rest of the afternoon off and spent most of it talking to Sheriff Long, who, unfortunately, I've met before, in my drinking/driving days. The day turned cold and gray and sleet started falling—that's spring in New Hampshire—and I felt sorry for the firemen and ambulance and police guys who had to work out there, taking pictures and whatever else they do, then hauling the sack of bones out of its pool. I heard that some poor guy in a wet suit had to go into the pool and lift the body out—bone by bone—because by then some of the ligaments had given way and things were falling apart. Trust me, I didn't want to hear any of that, but since I was sitting in the sheriff's office, sipping hot coffee and wishing like hell for whiskey, I couldn't help overhearing. The whole place was buzzing with excitement. A dead body really wakes up small town law enforcement types. I told my story over and over, shivering and sipping, until finally they decided that I didn't know anything else and the deputy drove me back to my cottage, watching that I got inside okay. They're not bad guys, really. Probably saved my life, if I care to admit it, the last time they pulled me over and took away the keys to my truck. Anyway, I got home and the dogs were really glad to see me.

Dogs are the best things in my life. Sad but true. Alex is a big old quasi-lab, the strong and silent type. Mags is a short-legged Jack Russell with enough bounce to get us all through the day, most of the time. The dogs tolerate each other and love me—what more can you ask? This day, both of them seemed to get the idea that something was not exactly right. I was shivering and sweating, all at the same time—shivering from cold, sweating from needing a drink and not having one. I went into the living room—there are three rooms in the cottage: living, bedroom, kitchen, plus a bathroom with a tin shower—and stoked up the wood stove. I was running low on wood so I usually parceled it out like gold coins but what the hell. I was too cold to care. I sat down in the old wooden rocker and wrapped Grandma's bright orange and dark brown afghan around my whole body, head and all. Alex leaned his chest against my legs and plunked his big square head onto my lap. Mags leapt over his head and landed on my solar plexus, quivering and circling. I wheezed for a minute, then we all settled down. When the knock came, I just yelled, "Come on in, Guy." Because I have only one human friend left. So who else would it be?

Alex stayed where he was, tail thumping, and Mags jumped off my stomach, nails digging in as she went. I could hear Guy's boots being wiped on the kitchen mat and his greeting—"Good evening, small dog"—then he was in the living room with me, sinking onto the daybed that serves as a couch.

It's the only piece of furniture wide enough for Guy Favreau's butt. The man goes, I don't know, three hundred pounds. He's half French-Canadian, half Abenaki Indian, six foot four, gray-streaked black braid down his back. He talks slow and sounds, most of the time, like a back-country halfwit. But, really, he's the sharpest person I know. He's also a lawyer, albeit not a very energetic one. A strange man but a good friend.

"Hello, large dog," he said. Alex's tail whacked the floor double-time. Even through the wooly afghan, I could smell Guy: wood smoke, cigarette smoke, and the spearmint tea he drinks all day. "Hello, Sophie," he added. "You've had an interesting day, I hear."

I nodded.

"It's almost certainly Robert Weston, you know. Man who went missing in the fall, October? The one everyone decided just ran off, left his nutso wife and who would blame him? Or maybe shot him-

self in some woebegone piece of the woods? Sad man, always hang-
dogging around the place, big circles under his eyes? Remember?"

I did. I hadn't known Robert, personally, but he'd come into the
store now and again, buy some household thing, and moan about
having to do some minor repair. "Yep. Kind of guy who makes
breathing look like a chore." That thought stopped me. I pulled the
wool off my eyes and looked at Guy. "Well, I guess he doesn't have
to worry about that anymore."

Guy looked tired himself. His flannel shirt was pulled tight
across the shoulders and belly. His hands were folded on top of
Mags, who lay curled between his legs like she'd grown there—a
doggy Athena from the thigh of a weary Zeus. "Nope. They say he's
probably been in the water since he disappeared. Not a lot left of the
man. But he was still wearing a necklace his wife gave him. She
ID'ed it."

"Huh." I sat up. "What water was he in, all that time?"

He looked at me. "Think it out, Miss Ex-Assistant Professor."

Now, that's true. Not many people around here know about it
but I was, for a brief while, Dr. Sheridan, Assistant Professor of
British Literature at Bates College. But no more—long story. Had a
lot to do with my friend Johnnie Walker. So, yeah, ex-assistant professor hardware saleswoman, at your service. And, you know, I like
selling hammers and nails better, overall. A whole lot more honest
way to live. But I do have a brain and I did think it out. The man's
body tumbled down the fast-moving falls just a few days after ice-
out. And the falls came from the canal and the canal came from—
holy shit, the canal came from the lake just outside my front windows. "He drowned in Waukewan," I said. I stood up, pushing
Alex's nose from my legs, and pointed out into the dark. There was
just enough silver left in the sky to show where the water was—and
if you listened, you could hear it, lapping up against the granite
stones. "Jeez. Right here."

Guy nodded. "If he drowned."

I had to think about that for a minute. "You mean, he might have been already dead when he went into the water? As in, not breathing?"

"Yep. That's what his wife says, anyway. No way her Sweet Bobboo—I swear to God, that's what she calls him—offed himself. No way a'tall." I started to speak, but he held up his hand. "No. Listen. She has a theory. She's coming to my office tomorrow, early. I told her my assistant would be there, too, to hear it."

"Your assistant?"

"Yes. I'm too well known around town to do what she wants done. You, well, you're not. You're low profile."

He was right. I kept my head low. "Great. So what does she want done?"

Guy stood up and Mags rolled straight down his legs, landing in an undignified heap of dog-feet and belly. "Ms. Weston says her Sweet Bobboo couldn't sleep and he was going crazy. She thinks he went to that new clinic, up at the end of Waukewan, where Porter's farm used to be. You know, the place that calls itself Perchance to Dream?"

I knew the name. Made me want to puke.

□ □ □

I'll spare you a blow-by-blow of the meeting with Ms. Weston. One crazy lady. Spoke three hundred words for every one that meant anything. Took a whole lot of listening to get what she was getting at. I sat in one of the ratty chairs in Guy's office and she took the other, jaw flapping. Guy sat behind his ancient oak desk like a Buddha, silent, smoking and sipping his spearmint brew. Gist of story: Robert Weston had been a National Guardsman, served a tour in Iraq. When he came back, the man couldn't sleep for shit. Walked around for three months—all of last summer—with circles the size of the Big Lake under his eyes. Then, in early October, prettiest day of the year, she swore, Ms. Weston came home from work and found a note, handwritten by her Sweet Bobboo: Hey. Got to split. Got to get some rest. And she never saw him again.

Now, I was thinking that who would blame him for up and leaving? Finding rest from her nonstop motor-mouth? But, no. She swore that he wouldn't do that. And when the police took his note to mean "rest," as in "rest from living," as in suicide, she wouldn't accept that either. No—her Bobboo had gone to that weird new clinic at the end of Waukewan, hoping, exactly as he'd said, for some rest. And he'd never come back. She started to bawl, still talking: he would never, not ever ever ever ever in this or any other lifetime ever ever ever leave her and—

Guy finally broke in, speaking over her. "The sheriff checked out Perchance, Soph, at the time. Staff there never heard of Robert Weston and never had him for a patient, they assured him. According to Sheriff Long, it's an oddball place. Sleep disorders clinic. I mean, what the hell is that? But it seemed harmless and there was no sign of anything illegal going on. Run by some doc from Boston. Had about five patients, all up from the city, all trying to cure their insomnia. All pleased with their treatments. All legit. I told her we'd check it out, though."

I shifted. His chair had a loose spring and it was twanging against my butt. "We?"

He smiled. "You do have trouble sleeping, don't you, Soph? I already cleared it with your boss. Think of it this way—you're going on a nice restful little vacation. You look like you could use some good zees."

□ □ □

So, yeah. Next morning, as raw a March day as you never want to see, I rubbed the dogs' ears and told them that Guy would come over to take care of them. They yawned and went back to the wood stove, curling up like doggie doughnuts, noses under tails. Talk about good sleepers. Guy's truck pulled up and his horn sounded. As I stomped my way through yards of semi-frozen mud, the cat—pure black, unnamed, half-wild, suspiciously chubby all of a sudden—dashed out of the woods and curled herself around my ankles, meowing like mad. Now this was strange. Cat doesn't much go in for public—or private—displays of affection. Should have taken heed. Cat thought I wasn't coming back.

Guy was more cheerful. "It'll be fun, Soph. Soft beds, down pillows, comforters a mile wide and foot deep. That's what they advertise. All you have to do is keep your eyes open, okay?"

As it happened, that "eyes open" thing turned out to be a real challenge.

□   □   □

Guy was right about the comfort, though. There I was, that very evening, sitting in what would have been one of the bedrooms of the old Porter farmhouse, now renovated to within an inch of its life. Outside, a full moon floated in an icy-cold sky. But in here it was warm and cozy. The walls of my assigned room were painted sage green and the one-shade-paler green carpet was so soft that my bare toes were smiling. My toes were bare because the nurse had asked me to disrobe and put on one of their 100% organic, 500-thread count, ecologically responsible, woven-from-bamboo nightgowns. Pure white. I felt like a Victorian bride. The nurse had said, for this first night, I was just to try to sleep, as usual. No monitors, no nothing. Just sleep naturally, she'd said, and report how it went in the morning. Sleep tight, she'd added, as she gently closed my door.

Right. I waited until the whole place was quiet, with actual contented snores rising from the other rooms on my floor. Then I tiptoed, barefoot, down the stairs and into the office where I'd first met Dr. Woodruff, a genial bald man with hairy hands who'd explained the treatment: evaluation of my disorder, repatterning my brain to a natural sleep rhythm, drugs only as a last resort. Sounded like bullshit to me, but then my brain always has resisted repatterning. (Ask the folks at AA.) Anyway, the whole house was dark. I'd learned that the staff all slept on the third floor, far enough away so that I wasn't worried about waking them.

I have a knack for picking locks, a skill acquired in my youth when we used to break into Saint John the Divine and raid the cabinet where they kept the communion wine. The office door was a cinch. When I opened the heavy drapes over the picture window—this must have been the front parlor, once upon a time—the moonlight was bright enough to let me see where everything was. I started to search desk drawers, file cabinet and so on. A bunch of patient records. Nothing with the name Robert Weston anywhere to be found. But when I closed one of the metal file drawers, it jangled. I reopened the drawer and lifted out the file folders. Underneath, partway caught in the metal glide bars of the drawer, two oval shapes. I pulled them out and held them in my hand. Dog tags. I piled the files back in the drawer and carried my find to the window. There in the moonlight, I could read only the capital letters of the name on the tags: RW. Close enough for government work, I thought, and hustled my butt out of the room, up the stairs and back into my room. Mission accomplished—and I wanted out. Out of the perfect warmth, the perfect décor, the whole creepy perfection of that sleeping house. It wasn't that long a walk back to my cabin. If I followed the shoreline, just about a mile.

I was about to slip the perfect nightgown over my imperfect head when three people stepped through my door: the nurse, a large guy in blue scrubs, and Dr. Woodruff.

Dr. Woodruff stepped forward, shaking his head. "I am sorry," he said. "You shouldn't have."

I stood up, the dog tags clutched in my hand. "I was looking for the kitchen," I said. "I was hungry."

He shook his head. "My dear, there are cameras. Do you think we would leave our patients unmonitored?" He gestured toward the corner of the ceiling.

Well, duh. Not much I could say, was there?

Dr. Woodruff turned to the nurse. "I will insert the IV line. You prepare the medication."

Without being asked, the large orderly stepped forward and held onto my arm. I tried to push him away, but, really, I didn't have a chance. In about three seconds, I was on my back on the bed, a needle perfectly placed in the crook of my left elbow, neatly secured under a square of gauze, all carefully taped to my flesh. A bag of saline was hung on a hook above my head and the whole contraption was running perfectly. The orderly was sort of sitting on my legs and Dr. Woodruff was drawing two different liquids into a syringe. He must have noticed the horror on my face, because he spoke gently. "This, my dear, is nothing harmful. It's the same mixture your gastroenterologist gives you before a colonoscopy. Fentanyl and Versed. Controls pain and deletes memory. Brings dreamless, perfect sleep. Utter oblivion. We use it, occasionally, on terribly sleep-impaired patients. Only once, I swear, was an overdose delivered, a terrible error. Only once." He glanced at the nurse, who turned white as powder. "You may leave the room, Ms Ellert," he said. "I know this upsets you."

The nurse scurried out the door, leaving just me, the doctor and the orderly camped on my legs. There was only the briefest second, while Dr. Woodruff's eyes were focused on his syringe and the orderly's eyes were focused on the doctor, when I could do anything at all. So I did what I could. I jerked the IV tubing just above the taped gauze, hoping to dislodge the needle from the vein. I felt it pull out, the tiniest bit, and I felt the burning in my arm where the vein tore. And then the doctor pushed the syringe into the port of the IV tubing, up above my head. And then things got awfully bright, for one millisecond. And then awfully blurry.

□   □   □

You'll have to excuse the fuzziness of the rest of this. I was, I heard later, a zombie. I may not have gotten the full dose of that stuff but I'd definitely gotten some. I'd heard, as if from very far off, the doctor curse when he'd pulled the gauze off my arm and saw, I surmised later, the precious drugs flowing not into the vein but into the tissue of my arm. But then—perfect oblivion. Except when I got very cold. That woke me, a little, and I fought up through the mists in my head. I was naked and it was windy. My hands were bound behind me and my ankles were tied, too. I remember only the embarrassment of being trussed like a turkey, complete with goose-bumped turkey-blue skin. And then I was in the lake.

Now, March may be ice-out but that doesn't mean the water is exactly hospitable for human flesh. That water shocked me awake. But there was not a damn thing I could do but wriggle as I sank. Here's what I think I saw. Streams of silver moonshine in black water, like lovely strands of tinsel. Bubbles rising above my head, first in a burst, then in a slim, fading line. Deeper: fish eyes. Cold, silvery, greedy. Pike, I thought. Teeth. Deeper: nothing. Nothing at all. Utter blackness. Terrible tearing chest pain. Ice water in my lungs. The last thing I thought: how sad my dogs would be. Because somewhere in the night, high above me, a dog was barking.

□   □   □

Here's what Guy told me, much later, when I was in my gloriously imperfect room in my wonderfully imperfect cabin, the wood stove glowing orange, he'd cranked it so high. Both dogs were under the covers with me and Guy was perched at the end of the bed, wrapped in blankets. We'd even let Cat in. She was licking her feet in a corner, clearly listening to the story Guy told to us all.

Guy had decided to have a sleepover with the dogs in my cabin. But Alex wouldn't settle down. He whined and scratched at the door and whenever Guy let him out, he raced to the dock and stood out there in the cold, head cocked, ears blown back by the wind. Mags retreated under the wood stove and wouldn't come out. But from her warm spot there, the small dog yipped, once every three seconds. Finally, Guy let the dogs have their way. "All right, all right, we'll go check on her." And they'd all piled into his truck and driven to a bit of sandy woods, just outside the boundary of Perchance to Dream, and there they'd parked. It was dark and it was cold. The dogs, in close quarters, didn't smell so good—and they paced and whined and drooled and farted, never once lying down. Guy was cursing the Abenaki blood that led him to believe in the instincts of animals when he heard voices and then a splash. Something going into the water.

Alex went absolutely nuts, clawing at the truck window like a demon. It took Guy a minute to understand, to let the dog out, and to grab his phone to dial 911. By the time he got himself out of the truck, the small dog whizzing like a flash of white lightning between his legs, there wasn't anything to be seen or heard in the moonlight. Except the silver wake of a black dog, swimming with all his might, arrowlike, unwavering, in the direction of old Porter's dock. Then the dog dove and disappeared.

What Guy saw next, he swears he'll never forget, all the days of his life. Out in the water, a hundred yards away, an arm was rising from the glimmering silver surface. The arm was pure white. The jaws around it were pure black. The square black head of the dog was just barely above the surface and it was clear that the beast was exhausted. But he was still trying. The dog was pulling the blue-white body behind him, the body of a woman, floating on her back, breasts bared to the moon.

Guy is not a swimmer, not a fan of any physical exertion. But he tore off his boots and went into the lake. He could walk for a while and then he swam. It wasn't far; the dog had done a good bit of the journey. Guy reached the tired dog and the naked woman and he wrapped both between his tree-trunk legs and he turned onto his back. ("Fortunately, fat floats," he'd said.) He back-stroked his way to shore. By the time the humans and dog were piled on the sandy beach next to the dock, a small white hurricane leaping on the top of the heap they made, the woods were alive with sirens. Blue, red and white light streaked across them. They all, for a moment, went blissfully to sleep.

❑ ❑ ❑

The rest was easy, comparatively. The sheriff took care of the arrests. Dr. Woodruff and the orderly had held their tongues, but the nurse cried and talked. No one, she swore, had meant for Robert Weston to die. It was a terrible mistake—somehow, she had given him triple the dose. He'd fallen into the deepest of sleeps. And he had not awakened. Dr. W had remembered that Robert had said no one knew where he was. No one had to know. They could all keep their jobs, their investments in Perchance to Dream. Easy enough to dump his body in the lake, hands and feet tied, like mine, with the stuff they use for self-dissolving stitches, that strong surgical thread that disappears on its own, over time. The body was weighted with stones in its pockets: even if it surfaced, Dr. W had assured them, it would look like suicide. And then the lake had frozen and kept Robert's body to itself. Until ice-out.

❑ ❑ ❑

Story over. I was feeling very sleepy myself. Warm and safe. The dogs snuffled and twitched in their sleep. I yawned. So did Guy. Finally, I said to him, "Listen. Why don't you get in here with us? We'll keep each other warm."

My bed isn't big, but somehow or other, we all fit. I fell asleep against Guy's wide chest and, in my dreams, I was floating, buoyed up above black waters, moonlight in my eyes.

That's it, I guess. Except for this. Sometime in that night, Cat gave birth to three kittens. Silently, on her own. No fuss.

Just, poof, there they were in the morning: three damp gray ovals against her pure black belly, mewing and kneading. The dogs were fascinated.

Life, you know, goes on. Spring comes, every single year.

The Gas Leak

Mike Wiecek

When Sue Ann in dispatch got the 911, she called out the fire department, then immediately rang up the sheriff. Sue Ann knew that any action at the Granger place was unlikely to stop at firefighting. The sheriff didn't answer, not surprising considering it was lunchtime, but instead of phoning down to the diner, Sue Ann hunted around on the radio until she scared up a deputy. And that's how Carleen Boyd, twenty years old and the town's first-ever female officer, came to show up with the pumper and the ambulance and the fire chief's old Blazer.

The vehicles screamed to a halt, sirens winding down, and the volunteer firefighters disembarked in no great hurry. No smoke, no flames, but three junked cars in the way if they really had to haul hose.

"Hi, Carleen," said the chief, shrugging into his turnout coat. "You know what the problem is?"

"Sue Ann just told me to show up," Carleen said. They waited, and nothing stirred.

Just as the chief sighed and started forward, a man came running around from the back of the house, overalls flapping and one boot untied.

"No! Stay there!" He started to push Carleen back, then glanced at her face and stopped, rather surprising both of them. "Gas," he said, and wiped a dirty hand across his nose. "Got a leak."

Carleen took her hand off her sidearm. "You're the one that called for help?"

"Yeah. I didn't expect you so quick."

The chief squinted at him. "Wayne, you don't have gas lines out here."

"The propane. We just got a new tank. One of the fittings must have come loose."

"How'd you know it was leaking?"

"Saw the valve, and I could hear hissing in the kitchen. I got out quick."

He sneezed, spraying drops in a wide arc, and both Carleen and the chief stepped back.

"Were you raised in a barn, Wayne?" The chief frowned at his coat. "Cover your nose next time."

"I got a bad cold," Wayne said.

"I guess," said Carleen, and they all looked at the house for a while.

"Tank'll run out eventually," said the chief thoughtfully.

One of the volunteers was smoking, leaning against the pumper. "Hey, chief," he called. "I could use another engagement or I'm going to miss the re-certification this year. How about, like, a contained burn?"

The chief looked at him. "You're not going to toss in that cigarette, are you?"

The firefighter appeared to take the question seriously. "Naw, I was thinking, maybe a road flare."

"Holy jump! Keep your ideas to yourself, Billy."

Wayne fidgeted. "Can I go, chief? Deputy?"

"Stay here," said Carleen. "Wait and see if your house blows up or not."

Birds called in the locust trees past the house. Cicadas hummed.

Carleen kept her feet away from the scraggly crabgrass, wary of scrub mites.

A pickup truck came along and stopped, pulling in ahead of the pumper. The man who got out looked like an older, cleaner version of Wayne, dressed in khakis and a polo shirt.

"What's going on?" he asked, frowning at the emergency vehicles.

"Tuck!" Wayne came from around Carleen. "You maggot!" He swung a wild fist. "You get yourself gone, right now, hear?"

Tuck avoided the punch, but stumbled and swung his own arms up. The two men collided, fell, and rolled around in the gravel, snarling and raking each other.

Carleen blinked. "Aren't they brothers?"

"Yup." The chief watched the scuffle. "Want to break them up?"

"Not particularly."

"Me neither."

Wayne got Tuck in a clinch and started banging his head on the ground. Tuck twisted around, breaking the hold, and cuffed Wayne in the nose. Blood spurted.

"Oh, for—" Carleen popped the patrol car's trunk and pulled out a fire extinguisher, yanking the lockring free as she aimed. The first spray of foam distracted the brothers, but they didn't separate until she'd blasted them several times more.

"What'd you do *that* for?" Tuck clambered to his feet, wiping foam from his shirt.

"Putting out a fire, dummy," said one of the volunteers.

Wayne got up more slowly. He sneezed again, fanning blood and snot everywhere. Bystanders yelped.

"Hey!"

"Watch your nose, Wayne!"

"We're gonna need the damn hazmat truck here."

Carleen pointed. "Tuck, right? You go stand over there. Wayne, you stay put." When they'd separated, glaring at each other, she turned to Wayne. "What's going on with you two?"

"That two-timing weasel knows he ain't welcome round here. Ruby don't want to see him no more."

"That's a lie!" Tuck called. "She's *done* with you and this dump."

"Shut up!"

"And that ain't *all* she's done with, what she tells me—"

The shouting rose. Carleen wondered why she'd been issued only one pair of handcuffs. The crowd of firefighters watched and murmured—it was better than Saturday night wrestling, down at the armory.

Just when it looked like coming to blows again, a woman came tottering around the side of the house, holding her head and moaning as she zig-zagged through the yard.

"Ruby?" said the chief. "What—hey, are you all right?"

"Someone hit me on the head!" the young woman said. She wore a velour sweatsuit and running shoes, and Carleen thought she looked fit, like maybe she actually used the sweatsuit for TaeBo or Jane Fonda or something. But when she pulled her hand away, they saw blood matted on her scalp.

"Medic!" hollered the chief, like they were all in a war movie. The EMTs swung into action, lowering the woman to the ground, cautious of a neck injury.

"You two stay put," Carleen said, with a look each for Wayne and Tuck, then knelt beside Ruby.

"What happened?" she asked.

"I was in the sitting room, doing some sewing," Ruby said, "and someone must have snuck in behind me, because I don't even remember getting walloped. I woke up on the floor when I heard your sirens. I was so woozy it took time to get myself up and going. Ouch!" She slapped at the EMT attempting to bandage her skull.

"Looks like this is turning into your business after all," said the chief to Carleen, and she radioed in. The sheriff told her not to mess anything up and he'd be right along.

"He doesn't want the scene disturbed," she told the chief.

"Fine by me." He glanced at his crew, many of whom had taken considerable interest in the woman, gawking as the EMTs, following protocol, lashed her to a wooden backboard. "Of course, if the gas ignites, even state CSI won't be able to learn much."

Ruby had just been loaded into the ambulance when the sheriff's car roared up, spraying gravel as he skidded to a stop alongside the pumper. One of the firefighters, standing too close, jumped backwards and fell down, swearing. The sheriff hauled his six-eight frame out of the cruiser, added the bear hat to make it an even seven feet, and slammed the door.

"Hiya, chief." His voice carried. "Carleen, you have to shoot anyone yet?"

"No sir." She glanced at Tuck and Wayne, who'd finally stopped squabbling.

"Tell me about it."

While Carleen summarized, she noticed how everyone had quieted down, and not just because they wanted to eavesdrop. The sheriff had a Marshal Dillon complex, but he really was a presence. Carleen wished she could command even a tenth of the respect he got just standing there.

"Bad blood between Wayne and Tuck," she said, trying not to be overheard. "It's not clear who struck Ruby, but tampering with the gas line could make it attempted murder."

"Hmm."

The ambulance drove off, lights but no siren. The sheriff studied the house with his eyes creased, posed like a cavalry scout in the old west, then turned to the fire chief.

"You boys'll keep watch, right?" he said. "Until the gas is gone.

Let me know later."

"Sure, sheriff."

"Meanwhile, Carleen, why don't you take Tuck and I'll transport Wayne. We don't want them making up a story together."

"Are we arresting them?"

"I reckon." He lowered his voice enough so only she could hear. "We'll stick them in opposite cells and hope one of them cracks before they think to call a lawyer."

"Yes sir."

"The last thing I want to do—" he looked at the junked cars, the dilapidated house, the overgrown lawn— "is waste *any* time investigating this sorry litter of idiots."

□ □ □

Carleen carefully backed the patrol car out onto the road, nodded to the fire chief, and started toward town. The sheriff's cruiser was already far ahead, disappearing around the wooded slope of Bucktop Mountain. Heat shimmered above the blacktop.

"Sorry about the cuffs," Carleen said, glancing in the rearview at Tuck.

"No problem, ma'am."

"If you hadn't attacked your brother—"

"Yeah, I know. He just gets on my nerves. Always has."

They drove in silence for a few minutes.

"Think Ruby's going to be okay?" Tuck asked.

"She didn't look that bad. I'll call St. Mary's when we get to the station, if you like."

"Maybe she'll finally divorce him. He oughtn't get away with knocking her around like that."

"Wayne, you mean?"

"Yeah." His sigh was audible to Carleen, even through the Plexiglas partition. "Still can't believe she married him."

"Were you and she—"

"Once upon a time."

Carleen slowed at a stop sign, where Route 3 crossed, but there was no other traffic visible, and she continued through.

"What about lately?" she asked. "You and Ruby?"

"Oh, hell." Tuck sounded resigned. "We might of stepped out, once or twice. This town, someone's sure to tell you."

"Uh-huh."

"I didn't do it."

"What, Ruby?"

"I know you're thinking—I could have knocked her out, then driven around the mountain once. It ain't true."

"Of course not."

"If I was going to blow someone up, it'd be that dirtworm lowlife Wayne, and no mistake."

"Maybe you shouldn't—"

"Not Ruby." He paused, and Carleen glanced back, caught his eyes in the mirror. "Never Ruby. You believe me, don't you?"

They were approaching the outskirts of town—a few houses, a shuttered farm equipment reseller, the Dairy Queen.

"She's going to be fine," said Carleen. "Don't you worry about her."

□ □ □

At the station, the sheriff had almost finished processing Wayne into the drunk tank when Carleen brought Tuck inside. The air conditioning was strongest in the front, where Sue Ann had her radio station. Back in the cells it was humid and warm, a faint smell of barf and tobacco in the air.

"Hi, Carleen," said Sue Ann.

"Put yours down there." The sheriff pointed to the end of the hall. "I opened number four."

"Yes sir." As Carleen closed the door on Tuck, looking so forlorn, she couldn't help telling him, "Sorry about this."

"That's okay. Just make sure Ruby's okay, could you?"

Out front, the sheriff dropped into his chair, leaned back and thumped his size-fourteens onto the desk.

"Don't suppose Tuck confessed?" he said.

"He more or less admitted he was having an affair with Ruby."

"I figured. Wayne's none too happy. I got to say, I'm figuring him for it."

The front door banged open. Carleen looked over, across the room, and saw a familiar-looking man walk in.

"Help you, sir?" Sue Ann doubled on reception, most days.

"I heard my brothers were here." The family resemblance was strong—the same big nose and windmill ears—but he walked straighter, and had fewer marbles in his mouth when he spoke.

"Brent Granger." The sheriff got up and walked over to shake hands. "When'd you get into town?"

"I stop by to see Pop once or twice a week." He nodded at Carleen. "Afternoon, miss."

She tried to turn off her natural reaction, with small success. Brent was clearly the educated, successful, worldly, *hunky* Granger brother. He wore a button-down white shirt, the sleeves rolled halfway up his tanned and muscular forearms.

"Pleased to meet you." She could hear Sue Ann smother a laugh behind her.

"How's the old man?" asked the sheriff.

"The terror of the nursing home." Brent grinned. "Every lady there's in love with him, including the staff."

"He always livened up a place."

Carleen spoke up, a little hesitantly. "Do you live nearby, Mr. Granger?"

"Nope—down in the city, nowadays. But I'm often here, like I said. Have to keep an eye on my brothers." He glanced at the door to the cells. "Speaking of which . . ."

"Ruby got whacked on the head, and they almost lost the house," the sheriff explained.

Brent shook his head. "No chance it was an accident?"

"Not the way she was bleeding. And we could all smell the gas."

"I still don't—it's hard to believe anyone could have done that intentionally. Especially not Tuck or Wayne."

"Well, maybe it was a drifter, or a burglary gone wrong." The sheriff might as well have said, *or maybe a meteor crashed out of the sky onto Ruby's head.* "We'll conduct a thorough investigation."

"Thank you." Brent turned to Carleen. "I appreciate all your help."

"Anything I can do," she said. Sue Ann whuffled again.

"Brent, I have a few questions," said the sheriff. "And Carleen, maybe you could run and check on something for me?"

□　□　□

She'd only been to Crestview Manor Rehab once before, when an Alzheimer's patient clocked an attendant and the night manager called 911. That experience hadn't left a good impression. But now, sunlight streaming through the dayroom, ladies knitting and watching TV, the facility had a warm and pleasant feel.

Carleen asked at reception and found Pop Granger in a wooden chair outside, sitting near the parking lot. He was reading the weekly *Clarion-Bugle* and spitting tobacco into a planter by the door.

"Mr. Granger?" Carleen introduced herself and sat in the other chair.

"A girl deputy, how about that." Pop seemed tickled. "What brings you out here? Someone lose their wallet again?"

"Not exactly—"

"Happens all the time, you know. Usually turns up in the microwave, or the backgammon box. I don't recollect one ever actually being stolen."

"I see—"

"The wonder is, why would any of us inmates even *carry* a wallet anymore? Not exactly a cash economy inside here. Kinda like Red China—iron rice bowl and all that."

"Uh, rice bowl?"

"Though they'd be doing *right* to serve us Chinese now and then. I used to like a good Egg Foo Yung. Back when I had my teeth, you know. All we seem to get here is stewed tomatoes and farina." He spat, accurately striking the base of the potted juniper bush. "Tell you what, honey, nothing like Moo Goo Gai Pan and a cold beer."

"Sorry, I can't help you with that." This time Carleen kept talking, even though Pop had opened his mouth again. "Your sons, Wayne and Tuck? Have you seen either of them today?"

"Huh? My boys? No, not them. But Brent was here this morning. Told me all about his company's new building. Brent's in wholesale plumbing, you know."

"There was an accident out at your house, an hour ago." Carleen got the story out.

Pop, for once, sat silent. "Almost too bad it didn't blow up," he said finally. "Not Ruby, of course. Nothing against her."

"What do you mean?"

"I love all my sons. Don't have to tell you that, do I? I love all three." Pop spat, with less energy, and some of the juice hit the pavement. "But between you and me, Wayne, well, he's always had trouble with the complicated parts of life."

"Excuse me?"

"You know. Like the part where you have to get a job and earn a living. And the part where you roll up your car windows so it don't rain inside and ruin the seats. And the part about doing laundry more'n once a year. And if you really *have* to play a few racks at Sully's Billiards every Saturday, you don't bet any cash money on it, especially money you don't even have." Pop shook his head. "Tell you the truth, I don't know how Ruby puts up with him, sometimes."

"Why did you say it would be okay if the house blew up?"

"Wayne needs a good kick in the pants. I never gave him one, sure enough."

"I don't think—"

"I'm working on my will, you know."

"Your will?"

"And testament." Pop folded his newspaper and tucked it under his chair. "If you'd told me the house was gone? Flaming rubble, all that? Then I could go ahead and leave the property to Brent, like I wanted to. He'd make something of it, no biggety. Dam up the crick and generate electricity, or run buffalo, or grow mary-juana—hell, I don't care, but it wouldn't be all run down to weeds like Wayne let it go."

"I see." Carleen paused, aiming to keep casual. "Did Brent know that?"

"I might have mentioned it to him."

"What about Tuck?"

"Oh, Tuck's all right. Got his own interests . . . he ain't come round on to you, has he? Tuck's surely got an eye for the pretty ones."

"I'll keep that in mind."

The conversation meandered. Pop recovered his energy and started hitting the juniper clean, again.

"You might as well let those boys out of jail," he said. "Ain't none of them dumb enough to do what you said, with the propane."

"It's not really up to—"

"Tell them to come visit me." Pop nodded. "And bring some Chinese. With fortune cookies."

□ □ □

When Carleen drove up to the stationhouse, she saw Wayne walking down the street one way, Tuck going the other. The day was hitting its peak heat, grass wilting in the glaring sun, few other people around. Tuck might have had slightly more spring in his step, but neither brother was moving fast.

Inside Sue Ann was on break somewhere, the sheriff himself perched in her chair, flipping through a Galls catalog.

"You let them go," Carleen said.

"Ruby's not interested in charges. The house didn't blow up. The fire department went home. Everyone's happy."

"It might not have been Wayne." Carleen's sense of justice was still young and strong. "Pop told me he always wanted to give the property to Brent. If the house was gone, and Wayne and Ruby moved away, Brent might get it all to himself."

"I know." The sheriff studied a page of tactical armor. "Cooley Dawt—the lawyer, always see him at the courthouse? He's rewritten and filed four different wills for Pop, just since last year when Pop went into Crestview. I heard all about it."

"So why don't we—"

"Because there's nothing to it. Brent's running his plumbing empire, the last thing he wants is a few acres of unimproved dirt. Only reason he comes back here at all is family obligation. Once Pop's gone, we'll never see him." The sheriff paused, glancing up at Carleen, a little bit of a grin showing. "Of course, that's not likely to be anytime soon."

Carleen rolled her eyes. Small towns.

"So we're just going to wait for next time?" she said, exasperated.

"Could be." The sheriff closed the catalog. "But maybe you ought to know. Once the propane had drifted away, Billy checked the valve."

"Billy?"

"One of the firefighters. He's an apprentice with the pipefitters, so I reckon he knows what he's doing. He said it could have come loose all by itself—maybe the deliveryman just hadn't tightened it up right when he swapped tanks."

"Oh."

"No big plot. If the Grangers had ended up minus one house today, it would have been an honest accident. Ruby's plumb lucky."

A call came in, the alert buzzing on Sue Ann's panel. The sheriff picked up her headset and held it to his ear, swinging the mic down. "Sheriff's office," he said. "Uh-huh . . . yup . . . stopped there how long, did you say?"

He put one hand over the mic and said to Carleen, "Someone's double-parked in front of the post office. Want to go roust them?"

Carleen looked at him. "Aren't there any other threats to the republic we could deal with?" But he was back on the call, and he just waved her away impatiently.

"Fine."

Maybe she'd run into Brent downtown.

□   □   □

Not Brent. But after finding the car's owner—Mrs. Earl, come to mail a package to her son in Iraq, who then stopped to gossip with friends for about an hour—Carleen saw a familiar velour track suit going into the Heavenly Glow nail shop. She waved goodbye to Mrs. Earl, who was pulling away from the post office, and walked briskly down the block.

Ruby was just settling into one of the chairs, leaning back with a sigh. A patch of folded white gauze was taped across her forehead.

"How are you feeling, Ruby?" Carleen asked.

"Oh, I've got a headache to beat all."

"No concussion? You're lucky."

"That's what the doctor said. She told me to go home and lie down, but Wayne has to get the truck and pick me up."

Carleen thought of him trudging all the way out to the house. "If someone doesn't give him a ride, that might take a while."

"Exactly. And I needed a little pick-me-up, so I thought I'd let

Marybelle pamper my hands. Right, sugar?"

"Sure thing." Marybelle, who Carleen had known in grade school, smiled and massaged Ruby's hands briefly. "Excuse me, I need to get some clean brushes."

When she'd gone to the back of the shop, Carleen lowered her voice. "Nobody's being charged," she said. "But that doesn't mean nothing happened."

"Of course not! Why, look at this knot on my head."

"I have been." Carleen paused. "How'd you do it, Ruby? Piece of firewood?"

Ruby's mouth thinned, but she didn't answer.

"The way I see it," Carleen said, "if you got hit from behind, the injury wouldn't be on your forehead. But don't worry. The sheriff's not interested."

"Maybe he should be."

"I talked to Pop Granger earlier. He told me about his will."

"Oh?"

"You know, if the house had burned down, Pop wouldn't have rebuilt it for you. I figure that's what you hoped—Wayne doesn't strike me as our town's own Bob Vila, and that shack must be falling to pieces around you, so why not start over on Pop's nickel? But he's more likely to send you packing and give the whole lot to Brent instead."

"He *told* you that?"

"Maybe you should have talked with him first."

Ruby said nothing for a moment. Her face slowly scrunched up, and a tear started from one eye.

"I might have made a mistake," she said.

"Yes—"

"No. I mean, marrying Wayne in the first place."

"Oh."

"He's a great guy and all, but he's about as ambitious as a pill bug,"

"Is that why you and Tuck . . ."

"Oh, you don't believe that, do you? Tuck's just a friend." Ruby sighed. "This town, I tell you."

Marybelle came back, carrying her kit of bottles and scrapers and applicators.

"How come I never see you in here, Carleen?" she asked.

"Police rules. Closely trimmed and no polish." She shrugged. "The sheriff's a stickler."

Ruby dried her eye. "You going to . . . do anything?" she asked Carleen.

"No." She shook her head. "The case is closed. Nobody's interested."

"Okay. Thanks. Really."

Carleen stood to leave, but turned back once more.

"Talk to Pop, okay?" she said. "He might be more sympathetic than you think. I bet you can work something out."

"Maybe I'll do that."

Marybelle looked up from her work. "You sure you don't want to sit a while? We haven't caught up lately."

"Wish I could." Carleen looked out at the summer-blasted main street. "But Wayne probably needs a ride."

Trust to Dust

Ruth M. McCarty

Erin Donnelly sat in the back booth at Perigini's reading the Prosperity *Daily News* when Wilfred Dunbar strutted in and plopped down on a seat across from her. She had just come off a twelve-hour shift and only wanted a bowl of pasta, a glass of merlot, and a little time to unwind before heading to the Hilltop Nursing Home to visit her mother. She knew that wasn't going to happen now.

Dunbar pointed to the front page of the paper, and yelled, "First they take over our town, and now they want to tell us how to rest in peace!"

Erin had just finished reading the article about the Eco Woods Depository's grand opening planned for the next day, so she knew why he was sputtering. Dunbar had conveniently forgotten that he'd talked most of the town into supporting Serenity Springs, an upscale, gated community on Still Water Lake, geared to attract boomers with money—lots of money.

Jonathan Truscott, one of those boomers, had bought much of the open land left in town and had scooped up fifty acres on the outskirts, directly adjacent to the public cemetery for a laughable amount of money because thirty or so of the acres were on a wooded slope. It would have been impossible to build anything on the land without removing truckloads of dirt and trees, and besides, even if developed, who would want to live next to a cemetery?

She'd heard Delphis Fournier, the previous owner, had his own laugh as well—all the way to the bank. No one in hell would have paid that much money for the land before Serenity Springs, so it was a win-win situation all around.

Truscott had turned most of the slope into a green burial reserve and used the remaining acres to build a peaceful park with a Pagoda-like building. The article showed an architect's rendering of the building. Erin had followed its progress and thought it looked more like a spaceship that had touched down and was ready to literally take you into the afterlife.

Always willing to get Wilfred Dunbar going, Erin said, "Green burials are the up and coming thing. Saves the environment and saves you money too. Are you going to the grand opening?"

"I wouldn't be caught dead there," Dunbar said. "You just watch. They'll put Fred Bruckner out of business."

The Bruckner family had been in Prosperity for generations and had taken care of the dead for at least that long. Erin folded the newspaper and put it on the table. "I doubt that, Wilfred. Most of us locals will stay with Bruckner's. Besides, this green burial shit will only work when there's no frost in the ground."

Mandy Fournier placed Erin's glass of merlot on the table. Erin knew she'd just turned seventeen and could now serve alcohol. "Thanks, Mandy."

Mandy turned to Dunbar. "You want something?"

Erin prayed Dunbar wasn't going to hang around and ruin her meal. She reached for her glass of wine, took a sip and glanced at the clock. She had about an hour to eat, and then she'd head to the nursing home to visit her mother before going home. Her visits always left her feeling empty, especially knowing her mother might need Bruckner's sooner than she was ready to let her go.

Dunbar scowled at Mandy and said, "Just fix my usual to go."

He stood, turned back to Erin and said, "It's creepy, I tell you. First cremations, now this!"

Erin watched as Dunbar left her table, spotted Delphis Fournier, Mandy's grandfather, sitting at the bar and began shouting, "You had to sell your land to Truscott. And now look what's going there! A freaking playground for rotting corpses."

Erin had heard enough. She got up, tapped Dunbar on the shoulder and said, "Delphis had every right to sell his land. Let it go."

"This isn't over yet." Dunbar shook his fist at Fournier. He mumbled something else then moved to the other end of the bar to wait for his order.

When Mandy brought her pasta, Erin asked her to bag it. She'd take it with her and eat it at home after her visit with her mother. She didn't have much of an appetite after Dunbar's rotting corpses comment. She drank what was left of her merlot, dropped some bills on the table and headed out.

◻ ◻ ◻

Mary Catherine Donnelly pulled the covers up to her quivering chin and cried, "Am I under arrest?"

Erin saw the terror in her mother's eyes and could have kicked herself. She should have changed out of her uniform before coming, but she just didn't have the energy after her shift. Prosperity needed more police officers, especially with the tourist season approaching.

"Hi, Ma. It's me, Erin," she said in a quiet, nonthreatening voice.

Her mother let the blankets drop. "Erin? Do I know you?"

Erin couldn't bear looking into her mother's empty eyes. She wanted to grab her by the shoulders and shake the shell of the person before her until her loving mother returned. Instead, she put her arms around her mother and rocked her like a baby. "It's me, Erin, your youngest daughter. It's my night with you. Megan came yesterday with the girls."

"Oh," she said. "Who's Megan?"

In less than three years, Mary Catherine Donnelly had gone from a vibrant woman and hip grandmother to the woman now wasting away in this bed. Erin's earlier conversation with Wilfred Dunbar crossed her mind. He wouldn't be caught dead in Eco Woods, but Erin thought it might not be a bad thing to be buried among the pines and hemlocks. "What would you want, Ma?" she asked. "I wish we thought to ask."

□   □   □

Sunday turned out to be one of those spectacular spring days that people count on their fingers. Erin wished she could just stay home and read, or do some spring-cleaning, or maybe even do a little fishing on the lake, but instead she headed out to Eco Woods, along with most of the town.

Jonathon Truscott and several residents, including Prosperity's mayor, stood in front of the double doors of the building holding a wide blue ribbon and a super-sized pair of scissors. Bobby Halloran from the Prosperity *Daily News*, digital camera in hand, stood ready to record the event. The local cable television crew had been taping the speeches and everyone seemed excited to finally see the inside of the building.

With the ribbon cut, Truscott smiled and said, "Before we start the tour of the Eco Center, I'd like to take you to see a sample resting place." He turned to the cameraman and said, "You can stop rolling for now. We have a short trek to the burial site."

Erin walked on the path behind the crowd, enjoying the peace of the woods. Sunlight poured through the trees forming beautiful patterns and she wished she'd brought her own camera.

They came to a natural clearing where several large rocks stood. Erin's trained eye noticed the prepared site.

Truscott faced the crowd and said, "Come a little closer and I'll explain the process to you."

Erin moved to the left of the crowd, closer to the rocks. From where she stood, the grave looked more like a deadfall trap than a final resting place.

"Green burials are a natural way to return to nature," Truscott began. "We use no chemicals. No caskets. No nails. No cement vaults. We bury you in a shroud, your grandmother's quilt, or your favorite blanket. Everything goes back to nature." On that he turned to the site, pulled up the raftlike covering, looked into the grave, then stumbled back, a shocked look on his face.

Erin stepped forward and looked into the hole. Lying at the bottom was what appeared to be a body wrapped in a cloth with ties at the head, arms and feet.

"What the hell is that?" one man said loud enough for the whole crowd to hear.

"Is that a real body?" a woman in front whispered.

Another man laughed nervously. "Boy, this guy really puts on a show."

Erin crouched, took her pen from her pocket, then carefully lifted a corner of the cloth tied around the head and looked inside. It definitely was a body and a dark stain behind the ear was probably dried blood. Erin got down on the ground, reached her hand into the cloth, and felt for a pulse. Nothing. She hadn't expected one. The skin felt cool, and judging from the very faint odor, the person hadn't been dead too long. Rigor hadn't set in.

Erin stood up, brushed the dirt from her slacks and said to the crowd. "Everybody back up now." She turned to Truscott. "I think you'd better bring the guests down to the Eco Center. We definitely have a body here. I'm not sure what we have, but I'll need to call in C.I.D."

Truscott looked puzzled.

Erin said, "The Maine State Police Criminal Investigation team from Alfred. They're responsible for investigating all homicides and suspicious deaths. I'm not saying it's a homicide, but it's damn suspicious. I'll get them here as soon as possible, but for now I'm officially calling this a crime scene until we know different."

Truscott didn't look too happy but he led the group away.

Bobby Halloran walked up to the hole and shot a couple of photos before Erin could stop him. "Hey, Bobby, back up, will you? Don't need any more footprints here." She climbed onto the rocks for a better look. "And you hold off on printing those photos. Download them for me. Heck, download all the photos you took today. I'll need to take a look. You did get some crowd shots?"

Halloran said, "Yeah. I got a bunch for the newspaper."

"Can you e-mail them to me? And copy them to a disk?" She nodded toward the crowd already making their way down the path. "You'll have to go with them now, but I'll give you first call when I know what's going on here."

She pulled out her two-way radio and called in the specifics to one of her officers, Ian McDermott. He'd make the call to Alfred, and bring the team up to the site when they arrived.

Erin squatted and stared at the shrouded body. From the newspaper articles, she'd expected it to look like a mummy and to be wrapped in white cloth, not tan with ties and looking like a wonton. Could it be a prank by the med students from UNE in Biddeford? They often had cadavers to work on. From this angle, she guessed the body to be five foot ten inches to six feet tall and heavyset. Probably male.

She jumped down from the rock. She wished she could turn the body over. See what she had. Maybe even unwrap it. But she knew better. She'd have to wait for C.I.D. She'd dealt with them a couple of years earlier when a woman's body had turned up on Still Water Beach. Erin had solved the murder that very night, her first and only murder, until now. Well, maybe now. If it was a murder and not a prank.

She took out her notebook and jotted down the time, and a description of the area, then estimated the number of people who had walked up the path to the site. Any footprints or marks in the dirt had been trampled on by at least fifty people. She'd have her officers search the woods on each side of the path for any scraps of cloth, cans or debris. Maybe she'd be lucky and get DNA from whatever they found. She made a note to ask Truscott just how much he'd prettied up the site for today's showing. She sure hoped his people had done a thorough job.

Truscott had let the cover drop to the side of the hole. Erin could see it was made from branches tied with cloth and would degrade overtime. She described it in her notes, but doubted if there'd be any fingerprints. With all the CSI shows on television, no one but the stupidest criminals committed a crime without gloves, but they'd still look it over carefully for trace evidence, like hair or fabric. She added a note to find out what material the shroud was made up of, and if Truscott had any shrouds missing from the Center.

Erin heard McDermott and the C.I.D. team coming before she spotted them. McDermott's burr stood out from the other voices. "Well, here we are, now," he said.

Before anyone walked into the area, one of the men started taking photographs. Erin shook hands with the team, then took out her notebook and read them her entries. After several minutes, and hundreds of photos, the team was ready to turn the body.

The photographer crouched by the hole and took several pictures as two of the team turned it over, then pulled open the side of the material tied around the head, exposing a wound.

Head trauma. Definite head trauma. Erin itched to get a look at the body, but that wasn't happening now. She was sure they'd call in an expert to look at the knots that kept the shroud together. She took out her cell phone, took a photo, e-mailed it to McDermott, then sent him a text message: "Show pix to Truscott."

Not five minutes later, Erin's cell phone rang. "Donnelly," Erin answered.

"I'm with Truscott," McDermott said. "He said it's a Kinkaraco shroud. Purelight. Plain muslin, unbleached. They go for around $300. He ordered twenty of them. I have him counting them now to see if one's missing."

"Good work."

Erin overheard Truscott say there were only eighteen, and he hadn't used any. Before McDermott could repeat it she said, "Got that. Ask him who had access to them."

After McDermott asked Truscott, he repeated to Erin, "He said he'd be the only one with access, but a bunch of high school kids helped with cleanup yesterday. One of them could have taken them without his knowing."

"Okay. Tell him to make a list of their names, then come back up." She took out her notebook, wrote down everything about the shroud, and then went over to the lead officer and filled him in.

He lifted an eyebrow and said, "Could be a miscount from the factory."

"Could be. McDermott and I will take a look around, just in case."

Erin looked for natural paths through the trees. She'd learned tracking from her grandfather when she was a kid. He'd taught her how to find her way out of the Maine woods by following her own tracks back out. She knew to look for footprints, broken branches, disturbed pine needles, and anything else that didn't fit into the quiet beauty of the woods.

It didn't take Erin long to notice that the trail north of the rocks appeared to have been swept with something like a pine branch. She doubted that Truscott would have had his help groom more than needed. She yelled to the state police photographer, and waited while he took photos before she proceeded along the path and found a freshly dug area covered with pine branches.

"Looks like another one," she said to the photographer. "I'll get more of my guys here and start a grid search."

At sunset, they called off the search. They'd only found the two sites and both bodies had been taken to Augusta.

□   □   □

Erin arrived at the Crime lab as the expert on knots was finishing his part of the investigation. "Amateurs," he said. "Looks like two different people tied the knots, but neither knew what they were doing."

The two shrouded bodies were on cold steel tables in a large room. C.I.D. requested Erin to be there when they removed the shrouds to help with possible identification. On the drive from Prosperity to Augusta, she'd gone over several possibilities and recorded her thoughts on a small cassette player she kept in her squad car.

The big question had been why there and why then. Did Truscott have enemies from the past? Had he ticked off someone who wanted to embarrass him now? She'd have someone look into his past real estate deals. According to the newspaper, he owned two other Eco Centers. One in California and one in New Jersey. Maybe he'd pissed off the Jersey mob and they were sending him a message.

One of her officers had already taken a ride to the University of New England and reported back that no cadavers were missing, so that ruled out a prank by the med students. And there hadn't been any recent deaths in town, so she doubted Bruckner's would have any bodies lying around. Then again, Fred Bruckner couldn't be too happy with the Eco Center opening, especially since his price for a burial was three times the price of a green burial. She doubted he'd do anything so stupid and possibly lose his license and his life's work, but that didn't rule out his kids. She'd have to talk to them when she got back into town.

Erin watched as the knot of the first shroud was untied at the neck. She moved a little closer as the lab tech lifted the corners out to the left and right, much like an old-fashioned triangular diaper. When the tech lifted the last flap and the face was finally exposed, Erin felt like she'd been sucker-punched. It took all her strength to calmly say, "That's Wilfred Dunbar."

The tech nodded, asked for the correct spelling of his name, then walked to the other table. Erin took a minute to compose her thoughts before joining him there. Dunbar was a pain in the ass and a loudmouthed drunk, but he had never seemed offensive enough to lead to murder.

She concentrated on the tech's hands as he untied the knot on the second shroud and was stunned a second time when she saw the victim was Delphis Fournier.

She didn't know how she was going to tell Mandy her grandfather was dead.

☐ ☐ ☐

On the drive back, Erin picked up the recorder and noted the time she'd arrived at Perigini's the night before and started a list of who was in the restaurant at the time of Dunbar's and Fournier's fight, if you could call it that.

Dunbar had sat with her, ordered from Mandy, and that's when he spotted Delphis Fournier at the counter, where they'd had words. More like Dunbar had spewed heated words at Fournier.

The owners of the restaurant, Rosa and Tony Perigini, had been working the kitchen. They'd popped out to say hello to Erin when she'd first arrived. Jimmy Lamothe and his wife, April, were seated in a booth near the door and a couple of teens sat at the counter.

That left the bartender and Mandy.

Erin made a note to ask Mandy if Dunbar had talked to anyone else after Erin left for the nursing home and, more importantly, how long had Dunbar and her grandfather stayed at the restaurant. Did

Dunbar leave after his meal was ready? Or did he start on Fournier again? There had to be more here though. It certainly wasn't a murder-suicide.

□ □ □

Erin called McDermott just outside of town and told him she'd swing by and pick him up. Technically he was off duty, but she knew she could count on him to come with her when she broke the news to Wilfred Dunbar's wife and Mandy Fournier.

It was nearly 1:00 A.M. when they pulled up in front of Dunbar's house. The porch light barely lit the path to the front door. Erin took a few deep breaths, and went over in her head what she would say. When she rang the doorbell, Dunbar's dog started barking, and she saw a light go on through the side panes. Erin looked at McDermott, who was standing behind her. He looked as pale as she felt.

The door opened, and Evelyn Dunbar took one look at them and said, "This can't be good. Come in."

They followed her into a small living room off the entryway. She sat in a wingback chair, and gestured for them to sit on the sofa.

Erin started. "Mrs. Dunbar, I'm afraid we have very bad news."

The woman pulled her robe tighter and held onto it for dear life as if to shield her body from what was to come. Erin noticed the blue veins bulging in her pale white hands. "I'm afraid your husband is dead."

"Oh, my God." Her hands moved from her robe to cover her face.

Erin waited a moment before saying, "Mrs. Dunbar, have you heard about the, ah, finds at the Eco Center?"

Mrs. Dunbar nodded. "It's been on the news all night."

"Your husband was one of the victims."

"But why would he be there? He ranted about that place the whole time it was being built."

Erin remembered Dunbar's feelings about the center. He

wouldn't be caught dead there. "Mrs. Dunbar, when did you see your husband last?"

"I guess Saturday night. No, afternoon. I had a migraine, so Wilfred said to go ahead and take my medicine, and then go to bed early. He had errands to run, and he said he'd get his own dinner."

"Did you hear him come in?"

"No. The medicine I take really knocks me out. When I got up this morning, I thought he'd left early. He does that sometimes. Goes to the office and works all day on cases he has coming up in court."

Erin had nearly forgotten that Dunbar was a defense attorney. "Has he had any problems with any of his clients?"

Mrs. Dunbar shook her head. "He doesn't . . . didn't discuss his cases with me."

Erin made a note to have his cases looked into, but her gut told her it wasn't a drunk driver or petty thief that smashed him in the back of the head. "Is there someone we can call for you?"

"My sister." Erin dialed the phone number Mrs. Dunbar gave her, then handed the phone to McDermott, and tipped her head to the right. McDermott got her message and walked out of the room to make the call.

"Mrs. Dunbar," Erin said, "the other victim is Delphis Fournier. Can you think of any reason why the two of them would be targeted?"

"Just that they were best friends. That is before the whole green burial thing."

□   □   □

McDermott was quiet on the way over to Delphis Fournier's house. Erin knew he was giving her space to think about how to tell Mandy. They had waited with Mrs. Dunbar until her sister got there, so it was nearly two-thirty in the morning now. All the lights were out when they pulled up to the old farmhouse.

Erin pulled her flashlight from the Velcro tab on the side of her cruiser door. It was pretty isolated on this section of road. The town cemetery was directly across the street from the house, and Eco Woods was further down the road. Erin knew Fournier's Farm had been quite an operation in its heyday. All that remained after the Eco sale was the house and about an acre of land. Erin guessed the property would go to Mandy now that Delphis was dead. She hoped he'd had enough sense to make a will so Mandy's mother couldn't show up and claim it after all these years.

Erin knocked on the door and listened for any sound inside the house. After a while, she rapped the flashlight handle on the wood. A light finally came on above, and she heard sounds from within and finally saw a light in the downstairs. The door swung open and Mandy stood there looking at them. She had on a white tank top, and gray boxer shorts. A short black silk robe hung open over them. Her jet-black hair, usually tied back at the restaurant, hung freely over her shoulders and her bare feet sported black nail polish. Smudged mascara ringed her eyes, and her lips looked strangely pale. She wore a black leather string around her neck with a heavy silver cross hanging from it.

"Mandy, can we come in?" Erin asked.

"I was sleeping."

"Yeah, we know. We have some bad news to tell you."

"Bad news," she repeated.

"Yeah, Mandy. It's about your grandfather."

"What about him?" She grabbed the door and looked behind her. And pulled it closed.

Erin looked over at McDermott and raised one eyebrow. McDermott said, "We'd rather talk to you inside."

Without a word, Mandy opened the door and they followed her to the back of the house. Erin had never been inside before so she made mental notes as she walked behind Mandy.

Mandy reached for a light chain and gave it a pull. She'd led them to the kitchen. She sat at the table, and then McDermott turned a chair around and sat down, too. Erin walked over to the sink, glanced at its contents and looked out the window. "Mandy, your grandfather. When did you see him last?"

She shrugged her shoulders. "I don't know. Yesterday some time or maybe Saturday. You know I work nights at the restaurant and he's in bed before I get home."

"Did you hear about Eco Woods?" McDermott asked.

Mandy yawned, got up, grabbed a glass from a cabinet, then poured herself some milk and sat back down. "Course I've heard about it. Everybody knows about it."

"I mean about what happened yesterday. They found two bodies there."

Mandy drank down the milk, then wiped her mouth with her sleeve. "Yeah, so? Isn't that what it's for?"

Erin said, "One of them was your grandfather. Whose vehicle is that out back?"

Mandy got up and started pacing like a caged animal looking for a way to escape. Erin had seen this pose so many times. She knew McDermott hadn't caught on yet because he hadn't seen the vehicle parked on the grass in the back yard. Erin could only make out the front bumper in the light from the window, but she was sure of what it was. And McDermott hadn't seen the dishes in the sink. Dishes for two with pretty fresh food clinging to them.

Mandy's eyes grew big. "It's my boyfriend's."

Erin glanced at McDermott. From his tightened stance, she could tell he'd finally noticed the shift.

"Where is he?"

"Upstairs. He's sleeping."

McDermott rose from the chair, unsnapped the holster on his gun. "I'll get him."

Erin's phone rang. "Sit there," she said to Mandy, before

answering it.

Less than a minute later McDermott pushed a shirtless, barefoot kid into the kitchen. Erin would have recognized him even if his father's hearse wasn't parked out back. She just didn't know which Bruckner he was.

McDermott pushed him into a seat. Erin grabbed his chin, turned his head side to side, and then looked at his hands and arms. Even with the poorly tended goatee, she could see multiple scratches on his face. "Been running through the woods?" Erin asked.

He touched his face, looked down at his hands. "These scratches? I must have got them when I helped with the cleanup."

"You were at the Eco Center?" McDermott asked.

"Yeah. It sucks. I had to do it or get a failing grade."

Mandy tried to stand up, but Erin pushed her back into the chair. Erin turned to McDermott. "C.I.D. called. They found a note in Fournier's shroud."

The Bruckner kid whipped his head toward Mandy and yelled, "You put a note in the shroud! Why the hell did you do that?"

"Well, he was my grandfather," Mandy said to the kid. She turned to Erin, put her chin up and said, "Cause I loved 'im, ya know."

"You kids better not say anything more," Erin said. But she couldn't help herself; she had to ask Mandy one more question as she handcuffed her. "Why Dunbar?"

"He came here looking for my grandfather and saw what we did." Mandy started crying—looking more like the kid she was. "He was making me wait until I turned twenty-one to give me the money he got for selling the land. I'd be old by then."

"Don't say another word," Erin warned. "We're taking you in."

"He put it in a stupid trust," Mandy wailed.

McDermott said under his breath as he handcuffed the Bruckner kid, "Looks like your trust has turned to dust."

Lights Out

J. E. Seymour

It was six days into the power failure when we got the phone call I'd been dreading. I knew sooner or later I'd get the calls; we'd already had two people die of carbon monoxide poisoning. That happened only three days in. But this was worse.

"Hey, Chris, I need you out here."

I looked up at my sergeant, Bill Curry. Bill and I make up the full-time contingent of police officers in this town of Liberty, New Hampshire. We've got a part-timer too, but he was at home, sleeping. I was wishing I was home sleeping, but I was in my office, catnapping in my rickety chair, and when Bill stepped in and spoke I came down hard and almost tipped the old chair over.

"What do you need?"

"Albert Foss hijacked a PSNH truck out on Route 23. Made them go up to Trundle Bed Road and he's standing there now, holding a shotgun, telling them they've got to fix the wires."

"Shit."

"Yeah."

I could hear the phone ringing in the other room, our dispatcher doing her best to answer the calls. Marie was just as tired and overwhelmed as we were at this point, but she just kept talking as I walked past her, pulling on my parka.

"D'you call anybody else, Bill?"

"No, ma'am," he replied, "I wanted to talk to you first."

"That was probably the right thing to do. Old Albert might react badly to the Staties coming at him."

"They'll get wind of it soon enough."

"I know, but if we can get out there first, maybe we can keep it from escalating."

Bill and I piled into the Bronco and I stared out the window while he drove. Things were still a mess, even six days in, with trees all over the place, telephone poles snapped in half, wires down.

"How did it go over on Pine Hill Road?"

Bill had been out this morning putting sawhorses at the end of Pine Hill Road because some dope had plugged in a generator wrong and the wires, still down on the road, were now backfed and live. "The folks were a tad unhappy about not being able to drive in and out."

"I wish we could just move the wires ourselves."

"Some sort of union rules."

We pulled off Main Street onto Trundle Bed Road and stopped. It was a long straight stretch, and I could see the yellow truck about a half mile down, its amber light revolving slowly. Albert's plow truck was slewed across the street, with its own amber light on the roof. I couldn't tell from this distance if the PSNH guys were working or not.

"I hear the governor is going to send out National Guard troops to anyone who wants them. I guess New Falls already has a couple."

"We don't need them." I jumped down out of the truck, double checking my weapon, and pulled my winter hat down tight on my head. "Let's go talk to Albert."

As we walked in closer I could see the linemen were actually working, up in the cherry picker, doing whatever it is they do. Albert was standing by the truck, dressed in his snowmobile suit, smoking a cigar, holding a shotgun. He whirled and raised the weapon when he spotted Bill and me. I had to fight to keep from drawing down on him; I had to remind myself that this guy was my friend, that I didn't want to shoot him. Bill had no such compunctions and he pulled his semi-auto and held it out, stiff-armed.

"Drop the weapon!"

"Bill," I tried.

Albert's response was to drop the cigar and fire the shotgun over our heads, and I tackled Bill so that we both hit the dirt, just in case.

"You need to leave, Chris. And take that trigger-happy youngster with you. I don't want to hurt no one."

"Albert, you can't do this." I looked up at him from my position on the ground, wondering if I could get to my feet without getting shot at again. I spoke to Bill under my breath. "You put your weapon away and go back to the car. Let me handle this."

"Chris," he protested.

"Just go." The smell of pine was so strong down on the ground it was making my eyes water.

Bill got up, tucked his gun in its holster, and backed down the road, hands well away from his body. "Take it easy, Albert, it's okay, I'm just going back to the truck." To me he added, "I'll call in a 10-66."

"I'd rather you didn't," I muttered, but I wasn't sure he heard me. "Okay, Albert?" I stood up, made no move toward my own Sig, just kept a steady gaze on Albert.

Albert lowered the shotgun. "What'd you have to come out here for, Chris? I just wanted to get my power back on. I've been running a generator but, man, it only keeps the fridge going and I'm out of water." He lowered his voice. "I've got a hundred bucks riding on the Patriots game. I need my TV. These guys only have to fix a couple of wires, there's power down to the main road." He waved a hand in the direction of his log home, the big dark screen showing through the front window.

"Albert, this isn't the way to get things done." I took a couple of tentative steps toward the older man.

"I ain't going to jail."

"Has anybody said anything about jail?"

Albert cocked his head toward the guys in the cherry picker, who had stopped their work and were leaning over the edge of the bucket, looking down at us. "They said I'd go to jail."

As I moved closer I could see that Albert's beard had icicles in it. I was freezing, and I'd only been out here for about ten minutes now. I could imagine how cold he was. "It's not up to them."

He nodded and lowered the shotgun further, letting the stock slip through his gloved hands.

"You cold?"

He nodded. "A bit."

"Why don't we take a break? We can sit in the Bronco; it's warm there and you can watch these guys work. Just give me the shotgun, and we'll go down and sit in the truck, okay?" I took a couple more steps, my pac boots crunching on ice and a million pine needles.

"It's supposed to snow again tomorrow, you know that?"

"Yeah, I heard."

"What are we supposed to do?"

I was moving steadily toward him, counting on keeping him occupied. "I think we've got some hot coffee in the Bronco."

He actually lifted his head at that. Sniffled. Wiped his nose with the back of a glove. Dropped the shotgun. I picked it up and put a hand on his arm, glancing up as the guys in the bucket started applauding.

"You got any other guns on you, Albert?"

"No, ma'am."

"That's good. You know I got to put the cuffs on you, right? Just to make it look good?" I could hear sirens now, knew the state troopers must be on the way, and wanted to get Albert someplace safe before they got here.

He brought his hands behind his back and nodded as a drop of something fell from the end of his nose. I couldn't imagine old Albert crying, but I handed him a tissue and he wiped his nose with his left hand while I snugged my cuffs on his right. He tucked the tissue into a pocket as two state troopers came roaring up to the end of the road, all code three, loaded for bear. Two cruisers, by God. Practically the whole of Troop F.

Albert pulled away from me and grabbed for his shotgun. I hit the deck and rolled, coming up with my own weapon a good five feet to the right, with snow and pine needles in my mouth, yelling at everybody to just stop where they were, but Albert had a bead on the Staties and they weren't going to understand that I'd known Albert since I was a kid and he wouldn't hurt anyone. Albert actually squeezed off a round—it appeared he was using buckshot from the pattern it made on the side door of the Bronco. The recoil made his feet slip out from under him and he dropped like a tree coated in ice, down to the road, the return fire from the troopers going over his head. I threw myself onto him at this point, got the shotgun away from him, and pulled him back to his feet just as the TV in his front window burst into life.

On the House

Hank Phillippi Ryan

D o you think he's dangerous?"

"Ron, you mean? Or Cooper? Down, Cooper." I pushed the Lab's massive yellow paw from my bare leg. With a big-eyed look that meant "It was just this once," he curled up under my bar stool, nose on my sandal. I love Cooper. He's the only one whose feet are bigger than mine, and he might just hate Ron as much as I do. I took a sip of my ill-advised third glass of Shiraz and looked across the bar at Errol. Gave him a "one more" signal.

"I know, you mean Ron," I said to Jess. "And no, he's not dangerous. He's just a jerk."

"A two-timing, paranoid, self-obsessed moron." Jess was attempting to fish a stubborn green olive from the bottom of her martini glass. Failing, she stabbed it with her little red plastic sword, and held it triumphantly. "If I could do this to Ron the moron, don't think I'd give it a second thought. Head on a pike. Finally. Justice."

I stabbed my own sword into the little white straw I'd been fussing with. My napkin was already in shreds.

Giving me a patient smile, Errol swept up the shards and placed a new napkin on the battered zinc bar. Followed quickly by another glass of Shiraz.

"On the house, Rachel," he said. "Anyone who's had as bad a day as you have. As bad a couple of months. Errol's can provide one more glass of red."

"Thanks," I said, trying to keep the bitterness out of my voice. Errol meant well. And, true, he'd been hearing my Ron-laments for months now. But the phrase makes me wince every time. On the House was our dream agency. The one Ron and I were going to open to make us both real estate millionaires. Competing brokers, we'd met at an open house in Back Bay. Neither of us got the sale, but we got each other. For better, and not long after, for worse. Then much, much worse.

Cooper shifted under my stool, probably having some dog dream. My only dream was that I'd never have to set one more toe in divorce court again. At this point, whatever Ron wanted, he could have. All I wanted was out. But out was not in the cards. Tomorrow, we'd be back in a stifling probate courtroom in downtown Boston. And I knew my return to singlehood was not imminent.

"I'm going to be married forever." I stared into my glass of wine. Whine. "I'm going to be married to the mistake forever. He's like a—"

"Leech," Jess offered. My best friend could always find the right word.

"It's symbiosis gone all wrong," I agreed. "We used to live for each other. I remember that, don't I? Then suddenly, I was going to work. And he was—"

A drift of some floral scent overpowered the bar fragrance of salted almonds and beer and twists of lemon. I smelled—hair spray? And expensive perfume. And turned to see the Platonic ideal of blondeness slide onto the stool beside me. I scooted closer to Jess, giving the Prom Queen newcomer all the space she needed.

"Well, he told you he was going to work," Jess said. "He kissed you goodbye. And then went back to bed. How were you supposed to know he was blowing off his real estate job? With—what'd he say? Chronic fatigue?"

"Chronic fathead," I said, taking the last sip of glass three. "He's got enough energy to sneak around with other women and shop with my credit cards. He's got enough energy to criticize everything I do. He's got enough energy to file for divorce. Moron."

Cooper shifted position, stretching out his front paws and almost knocking over my red leather purse. Ron always called him "Klutz." Or "Galoot." Coop did everything a dog could do to insult him back. Planting mud-streaked paws on his Italian suits. Chewing his shoes. The incident of the sweater drawer.

Errol placed another glass in front of me. My brain sent warnings about tomorrow morning and puffy eyes and the harbor-side condo I was showing at the crack of ten.

"Back in court," I continued, shaking my head at the relentlessness of it all. My life seemed ruined before it had really begun. "I'm thirty-something. I'm in good shape. My hair is still naturally brownish. My dog likes me. I'm pretty successful, all things considered. And yet I'm—"

"Bummed," Jess suggested, clinking glasses. Her hair, scrabbly and almost-maroon, looked somehow hip instead of wacky. She was a good actress, established in local theater. And she could wear those little ankle boots with a short skirt. I'd look like I was in outgrown hand-me-downs. "He really asking you to pay alimony?"

Errol put a glass in front of the Prom Queen. Chardonnay, of course.

I turned my back on her, just a bit. But I couldn't avoid her face in the lighted expanse of mirror behind Errol. When she raised her glass at my reflection, offering a friendly smile, I managed a noncommittal one in return. No need to be a bitch just because I'm being taken to the cleaners by a weasel in a Prince Charming outfit. Whatever. I knew what I meant. Being on glass four now meant my metaphors might be turning unreliable.

"Yup. He wants me to pay him. Beyond ridiculous. Wish I

could, I don't know, do something," I said. I used Jess's little sword to stab holes in a cardboard St. Pauli Girl coaster. Right in the milk-maid's nose. Whatever she was. Beer maid. "Like, erase the condo listings from his computer. Change the speed dial phone numbers on his cell phone so whenever he called someone, he'd get someone different."

"Funny," Jess agreed, contemplating. "But it wouldn't get you a divorce."

True. That was the problem. All I wanted was a divorce. And Ron was doing everything he could to delay it.

"Why? Why? Why?" I asked, perhaps more dramatically than necessary. Cooper looked up, his cocoa eyes questioning, making sure I was okay. I blew him a kiss, and he flopped his tail once, understanding. "I realize he ridicules me to cover up his own fail-ures. But he knows he lied. And cheated. And stole."

"He's doing it to make you miserable," Jess said. She hooked those little heels over the rail of her stool, facing me. "That's all he has now. That's like his job, you know? He gets up in the morning and thinks of ways to make you miserable."

"Well, he's damn good at it," I said to my wine. "I'm miserable."

"Last call," Errol said.

I looked at my watch. "You're kidding. It's one-thirty on a school night?"

"A court night," Jess reminded me.

"Men are like that." The voice came from behind me. Not a bit-ter voice, not a sad voice. Just straightforward. Matter of fact.

I turned.

Jess leaned her elbows on the bar, curving herself to see past me.

"I've known too many of them," Prom Queen added. She lifted her almost untouched Chardonnay, toasting me again. Her pale lip-stick had not even left a smudge on the polished glass. "And they all want the same thing. Don't they? They all want their own way."

Well, that was interesting. Cooper lifted his head, sniffed, and gave her his most adoring look. That was interesting, too.

I looked up, catching Errol's eye. He was in classic bartender pose, towel and martini glass. He shrugged.

"Last call," he said.

□ □ □

"Do you think she's dangerous?"

Jess moved a stack of magazines with her foot, making room on my just-dusted coffee table for her legs. She leaned back against the puffy navy cushions of my couch, staring at the ceiling.

I swatted Jess's feet back to the floor, replacing them with a casual but thoughtful display of cheese and crackers. Prom Queen's name turned out to be Camilla Ayers. She was on the way. And she was offering an interesting proposition.

"No," I said. "Camilla's got a genius plan. And in a little while, we're going to find out if it can work."

Cooper snuffled towards the brie. I pointed sternly, an I-am-the-master-you-are-the-dog gesture to indicate that cheese was people food. Cooper pretended to be confused, the way he always does when I give a command. Most often, he does just the opposite of what I say.

It wasn't my usual Saturday afternoon. But yesterday had been my usual Friday. Court, arguments, and Ron's histrionics. He was representing himself after he'd refused to pay his original lawyer. Typical Ron: the rules don't apply to him. Oh, he was out of money. Oh, he was too sick to work. Oh, "the defendant" should give him alimony. Oh, she got the dog just to drive him crazy.

It was all I could do not to leap out of my rickety wooden chair. I couldn't believe the judge stood for it. Sat for it. But she did. And Ron got yet another continuance.

How could I have made such a life-ruining mistake? I'd longed for a husband. A partner. Maybe even a baby. But Ron soon decided everything wrong in his life was my fault. And never let me forget it.

I looked toward my front door, even though there's no way to see who's walking up the front path. I'm on the top floor, and you have to buzz to get through the main entrance. No buzz yet.

"Don't you think it's genius?" I said, looking to Jess for reassurance. "I mean, I'm not hiring her to kill him. It's not like she's some FBI agent entrapping me into a sting. And there are no hidden cameras here. It's my own apartment."

Jess swiped a Sociable through the brie, using one finger to cut her gooey cheese away from the white triangle. "There are no real hired killers," she said, licking her finger. "They're all FBI agents. I've never understood why people don't realize that. I mean, don't they read the paper?"

"Probably not," I replied. For the millionth time, I made sure I had pulled out everything Camilla said she needed. Family photos. Wedding and vacation pictures. Memories now so poisoned she could keep them all forever, far as I was concerned. But she said she needed anything that could give her insight into Ron's background.

"How do you suppose she'll do it?"

Cooper leaped up, tail flailing, paws scrabbling on the hardwood floor, yipping like an over-wound toy. As the snare of the bell hit our human ears, Cooper jumped up against the front door, his pudgy yellow paws leaving even more marks on the painted metal. Stretched out, nose to tail, he was taller than I was.

"Down, Cooper," I said, for the millionth time. He didn't care. "Down."

"Here we go," I said to Jess.

"Your funeral," Jess replied.

◻ ◻ ◻

Sitting cross-legged on my couch, listening to the best idea I'd ever heard, I briefly wondered if Camilla Ayers was some angel sent by a heretofore unknown society for the protection of cruelty to wronged women. An avenging angel.

"So I'll tell him," she said, finishing up her 'proposal.' "No sex with me until he's absolutely divorced. Signed on the dotted line, no more continuances, no more court dates, you out of his life forever. Believe me, you'll soon be rid of him."

"You think it'll work?" Looking at her effortless blonde hair, her no-makeup make-up, her toned biceps and graceful ankles, it was easy to imagine her getting anything she wanted. From men at least. Even Cooper was smitten, staring at her as if she were a morsel of bacon, placing his nose protectively near her delicately pink toes. I mulled Camilla's idea. Brilliant, but certainly a little out there.

"He's a jerk," Jess said. "He's a manipulative, megalomaniacal, selfish—jerk. My vote? If Camilla does her thing, he'll be toast. Jell-O. Mincemeat."

Cooper lifted his eyebrows toward Jess at the mention of meat. But he didn't leave his post.

Camilla nodded, one lock of blond falling across her brown eyes. And by brown, I mean molten chocolate. Everything about her was delicious. I had to admit, I could see how it might work.

"It'll work," Camilla said. "It's worked every time."

"You mean you've—?" I said.

"You mean it's a—?" Jess said at the same time.

Camilla held up a hand. "Let's just see what we have here," she said, stopping our speculation. She turned a few pages in one leather-bound photo album. "Wedding took place at a ski resort? So he skis?"

I nodded. "Double black diamond."

"School? Family relationships? How does he get along with his mother? Does he have sisters? Do you have his bank records? What's his favorite food? Was he married before?"

By the time we'd finished, all the brie and crackers were gone.

We'd given up tea for Chardonnay. Least I could do. And plan Get-Ron was under way. My divorce was going to happen. I was convinced.

What's more, Camilla had promised I could watch.

□   □   □

"Over there, behind the palm tree," I whispered, though I didn't need to, pointing Jess in the right direction. We were positioned on stools at the bar in Larissa, the chicest restaurant in town. Three tables behind us, reflected perfectly in mirror view, were Angel Camilla and Devil Ron.

"Why do men always fall for the hair flipping thing?" Jess whispered, too.

"Who cares," I said. We were dolled up in wigs from Jess's costume stash, Burberry scarves, and fake glasses. Camilla had promised she'd make sure he didn't see us, but Jess insisted we take precautions. "Look at him. He's literally drooling."

I felt happy for the first time in months. Camilla was in full flirt mode. Laughing, touching Ron's hand, twirling her hair. She was probably talking about skiing and having a younger brother. And loving Italian food and watching the World Cup. Just like Ron. Oh, what a coincidence.

He was a goner. And there was nothing illegal about it. The whole point was that she wasn't going to sleep with him. So it wasn't like she was a hooker, or even an escort. She was just on a date. Acting. Not a woman alive who hasn't done exactly the same thing. And no one was getting hurt. Except Ron. Who deserved it. And he would just be as angry as I was. Welcome to my world, I silently telegraphed across the room. How could I have thought he loved me? I'd made a huge miscalculation. He'd made me miserable. Now it was my turn. I could ruin his life. Just long enough to get free of him.

"Is it creepy that you're not paying her?" Jess asked. She adjusted her plaid silk scarf. "Or would it be creepier if you did pay?"

I had to admit that had been nagging at me too. When I'd asked, hesitantly, about 'reimbursement,' Camilla had smiled, waving me off.

"It's on the house," she'd said.

□ □ □

"You're lucky to be out of his life, I must say." Camilla's voice crackled through my cell phone.

"Why?" I asked, almost shrugging. I had Cooper on his leash, a cloth carryall of groceries over one shoulder, my purse over the other. We were walking home from the grocery in the quiet May twilight, one of those wonderful Boston evenings where the fragrance of the harbor smells like salt and sun, and summer is more than a promise.

Nothing Camilla could say could ruin my night. Our plan was working. And soon I would be single again.

"He doesn't like you very much," Camilla said. Her voice, even over the phone, was gentle and tentative. "I mean, did you have some quilts your grandmother made?"

"Gran's quilts?' I said, alarms suddenly going off in my head. "Yes, they're treasures. Made from her wedding dress. And her mother's. They're in my wooden chest, in the guest bedroom. In tissue paper."

"They're not, I'm afraid," Camilla said. "Ron told me he sold them. Your wedding china, too. He left the carton marked 'china' in the storage locker, he told me. And he was quite gleeful when he told me he'd packed it with old paperbacks and taped it up again. Said he wished he could be there when you opened it."

Tears came to my eyes, blurring the brownstones and Cooper and the emerging moon. I stopped in the middle of the sidewalk. Cooper sat, looking up at me, inquiring. Two twenty-somethings, all earbuds and miniskirts and pushing-the-season tank tops looked at me scathingly as they passed.

"He's crazy," I whispered.

"Maybe," Camilla agreed. "What did you do to him, anyway?"

"Nothing." I could hear the anguish in my own voice. I'd thought about this very question, endlessly. Was it the building I sold? He said, 'out from under him'? That I was more successful than he was? Suddenly, nothing I had done was right. He even hated Cooper, a squirming birthday present I'd chosen to charm him. First, Ron had gotten quiet. Then mean. Not physically mean, but still. I never felt quite safe. "Nothing."

"Well, it's almost over," Camilla said. "He's hooked. I'm sure of it."

□   □   □

I slit open the long white envelope, slowly, carefully, as if what was inside was so important I didn't want to risk ripping the paper. I pulled out a kitchen chair and sat at my little table by the sliding glass doors to the deck. Carefully drawing a folded piece of white paper from the envelope, I took a deep breath. And flapped open the top. Then the bottom.

"Decreed this twenty-ninth day of May," it began. In the middle, a lot of legalese that meant no alimony, no payments from the "defendant" to the "plaintiff," no obligations, no connections, no ties, no nothing. The condo was all mine. And by the power vested in the Commonwealth of Massachusetts, the document ended, this divorce is final.

All the blood rushed to my face, then rushed out again. I looked out my doors into the crayon blue sky and greeting card white clouds. I looked again at my third finger left hand, as if to reassure myself. Single, single, single.

Thank you, Camilla.

There was just one scene left to play out. And it was going to be even more satisfying than this life-changing piece of paper.

□ □ □

I pulled a little black wheelie suitcase behind me, just to make sure I blended into the hubbub of Logan airport. I could have pretended to be meeting someone rather than going away, but somehow the suitcase was a comforting addition to my disguise.

I smiled, like a cartoon cat, licking my chops as I walked to the pod of white plastic seats just outside the Starbucks in Terminal B. Camilla had suggested the nearby currency exchange booth would provide a good cover for me to watch the final episode of this soap opera. And suddenly, now that I was no longer an actor in it, it was my favorite show.

Baseball cap, fake brown ponytail courtesy of Jess's stash, big Jackie O sunglasses and a Life is Good sweatshirt. I was a fashion mess. But this evening wasn't about looking good, it was about feeling good. And I was about to feel great.

Jess had wanted to come with me. I almost said yes. In the end, we decided it was too risky. Camilla and I had planned to meet at my place after it was over. She would return my stuff. And we would say goodbye. I'd gotten her a little present, a silver bracelet from Tiffany, as a thank-you gift. Nothing could be reward enough for saving my life. But jewelry is always a start.

Five-fifteen is a busy time in Terminal B. All the day-tripping New York moguls flying between Boston and the Big Apple are walking purposefully toward the gates. Then there he was, pulling a black wheelie of his own, and looking rendezvous-ready in jeans, a starched pale blue shirt, loafers with no socks. Sunglasses perched on his sandy hair. I had the tiniest flurry of the Ron-I-used-to know. Which was instantly erased by the Ron-I-do-know.

I put the Boston *Globe* in front of my face.

Ron looked right past me, searching the streams of travelers for, I knew, the woman of his dreams. Dream on, Buster. I know what you don't. She's not showing up. There's no trip to Bermuda. No pink sand, no long-awaited night in a pink-pillowed canopy bed in the ultra-glamorous Breezewoods.

Was it unworthy of me to gloat? Sitting hidden behind the newspaper, I stared at the words, unseeing. Maybe this had gone too far. He'd fallen for Camilla's scheme. Our scheme. Maybe it should be enough for me just to know that. I should just live my life, Ron-free, without actually needing to watch his heart get broken. I would get over the whole thing, in time. And though he had broken my heart, it wasn't fatal.

It would be closure, Jess had told me. I supposed so.

I inched down the paper, just enough to see him plop down in a white chair, drawing his suitcase closer. He looked at his watch. Looked up. And looked at his watch again. He adjusted the sunglasses on this head. Retied the sweater around his neck. Took a newspaper out of the side pocket of his wheelie. Mr. Heartthrob.

I looked at my watch, too. Camilla wasn't really late. Yet. I was well hidden behind the currency exchange. I was out of view. I put the newspaper in my lap and brazenly watched the show.

Some of the fight went out of me as I saw Ron's composure disintegrate. As the time ticked by, he stood, craning his neck at the oncoming stream of passengers. He checked his watch. I stopped counting how many times he took out his cell phone. I stopped counting how many times he punched in numbers, becoming increasingly concerned. He stopped a blue-uniformed state police officer, pointing to his watch, waving his arms, obviously asking him something.

The officer shook his head, shrugging. The officer looked at Ron's suitcase. And then whatever the officer said made Ron look even angrier.

Ron suddenly looked down at his hand. Turning his back on the cop, he flipped open the phone he was holding. As he listened, I watched his face morph from relief, to shock, to anger. His face twisted. He said something, then slammed the phone closed. By that time, anger hardly described it.

I guess she had told him the truth. Enough of it at least. Camilla—had she given him her real name?—was not going to appear. Game, set and match.

◻   ◻   ◻

Camilla was late.

I felt like Ron, looking at my watch, checking my phone for messages. Calling her cell. I wasn't angry. But I sure was concerned. I looked out over the railing of my deck as if I could see someone coming. I knew I couldn't. The water beyond Boston Harbor was nicely visible, but straight down, it was just parking lot. Ron had insisted we didn't need the expensive all-water-view unit.

Cooper wagged his tail as if it were just another spring night, poking his nose through the wooden slats of the deck's waist-high redwood fence. Seagulls dived and swooped, lining up along the rooftop of the condo across the way. Red and green lights blinked in the sky, planes taking off and landing in the distance. Planes Ron and Camilla would not be on. I had to smile, remembering. I knew Camilla wasn't in Bermuda. So where was she?

"You were coming at nine-thirty, right?" I continued my latest message, leaning my backside against the rail. "It's ten. I'm a bit worried about you. Like I said, it was great. But call me."

I called Jess on my landline, keeping my cell open for Camilla. Jess was probably at rehearsal, I knew, and had to keep her cell off. I left her a message anyway. While Cooper single-mindedly wolfed down his dinner back in the kitchen, I picked up the robin's egg blue box with the white satin ribbon, and moved Camilla's gift, two glasses, and a cooler of Chardonnay to the little table on the deck.

I pulled out the cork and poured a glass, toasting myself. Why not? My condo. My life back. The balance was resumed.

When my front door opened, it took me a second to understand.

In one hand, Ron was holding his key. In Ron's other hand—was Camilla's hand. They were in matching pale blue sweaters, Camilla's tight and not quite meeting the waist of her white slacks. Her high heels were ridiculous. Camilla and Ron were both smiling.

"How?" I began. I edged away from them, farther out onto the deck. My mind was racing. Calculating. "What the hell—?"

"Hey, Rach," he said, giving me the twinkle I used to crave. Then he leaned down, and kissed Camilla on that spun-sugar hair. "We didn't want to leave without saying goodbye. Our flight to Bermuda leaves in two hours."

"But she told me—you were supposed to—" I looked at the little box with the bracelet inside. Then at Camilla. And then my brain went into lockdown.

"You got what you wanted, didn't you? The divorce?" Ron asked. "And now I have what I wanted."

"But—" I kept edging away, as far from him as I could.

Ron took three steps toward me, little Camilla glued to his side.

"You thought you were so clever," he said. "Concocting your little scheme to humiliate me. Cammie and I would roar with laughter at you. Every night. I couldn't believe you fell for it. You were never clever, Rach. You were boring and predictable. And a dupe to the last moment."

He draped one arm over Camilla's shoulder, his fingers grazing her chest. She turned toward him. I could almost hear her purr. And then she looked at me.

"Thanks for the china," she said.

I opened my mouth to say something. Anything. But my brain was chaos and my heart was certainly about to stop.

"Is that wine for us?" Camilla unwound herself and gestured at the glass. She stopped, fluttered her lashes. "And that little box for me?"

Without waiting for an answer, she crossed to the table and

picked up the box.

My brain kicked in. That night in the restaurant. They hadn't been faking. It was all real.

"No," I croaked, barely a whisper.

She pulled the white ribbon.

"No!" I yelled. Then threw my glass of wine. Straight at Ron. It missed, shattering onto the hardwood floor behind him.

Ron laughed, dodging a splash of Chardonnay.

In the airport. It had all been a ruse. "Just to, just to, make me miserable?" I was hissing, teeth clenched, everything clenched.

Camilla backed away, leaning against the deck railing, her laughter pealing. "I truly didn't think you'd fall for it," she said. "It's kind of funny, really, if you think about it."

She laughed again. Ron laughed too, deep and happy, moving toward her as if drawn into her orbit.

I whirled to face him; hate, horror, and humiliation twisting my stomach. My vision was a blur.

A yellow blur.

Cooper. Thrilled and befuddled by adoration, he thundered from the kitchen. He must have heard Camilla laughing. And, even at dinnertime, could not resist her.

With a final leap, he jumped, delirious with joy. Paws on the pale blue sweater. Another wine glass flew. Hers, almost in slow motion, arcing into the air above the parking lot.

"Down, Cooper!" I yelled.

And then Camilla was gone.

Her glass smashed onto the concrete. Cooper poked his nose through the slats of the deck's low fence, wuffling. Confused.

Ron was silent. We both looked down. Five floors below, right between two yellow lines of the concrete parking lot, Camilla was a rag doll. A very dead rag doll.

"Oh—no." My voice refused to work, rasping out in a whisper.

I clutched the railing, woozy.

A lone seagull wheeled and disappeared into the night.

Ron was still staring straight down, his hands clamped onto the railing. "You—" he began.

Ron was going to blame me? No. No. Never again.

"No," I said, shaking my head. "You. You killed her."

Suddenly, the world made sense. My turn. A swell of power filled me, and somehow my words came easily.

"You pushed her, Ron. When you found out she had led you on. Duped you. When you found out I'd asked her to humiliate you. To make you miserable. Now I have to call the police."

Maybe Ron said no. Maybe Ron denied it. He was certainly talking. Nonstop. But I wasn't listening. And I didn't care what he said.

"Guess Bermuda's out," I said, scratching Cooper behind one ear. "At least Massachusetts doesn't have the death penalty."

"You wouldn't." My ex-husband's eyes narrowed.

I wondered why I'd ever thought he was handsome.

"You couldn't." There was a twist in his voice, an edge I'd never heard before. It was fear. And humiliation.

He was miserable.

And finally, I wasn't. "Jess knows about the plan. So does Errol. I'm sure they'll be happy to tell it all to the police."

I turned from the fence, away from Ron and away from Camilla and away from the still-baffled Cooper, whose cold nose was worrying my leg. "Now I have to call 911."

By the time the police arrive, I'll have decided what to tell them. But Ron doesn't have to know that. Not quite yet.

"And Ron? Remember, I can testify against you, too, you know?" I pushed nine, then one, then paused, gesturing with the receiver. "Now that we're not married anymore."

All Set

John R. Clark

Mackey Lenfast tipped the amber bottle skyward, letting the last trickle drizzle down his eager throat. Taking aim at a nearby gull asleep on a well-spotted rock, he let fly, watching in half drunken satisfaction as the bottle exploded just beneath the startled bird, who flew off squawking like a banshee.

"There, I hope some puffy pants flatlander slices their foot open on the shards."

Chances of that happening weren't particularly good, he thought morosely as he fumbled in the paper bag beside him for another bottle. Damn red tide was lasting longer every summer, closing the flats and spooking off the tourists. Funny how something you could barely see was killing off two of the three sources of income in the Machias Bay area. Of course, come November, he could go tippin' but more and more woodland was posted every year, and besides, Mackey hated being away from the coast for more than an hour or two. There was something gawdawful unnatural about places without tide and seaweed.

It was that same fear which kept him a prisoner here in Clydesport. Hard to believe twenty-five years ago, he was valedictorian of his high school class. Sure, there had only been twenty kids, but he had been considered wicked smart and could have gone to school up in Orono. Yup, could have, but a weekend summer orientation left him as spooked as a coon cat in a room full of rocking chairs. Mackey had booked for home, gotten his lobstering license and never looked back.

"Frig!" His hand came out of the empty bag, which sailed off on a gust of July wind, settling gently on an incoming wave. "Double frig," he muttered, looking forlornly at the single dollar in his wallet. No way he was gonna gas up his boat, let alone buy more nasty-gansett. He stood, squinting out to sea as he waited to make sure his legs would cooperate before heading toward the lobster co-op beside the town pier.

Legs Skidgell grunted and tossed Mackey a can of Red Man as he sat down on a well worn bench in front of a grimy window. Even the multi-year accumulation of wood smoke and assorted grease couldn't prevent the sun from warming his aching shoulder. Damn it felt good. Not as good as the relief which came from a good six-pack buzz, but welcome nonetheless.

"You don't get out there in the next couple days, your traps gonna be full of half eaten lobsters and I'll be looking for another stern man job." Legs caught the tin of snuff as Mackey tossed it back to him.

"Don't you think I don't know that, Bub. I was countin' on making fuel money by hitting both tides every day this month, but the damn clam warden shut everything from Lubec to Cundy's Harbor down and that's a fact. If I hadn't wiped out the shaft on Hibbert's Ledge last month, I could probably scrape by."

"If you hadn't been three sheets to the wind and running full tilt after dark, you never would have hit the blasted thing in the first place."

Mackey didn't have a response to Legs's observation. Everything seemed like a Catch-22 these days. If he hadn't tried to break up a fight, he wouldn't have been stabbed in the shoulder. If he hadn't been partially crippled by the attack, he would probably earn enough to afford health coverage, but if he was that able, he wouldn't need health coverage. Cheap beer was a poor man's medical policy, but having enough of a buzz on to kill his pain also made him prone to doing really dumb things. Mackey groaned as he leaned forward and studied his quivering hands. This line of thinking was like watching a dog chasing its tail, and only left him dizzy and confused. Too bad he couldn't stumble on a cache of treasure down on the beach. That would solve everything.

"Guess I'll head over to the library and check that free e-mail account Ms. Peterson set up for me although all I seem to get is luncheon meat."

"Doncha mean spam?"

"Whatever," mumbled Mackey as he shambled through the door.

Truth was, Mackey had a crush on the town librarian and used numerous flimsy excuses to drop in. He didn't expect anyone to have sent him a real personal e-mail, but that was a minor irritation.

Amanda Peterson had graduated three years behind him, but lacking any phobias, she immediately left town and sailed through the university, followed by another stop at the University of South Carolina to pick up a library science degree. Mackey still couldn't figure out why such a smart woman would come back to downeast Maine after working at the Library of Congress.

Her welcoming smile as he entered the town library always made his knees weak. Mackey covered his additional beer-fueled unsteadiness by nodding slightly and sitting at the public access computer nearest the door. Spam, ham, baloney; whatever this junk mail was called, Mackey never ceased to be amazed at how many completely implausible messages he got. Today was no exception— thirty-three in his spam box and one in his inbox. He glanced at the single message, something about an emergency meeting to protest closing the clam flats. He snorted. Like anything a bunch of

Washington County rednecks might do would affect decisions in Augusta and Washington.

The spam folder was full of the usual junk—fake lottery wins, a couple Russian ladies who claimed to have fallen in love with his profile online, several offers of mail order potency enhancements and one of his favorites, the Nigerian oil scam. He read it and then re-read it as an idea began forming in the back of his mind.

"The best way to advertise for free? That all depends, Mackey. If you want to buy, sell or offer a service to people in a specific area, I'd use Craigslist. There are sublists for pretty nearly every city and county in the U.S. Say, you wouldn't be selling your boat and leaving town, would you?" Amanda's question, while joking, seemed to have something else underneath it.

Mackey spent most of the afternoon navigating the complexities of Craigslist for various cities along the eastern seaboard. At times, his ears threatened to melt as he read offers for physical relationships so bizarre he had trouble picturing them. After a while, he found the category which seemed best suited for his emerging scheme. He didn't post anything right away. He needed to work things out in his head and get enough poor man's medicine in his veins to be able to take that step.

"You think you can sucker some flatlander to do what?" Legs gave Mackey his undivided attention. While hare-brained, his friend's scheme was the most creative thing he'd heard in years.

Mackey re-read the ad he planned to post on the Boston Craigslist. "Of course I can hook someone. Those Massholes all think we're dumber than periwinkles. I stopped in at Lurleen's this morning and she's gonna let me borrow some of that junk jewelry she has in the front window to spice things up."

Legs shook his head and dipped some snuff out of a nearly empty tin. "Well, things can't get any worse. If we get caught, at least the county will feed and house us for a while."

"Trust me, Bub, we'll do better than that." Mackey finished his fourth beer of the day and headed for the library.

After reading his e-mail, Mackey laid out the paper with the ad he had written and rewritten three times the night before, and went to Craigslist. He clicked on the post button under business opportunities and started typing.

"Downeast entrepreneurs looking for silent financial partner to fund recovery of seventeenth-century artifacts. Cache located near tide line, so no need for dive equipment. 50% share offered to the right person. Looking for a man who has fiscal resources, is discreet and can keep a secret. Reply to lobsterdude@yahoo.com."

Mackey read it one last time and hit the post button. He might get a hundred replies or none at all, but it was his last best hope of salvaging things. If they did hook a live one, he hoped he had the stones to follow through.

After conning his great aunt Martha out of half her monthly check, Mackey laid in a supply of beer and focused on responses to his posting. He was starting to berate himself for utter foolishness when the responses started trickling in. Some were obvious loonies. Those he discarded immediately. A couple others sounded pretty legitimate, but aroused his suspicions. The last thing he needed was to get stung by some internet cop. There was, however, a reply from a guy in Marblehead which intrigued him. Mackey read the e-mail carefully, printed it off and left the library.

Legs took a well-used handkerchief from his back pocket and rubbed grime off the window pane. "There, I can see now. Hmm, he does sound like he's worth a good look. What ya gonna do next?"

"Dance with him a little to get a better handle on how best to play it out. There's a quarter moon this weekend. Enough light to make that crap jewelry look real if half buried. I'll see how things go."

Mackey took a deep breath and hit send. As the e-mail with

directions to the back cove south of Clydesport Harbor disappeared, he hoped he wasn't about to step in a big one.

Legs and Mackey fidgeted and swatted mosquitoes as they waited for the fish to arrive. The only sounds breaking the tense silence were the soft whoosh of the outgoing tide and a distant jet headed out to Europe. Mackey drained his third bottle of rapidly warming beer just as headlights appeared where the gravel access road met Route 219. Resisting the impulse to heave the bottle seaward, he set it down and nudged Legs. "You set on how we handle this?"

"Ayup. You do the talking and I'll do the watching. If anything smells like a mackerel, I distract him while you get the drop. You sure that Christly thing won't make him double over in laughter?"

Mackey took the rusty flare gun out of his pocket and aimed it at his partner. "Wanna put money on what happens if I pull the trigger right now?"

The increasingly loud crunch of tires on gravel cut short their nervous banter. Mackey tucked the gun in his back pocket while Legs moved far enough away to make ambushing both of them nearly impossible. They waited as the vehicle swung around in a circle, illuminating the entire area briefly.

The mark, evidently satisfied they were the only ones present, killed his engine and left the parking lights on as he stepped from what looked like one of those fancy foreign jobs only tourists could afford. He shined one of those high tech blue light flashlights on them. "Well, I'm here."

Legs and Mackey maintained their separation as they approached the car. They stopped as the bright light hit each of their faces, nearly blinding them.

"We can see that. You interested in dealin' or did you drive three hundred miles to be a comedian?"

The mark chuckled. "I didn't think you were born yesterday. Aren't many outside of Portland and maybe Bangor who ever heard of Craigslist, let alone know how to post something correctly. Let's see what you have and we can go from there."

Mackey grunted and turned on his own battered flashlight. "This way."

They had buried the stash of junk jewelry between two barnacle-encrusted boulders just below the high tide line. Mackey had scrounged some authentic looking bits of rotten wood at the dump so it would look like the booty had spilled out of a very old box. He sure as hell hoped the layout looked as real to this guy as it had when he showed it to Legs. He sure could use some more liquid medication right about now.

"I was lookin' to see if anything decent had washed up after the storm last month. Had to take a leak something awful and there were a bunch of kids playin' hooky further down the beach. Went between these two rocks and was just getting down to business when the sand collapsed under my foot. Damn near whizzed all over myself before I got straight. Looked down and there was this busted wooden box full of, well, you can see for yourself." He waved his light in the direction of the cache.

The mark let greed overpower caution as he moved between the rocks and bent over to check out the sparkly array half hidden in sand and rotten wood.

Mackey grimaced as the fellow's low rise pants revealed a very hairy Deer Isle smile. His nervousness grew as the mark tensed and used his light to examine a particularly gaudy bracelet. Without realizing it, Mackey pulled the flare pistol from his pocket.

"Last I knew, pirates weren't burying booty with Made in China stamped on it. I think you bumpkins made a big mistake." The mark started to reach for something in his pocket as he turned back toward Mackey.

Mackey panicked, firing the flare gun point blank at the flatlander, who stiffened, issued an anguished grunt and fell writhing on the sand as bits of flesh, gut and fire erupted from his midsection.

"Jesus in knee pants! Didja have to shoot him? We're gonna be in a wicked pickle unless we can figure out a way to get rid of him and his wheels real fast." Legs was white as a sheet as he watched the wounded man make one last twitch.

Mackey needed to wrap himself around three more warm beers before his mind would slow down enough for him to start thinking rationally. He knelt beside the corpse, grunting in disgust when he realized the mark had been reaching for his car keys. Too late for recrimination, he thought. Might as well salvage what we can. In addition to an expensive looking watch, there was close to a thousand in cash in his wallet. Mackey eyed the half dozen credit cards longingly, but knew sure as hell if they used any of them it would be an invitation to disaster.

"Well, I managed to muck this one pretty good, eh, Bub. I think we can sleaze out if we play it right. You know the Nadeau boys in Cherryfield?"

Legs nodded.

"Think you can drive his buggy up there tonight. Take whatever they offer. We're more interested in getting it pieced out as soon as possible than haggling over a few bucks. I'll get rid of the body in that beaver swamp out past the dump and then swing up to get you. You good with that?"

Grateful that Mackey was taking control of the situation, Legs nodded again and took the keys, vanishing unsteadily into the darkness.

Mackey hustled to the beater pickup he had hidden off the entrance road. He fumbled behind the seat, cussing at the burned out dome light. He was sure there were one or two trash bags underneath the accumulated empties he'd dropped over the seat back. He headed back a moment later, clutching a couple of the big ones he used to collect returnables in along the roads right after the snow melted.

Lightning was flashing off toward Bangor and scudding clouds were intermittently obscuring the moon. It looked like the line of storms predicted in today's paper was on schedule. That would cut down on what he'd need to do before retrieving Legs in Cherryfield. Mackey worked a bag over each end of the deceased, tying them together in three places before hefting the body over his good shoulder.

After covering the bagged body with a few evergreen boughs, he headed back to the boulders. He sure as hell didn't want to leave anything behind if he could help it. Mackey scooped all the junk jewelry into the bag his last batch of beer had come in and set it aside. Holding the flashlight with his teeth, he scooped every bit of bloody sand and tissue onto bits of rotting board, carrying them one at a time to the incoming waves where he made sure every trace was washed off before tossing the decaying wood into the surf.

After one last look to make certain he hadn't missed any blood or bits of flesh, Mackey took a last bit of wood and smoothed the sand as best he could. The first peal of thunder rolled in the distance as light rain began falling. By the time he turned onto the paved road, it was coming down in earnest.

It was nearing midnight when he pulled into the eerie landscape that was Nadeau Bros. Towing and Salvage. Rusting buses atop wrecked semis winked at him as lightning struck somewhere near the back of the property. Legs wasted no time hustling from the open garage where the brothers stood smoking the little black cigars that were part of their trademark image.

"We got lucky," Legs said as he opened a small canvas duffle bag. "I stopped to take a leak and figured I might as well give the vehicle a quick going over. The guy had another four thousand stashed under the rear seat along with a pistol. I clipped the GPS, too. It looks like one of those really fancy ones that does everything but fry bacon. You get rid of the body all right?"

"Yup." Mackey waited while a semi from the Prospect Harbor cannery flew by before turning toward home.

There was a pink tinge on the horizon as the two counted the money and divided it. Legs waved at the gun and GPS. "Want me to see what I can get for the unit. I think the gun better disappear for a while in case someone gets curious about the whereabouts of our friend."

Mackey nodded. "Okay by me. Hey, I'm sorry I lost it last night." He fell silent, not sure what else to say.

"Ain't nothing can be undone in a situation like that. Let's hope he wasn't too free about tellin' folks where he was goin.' "

Mackey and Legs were on tenterhooks for the next couple weeks, jumping when doors slammed and phones rang. While waiting for his boat to be repaired, Mackey made a point of stopping in at the library frequently to check Craigslist as well as online newspapers from the Boston area. He found no mention of a missing person fitting the description of the mark.

The red tide went away, tourists started flocking to Clydesport and Mackey's boat was seaworthy again. He and Legs went back to lobstering on a daily basis.

"Damn a clam, Bub, I haven't seen catches like we've been havin' since I was a teenager."

"Ayup, whatever you're puttin' in them bait bags got lobsters goin' wild to get at it. What'd you get anyway?" Legs rebaited a trap and slid it over the side.

Mackey took a swig of Diet Pepsi, having weaned himself off beer after seeing a real doctor about his bum shoulder. "Truth to tell, Bub, I call it flatlander supreme. See, I got ready to haul that Masshole into the swamp, but you know how spooked I get in the woods and with lightning, thunder and some of the most gawdawful shadows I ever seen, I said the hell with it and brought him down to the shed. Next day, it took about three hours to chum him up. Look at it this way, he'll last another week, we're makin' out like bandits and there's nothing to be found in the woods and trip us up down the road. Face it Bub, we're all set."

Finish the Job

Vincent H. O'Neil

The man watched while the girl worked. It was shortly after midnight on a late autumn evening in northern Massachusetts, but
enough leaves still clung to the trees to conceal them both. The man
occasionally swung his head from side to side, taking a slow look
around before shifting his attention back up the telephone pole. The
girl, wearing a set of brown coveralls identical to the man's, leaned
back easily into a lineman's belt and worked with a patient speed.

Set back from the deserted street, the pole was the first link in a
wooden chain connecting the Receiving Annex of the Swain-Carver
Museum of Art with the rest of the electronic world. The stone annex
itself stood two nearly windowless stories high a few yards beyond
the shelter of the trees. It had begun its existence as the small town's
only bank, but had been overtaken by the Swain-Carver's growth
many years before. Over the decades the complex had expanded to
consume several neighboring buildings that now branched out from
the central museum in the shape of a horseshoe. The Receiving
Annex was the only part of the horseshoe not actually attached to the
rest, which made the job assigned to the man and the girl that much
easier.

The girl came down the pole quickly but with great stealth, a
variety of electronic gadgets swinging from her utility belt as she
descended. The heavy coveralls and baseball hat did not conceal the

fact that she was athletic and pretty, or that she wore an impish smile when she finally touched the leaf-strewn ground.

"I know that look." The man turned his head as if expecting bad news, his dark eyes staying fixed on the girl. He was a good six inches taller and probably thirty years older, but he seemed to fear what she was about to whisper.

"Yes, you do. Looks like we need to switch to Plan B." The girl spoke in a muted voice while taking off the lineman's belt. She still wore the elfin smile, though, and her green eyes were vaguely feline in the darkness.

"There is no Plan B." The man chuckled deep inside a barrel chest as he spoke. "What happened? You couldn't find the right connection for the cut-out?"

"Oh, the cut-out's in place. No signal for the boys at Night Owl Alarms tonight. At least not from here." She stopped playing with her tools and looked up with real affection. "The problem is the alarm isn't turned on. How are we supposed to convince the guards we're answering a false alarm when the thing isn't even on?"

"It's off? I know it's an old system, but how could it be off?" The man kept his voice low while searching for a possible answer. "You don't suppose they wired into the rest of the complex, do you? Recently, I mean, to get the whole place on one system?"

The girl shook her head slowly, proud of the skills the man had taught her. "Nope. The alarm circuit is live. It's just not turned on."

The man reached up and adjusted the orange ski cap that covered his baldness, pressing his palm against his forehead as if taking his own temperature. The girl could see that he was turning over the various possibilities in his mind, and decided to head him off.

"We still gotta go in."

"Going in was Plan A. Plan A meant cutting the line, setting off the alarm for a few seconds, and using that as an excuse to get inside. Now we got no false alarm, and maybe a whole new security system to worry about."

"Come on." The girl was cajoling, a gloved hand reaching out to his arm and playfully pulling on it. "What did you teach me about running into trouble?"

"Don't start."

"Finish the job. That's what you always say."

"Yeah, but there's a smart way and a dumb way to finish the job—"

The girl was already walking back through the trees, toward their waiting van. When she didn't hear his footsteps in the leaves, she turned and fixed him with an expectant look.

"Come on, Dad." The smile was still there. "Let's finish the job."

□   □   □

They were still dressed in the coveralls when they rang the service bell at the front door of the Receiving Annex. The light over the door shone down on their outfits, revealing the emblem of the Night Owl Alarm Company on the right chest pocket, and a name patch sewn on the left. The man's patch identified him as Jack even though that was not his name, and the girl's said her name was Jillian with equal accuracy. They had picked two names that were easy to remember, but decided to change the second one because Jack and Jill sounded a little too obvious.

The girl had tucked her dark hair up under the baseball cap and donned a pair of ugly brown plastic glasses even though her eyesight was perfect. The man was still wearing the orange stocking hat, and they carried a small canvas tool bag apiece. As always, they were unarmed and had no plans for any rough stuff.

"So whaddya think? Everything we were told is wrong?" The girl muttered playfully out of the side of her mouth, mocking her father's concern while they waited for the door to open. "Maybe an entirely different alarm system on the inside? Maybe a hundred security guys in there?"

The man made a shushing noise, trying not to smile at her antics. A professional thief his entire life, he was still amazed at his daughter's composure under even the most trying circumstances. They had been working together for years, having started when she was in her early teens, and her question made him smile because it was exactly what he'd been thinking. He'd been questioning the accuracy of what they'd been told, and wishing there had been more time.

The job at the Swain-Carver Museum was a hurry-up, but even that was a testament to their reputation in certain circles. The man and the girl were known for their ability to think on their feet and their dedication to getting what they were after. There had been almost no time to conduct proper surveillance, and so they had been forced to rely on what they had been told. What they had been told had sounded pretty good, though.

An art museum associated with the Swain-Carver, a similarly ancient place just across the state line in New Hampshire, had suffered a fire a few weeks earlier. Although none of that museum's considerable holdings had been damaged, the structure had been compromised enough so that its entire contents, including several art masterpieces, had been shipped to the Swain-Carver.

The man had watched part of that shipment being moved around that very day. Initially delivered to the Receiving Annex, the special insulated boxes containing the artwork had been immediately shifted to the main building further up the road. The remaining boxes, wooden crates for the most part, had been left in the Receiving Annex to be sorted out later. The stone building and its older alarm system were considered safe enough for the New Hampshire museum's flotsam and jetsam, once the wheat had been sorted from the chaff.

Unfortunately for the Swain-Carver, a mover at the New Hampshire museum had placed one of its better paintings in one of the wooden crates now sitting in the Receiving Annex. This had not been an accident, and the painting had not been selected at random.

The man and the girl had been provided with a photo of the work, its exact dimensions, and the description of a special mark in grease pencil which would identify the crate in question. The masterpiece would complete the collection of a slightly nefarious buyer on another continent who had coveted it for years, and that buyer was prepared to pay handsomely.

"That's the best part, honey." The man had explained to the girl during the long drive to Massachusetts. "Fencing good artwork is hard, and you almost never get anything near what it's really worth. But in this case there's a buyer all lined up, and we stand to make a nice tidy bundle for one night's work."

The man had been assured that security at the Receiving Annex was laughable, and he'd taken the job when he'd heard the name and the vintage of the building's alarm system. The rest of the Swain-Carver was reputed to be tight as a drum, but the Receiving Annex, where the misplaced painting was stored, was wide open. At least it had seemed wide open, until the girl had come down the telephone pole with her news. No matter how old it was, the alarm system should not have been turned off at that hour.

Standing in the light outside the annex with his daughter at his side, the man wondered just what they might be getting into.

□ □ □

They found out a moment later, when the door swung open to reveal an old man in a blue guard's uniform. The uniform was partially covered by a dark gray cardigan sweater, and the guard looked at them from behind a set of large black-rimmed glasses. A thin white moustache sat on his upper lip, and the hair under his visored cap was the same color. When he spoke, his voice was rough and high-pitched.

"Hello! What happened to Bobby and Earle?"

The man in the coveralls was so surprised by this question that he initially failed to understand the words. He had been poised to explain why they were there when the old man had spoken, and so his mouth was still agape when his daughter came to the rescue.

"Bobby and Earle? Are they the guys who usually come out here?"

"Sure are. Every time there's a problem with this hanged alarm system. What, did they get the night off? Gone into town to see the Bruins maybe?"

The girl never missed a beat. The original cover story was designed to explain the presence of two unfamiliar Night Owl employees, and the two thieves had modified the rest of the tale while driving toward the annex. "Actually, we're not with the local department. We're inspecting all of the exterior lines across the state, but when we checked yours we didn't get a signal and thought we'd come knocking."

"You're checking the lines at midnight?"

"Best time for it. Less traffic on the lines, and if we find something that needs to be fixed, the maintenance teams can get out bright and early." The girl looked up at the building as if visually trying to determine what was wrong. "Like I said, we didn't get a signal from here. We didn't want to send a team out in the morning without first swinging by ourselves."

"Well, of course you're not getting a signal from here. If you'd talked to Bobby and Earle, they'da told you I turn that blamed alarm off every night when I come on shift. Silly thing used to go off three, four times a week . . . I'm sorry, where are my manners? You two must be frozen! Come on in!"

□ □ □

The Receiving Annex had been gutted and reconfigured at least once since its former life as a bank, so the man and the girl were led into a narrow hallway flanked by several administrative offices. They already knew that the front half of the building contained two floors of offices while the back half was a two-story open lockup for the museum's less valuable items. The watchman turned left at the end of the hallway and brought them into what was clearly the guard office.

It was a small room containing a large table, a phone, and the relay box for the alarm system. The table was covered with small hand tools, bits of soft-looking wood, and the hull of a replica wooden ship. A small painting propped up on the table showed a warship from the age of sail splitting the waves.

"Doing a little modeling here?" the girl asked, trying to keep up the rapport they had developed with the night watchman. He had told them his name was Charlie and that he was alone, and the girl hoped he would let them into the lockup where the crates were stored.

Charlie turned with obvious delight, extending his slightly shaking hands toward the ship as if warming his hands at a fire. "You know what this is? The *Constitution*. Old Ironsides herself. I make these from scratch, and sometimes they use them as part of the displays in the main museum. I was a guard there for thirty years, know as much about the New England side of the house as anybody—including that new curator of ours."

The girl's father gently cleared his throat in an attempt to signal that time was wasting, but Charlie heard him and took the hint.

"Well, the control switch is right here on the wall, so you want me to turn 'er back on?"

"Actually, Charlie, we don't need you to do that. Like we said, we're checking the lines themselves, and the readings outside the building were all okay. If we can do a few spot checks on your interior cables that should be plenty. Can you take us to a couple of the alarm boxes?"

"Sure thing. And I can tell you a whole lot about this building while we're walking. Did you know this was once a bank?"

□   □   □

It didn't take long for the trio to reach the lockup, as the storage area took up the back half of the building. The man and the girl pretended to test the system's interior circuit at each alarm box they encountered, all the while listening to Charlie's observations about the structure's history. The night watchman's knowledge of the premises was encyclopedic, but the tantalizing proximity of their prize kept the man and the girl from making much of it.

"Now here's the most interesting part of the entire annex," Charlie stated with pride when they reached the wall separating the administrative segment of the building from the lockup. Set into the center of the wall was an old-fashioned vault door. It was taller than a man, with a massive set of hinges on one side, and what looked like a steel ship's wheel on the other. "Yep, this was the door to the original bank vault, and when they gutted the place in '81 they couldn't bring themselves to part with this door. Back then we used to store all the real valuables here, at least the items that weren't on display, and between this and that big loading dock door the place was tighter than Fort Knox."

The girl's father had watched forklifts carrying crates and boxes into the annex through a large sliding door that afternoon, and he did not share Charlie's faith in the outer door's invulnerability. He had considered cutting the alarm circuit and gaining entrance through the loading dock, but large floodlights on that side of the building had finally made him reject the idea. He and the girl had then decided to talk their way into the lockup and find the special crate while pretending to do work on the alarm system. The man experienced a sinking feeling just looking at the bizarre door, and he waited for the latest snag in their plans even as his daughter angled her way toward the obvious question.

"This door is simply amazing, Charlie. How thick is it?"

"Three feet front to back, with locking teeth bigger than your thigh." The night watchman was practically beaming.

"Can you open it?"

"Oh, mercy no, little lady. It's a time lock. Won't be able to get in there until 9:00 A.M." He turned and looked back the way they had come, as if the model of the *Constitution* were calling him. "Besides, there's no need for you to go into the lockup. No alarm boxes in there."

□ □ □

"This is the weirdest job I have ever been on." The man leaned back against the van. He and the girl had driven back to their earlier vantage point in the trees after exchanging farewells with Charlie. "First the alarm isn't even on, then the lone night watchman takes us on a guided tour of the place, then there's a bank vault door with no bank vault, and even though there's no vault, the door is still set on a time lock. We're no closer to that painting than before we left home."

"You know what we have to do."

"Don't tell me to finish the job. Heard that one enough already tonight."

The girl leaned into the van through the open side door and came back out with her arms wrapped around a large canvas bag. The man seemed intrigued by the sack until the girl dropped it between them. The top of the bag opened enough to reveal a rope ladder with wooden steps, and the very sight almost made the man jump in surprise.

"Oh no. No way."

"Come on, it's only two stories up, and now we know the alarm system isn't even on. I'll climb the outside and drop the ladder so you can come up. We'll jimmy the skylight, use the ladder to get inside, and find the crate. Then we'll reverse our steps. Won't take even a half hour."

"Why did you bring that thing?"

"Because somebody taught me to bring every tool to every site. Because somebody taught me to finish the job."

"No."

The elfin smile was back, and the pixie bobbed her head in order to make eye contact with her father. "Now who's forgetting he got his start as a second-story man?"

"Who's forgetting I took a fall last year that almost killed me?"

"You're not gonna fall. You're gonna be on the ladder the whole way this time." She turned and looked through the trees at the looming building. "Unless you want me to go alone."

"You'd never be able to move the crates by yourself."

"I'll do what I have to, to finish the job."

The man exhaled heavily, shaking his head as he bent over and gathered up the bag. The girl selected some climbing rope and a few tools from the van, and then headed off through the trees. The man followed, whispering.

"I gotta have rocks in my head for doing this. Promise you'll bury me nice."

"It's only two stories. That last one was four, and it didn't kill you."

"I didn't fall the entire four. And that bay window slowed me down a lot when I bounced off of it."

The girl went on as if he hadn't answered. "Then again, it's amazing it didn't. You should have heard the noise when you hit."

"I did."

□ □ □

The old security bars still protruded from the building where the windows had been bricked up, and the girl used them to anchor her safety line as she climbed. Pressing her shoulder blades into a right-angled part of the building, she shinned up the wall as if giving herself an extreme kind of back scratch. Wedging herself firmly with her feet and back, she gently tugged her safety line loose from the lower bars and flipped it over the next higher set. On the ground below, the man held the other end of the line snugly across his lower back. If his daughter lost her grip he would simply sit down, holding her suspended by the line passing over the window bars and around her waist.

The girl used the safety line to pull the ladder up once she was over the flat roof's parapet. The ladder's wooden stairs unwound from the bag on the grass below, and once she had affixed it to the wall her father quickly ascended.

Though breathing heavily and looking quite pale, the man was energized by the brief climb. Normally he would have let the girl jimmy the heavy iron mesh protecting the pitched skylight, but time was wasting and he was slightly ashamed of his reluctance to scale the wall. With the alarm turned off, it was a simple task to pick the heavy lock and raise the skylight panel beneath it. Forgetting his earlier dread of the climb, the man reflected that they probably should have used this option right from the start.

The girl had already pulled up the ladder, accordion-folding it on the roof's loose gravel before carrying it to the skylight. The man gently lowered the ladder into the blackness below, and without a word swung over and onto the rungs. Once inside, he stopped long enough for his daughter to switch on the headlamp strapped around his stocking hat, and then he was moving downward.

The girl touched down right behind him, and their two narrow flashlight beams quickly located the light switch. Between the bricked-up windows and the floodlights trained on the loading dock, they were confident that the lockup's illumination could not be seen from outside. The weakness of the ceiling lamps further supported this idea and suggested that no one set foot in the lockup once the sun went down. Dim as it was, it was still enough to see that almost fifty wooden crates, stacked four or five deep, lined the walls of the lockup.

"That's strange. Why did they stack them like that?" the man whispered, looking around the basketball court-sized space. "They're going to sort through them here, and there's plenty of room, so why didn't they spread them out? They had at least ten guys working on this."

The girl understood his question when she remembered that the mark they sought was on the lid of the special crate. Reaching up, she used the palms of both hands to lift one end of the nearest stack's topmost box. It was heavy, but not immovable. "At least they're not monsters. We can unstack them."

The man had walked across the floor while she was speaking. She turned her head when he did not respond, and saw what had caught his eye. Five of the crates were spread out near the loading dock door, and they had already been opened. The girl quickly joined her father and helped to check the discarded box lids for the special symbol. After a few tense moments they were able to determine that the sign was not there, and that the box they sought had not yet been opened.

"That's why this was a hurry-up job. There was always a chance they might open everything when the shipment arrived. Lucky for us they quit when the sun went down," the man observed as he leaned the last lid against the wall. He noticed that the open boxes were still full of the document containers and other detritus of the New Hampshire museum's archives, but gave it no thought. Looking around, he made a rough estimate and then rubbed his hands together briskly.

"Okay, let's be organized here."

□   □   □

The van pulled out of the trees as the sun was beginning to rise. It rolled out quietly, but once on the road it roared off in an angry billow of leaves.

Charlie's partner Kenny, who had been walking a guard tour at the main building during most of the night, watched the van roll away as he got out of his car. He was a good-looking man in his early twenties, and his left arm was in a sling. He had separated his shoulder in a rugby match the previous weekend, but it had not kept him from going up to the main building when one of the other guards had called in sick.

He juggled a cardboard tray with two steaming Styrofoam cups of coffee while walking toward the door, and was surprised when Charlie opened it for him. The older man was smiling as if his Bruins had won the Stanley Cup again.

"What's up, Charlie?"

"Not much, Kenny." Charlie held the door open for his partner, but stayed in the entrance after the other man had started down the hall. Squinting in the cold fall air, he looked down the road as if fascinated by something in the distance. "See that van leave?"

"Yeah. Anybody we know?"

"Not really. Come on, let me show you something." The two guards walked to the office where they normally spent the night shift, and Kenny handed his partner one of the cups before they continued down the hall. When they got to the vault door, Charlie worked the combination and then guided the huge metal barrier as it swung back. Even before he hit the light switch, Kenny was able to see that something was wrong.

The floor was covered with neat rows of boxes, each with a large wooden lid carefully placed to one side. The contents of the containers, mostly documents, sat snugly within the crates.

"Well this is a nice surprise, Charlie. I didn't know how you and I were gonna do this job." He looked back in the direction of the street. "Did those guys in the van help you with this?"

"Sorta. You know that missing painting, the little one that the curator was all bothered about?"

"Yeah, the movers found it in one of these crates when it wasn't with the other paintings." The museum curator had inventoried the other gallery's artwork as it arrived, and had launched a frantic search when one of the most expensive pieces seemed to be missing. The movers had sorted it out quickly enough, finding the picture in a crate, which had then been whisked up to the main annex.

"That's the one. Last night a man and a girl showed up saying they were from Night Owl, and that they were checking the alarm lines in the area."

"Showed up?" Kenny's eyes took on a suspicious squint. "They're supposed to call ahead about something like that, even for here."

"Right. Well, they were a little too interested in the lockup—"

"They weren't robbers, were they?" Kenny was smiling even as he asked the question.

"Actually, yes. Good ones, too, and from the look of the girl I think they were a father-daughter act. They didn't know I was onto them, and when they asked if I could open the vault door I told them the time lock was set for later this morning."

"The time lock? We've never used that thing."

"They didn't know that. They left easy enough, and I was going to call up to the museum to report it, but then I remembered that little job the curator gave us."

"You mean this?" Kenny pointed at the open boxes on the lock-up floor. The curator had been badly shaken by the close call with the misplaced artwork, and even the completed inventory of the important items had not calmed him. Shortly before going home for the evening, he had ordered Charlie and Kenny to spend the night opening every one of the remaining crates.

"Yeah. I tried to tell His Highness we couldn't do it, not between your shoulder and my age, but he wasn't listening. So I decided to wait and see if my two visitors might help out."

"Charlie!"

"I know, I know, but they didn't look the violent type. In fact, they looked real professional, and that's what made me think they might come back." He waved a hand at the rows of open containers. "And they did! I was at the peephole watching and listening on the other side. I watched 'em most of the last three hours. Quiet as church mice, even prying up the lids, and look how neat they were! They were definitely after that painting, and when they didn't find some sort of mark that was supposed to be on one of the boxes—"

"Probably on the crate that got moved to the main building."

"No doubt. And now we know why that one mover found the picture so fast. I guess we have to mention that to the curator, but I'll tell you these two were pros. Look—they even shut the skylight and locked the cage around it when they left."

The two men looked up at the steepled glass over their heads, just beginning to show the first signs of daylight.

"Charlie, why didn't you call for help?"

"Thought about it, but there's nothing worth stealing in here, and they were definitely after that one piece. With the painting gone, I figured there was a chance they might open all these crates for us, and you can see they did. Saved you and me a big run-in with His Highness."

"That ain't it." The younger man looked at the older man with a smile. They had worked together for a long time, and he knew when Charlie was only telling part of the truth. Charlie looked back at him and finally broke into a broad grin.

"You're right, that's not it. It was that father and daughter. They were so . . . dedicated. No matter what they ran into, they just backed off and tried a different way. If they'd quit earlier, they'd never have known that the picture wasn't there. It's important for people to know they did everything they could."

"You really are an old softie, Charlie. Worried about the self-esteem of two thieves."

"Nah, it's not that. I just hate to see people leave a job half-finished."

Where There's Smoke

Nancy Gardner

As the dark January morning marches toward a sunless noon, Flo Dembrowski, a hefty, unkempt woman, releases a Shaw's shopping cart mired in the slush.

"What's the matter, Rosie? Seen a ghost?"

Rose Hernandez, a pint-sized woman shabbily dressed in layers of purple, shuffles foot to foot in front of a trash can. She holds the lid outstretched, rigid. Staring inside, she mutters into the moth-eaten scarf wrapping her neck to nose.

"You're scaring me, buddy. What's up?" Flo asks as she stomps towards her friend.

Rose drops her arm, drops the lid, winces at the slush-muted clang, stabs a lavender mitten toward the can rim. "Look."

"Look at what?" Flo ambles over, peers inside. "So?"

"Violet had one." Rose nudges her friend aside.

From a bed of stacked newspapers, she lifts a cherry-nosed, porcelain-faced doll. Lifts it like she's found the Holy Grail.

Turning it over, she winds a metal key, then hums along to the tinkling of "Send in the Clowns." Her voice trails off. The tinny music slows and slows and stops.

Flo scowls. "Hell's bells, Rosie. That there clown doll gonna mess with your mind? You don't need no setbacks. Let it be. Some things're best left alone."

She snatches for it.

Rose evades her friend's glove, stuffs the clown into her faded tapestry carpetbag, replaces the lid on the can, sloshes forward to the bulging, rusted shopping cart.

"All right then, Rosie, you win. Just don't blame me if you end up in the looney bin. Again."

Rose winces, flops her bag in the cart's child seat, grips the handle, heaves, goes nowhere.

"Goldarnit, Rosie, let me do that." Flo wedges her out of the way and drives the cart forward.

Rose follows.

"Sorry. I shouldn't of said what I said. It's just that—"

"Shh, Flo."

"You know me, Rosie. I just don't want . . . Maybe you can sell that thing to Sister Anne's junk-buying friend."

"Maybe."

"Get yourself a warmer jacket."

Rose shivers, crosses her arms to block a cut of cold sneaking under her tattered windbreaker.

They round Daniels Street onto Derby. The smell of low tide sharpens as it rides in off the harbor. They continue their trudge in silence, reach the front door of Jake's Liquor Mart and halt.

"Good haul," Flo says. "My guess, eight or nine bucks worth of empties here." She taps the lumpy plastic bag that threatens to overflow the sides of the cart, then hands Rose her carpetbag.

Rose shifts it hand to hand, takes a step backward, and nearly collides with a burly figure in blue.

He sails past without a glance and walks into Jake's.

Sucking in a raspy breath, Rose whispers, "P-p-policeman," as she curls back against the storefront.

Flo holds up a big, gloved hand. "None of that now, Rosie. That cop ain't got no reason to bust your chops."

"No." The little woman shakes her head.

"It'll only take a minute. C'mon with me. Get warmed up."

"Y-y-you go," Rose says, eyes wide, panicked.

"Calm down, girl. Ya don't wanna go in, ya don't have to. Just promise me ya won't go wanderin' off."

"Won't." Rose's gaze steadies as she focuses on her friend's face.

"Why don'tcha take a load off and wait over there?" Flo says, pointing across Derby to a retaining wall fronting the wharf.

Rose nods, shuffles her way across the empty street. At the snow-blanketed granite wall she elbows a clean swath, smoothes the back of her outsized corduroy skirt and takes a seat, mustering a limp wave for her friend.

Flo salutes, winks, hoists the clinking trash bag over her shoulder and disappears into Jake's, the tail end of her red stocking cap barely escaping the closing shop door.

Ignoring Salem Harbor's windy bite, Rose loosens her scarf, revealing a lined, once-pretty oval of a face.

"Hurry, Flo," she mumbles, setting off a vague cloud of frozen breath. She tucks wayward gray-red curls under the brim of her purple knit hat, rewraps the scarf, masking all but wary blue eyes. Eyes that flit to her lap, her mittens. Eyes that wince when she removes the mittens, reveals grotesquely burn-scarred hands, one of which she sets to work tracing a crimson rose embroidered on her bag.

A seagull swoops past. She watches it disappear, sighs, sinks a hand inside her bag, fishes out the day's Boston *Globe*, opens to the comics. "Calvin and Hobbes?"

When she doesn't find what she's looking for she folds the newspaper back inside, continues digging, reclaims her treasure. Outfitted in silk pajamas, white with rainbow dots, and matching peaked hat, the clown seems to contradict the stern winter sky.

She smoothes the red yarn curls, examines a tight loop of stuffing jutting from a small tear in the silk, prods the stuffing back inside. "Easy fix. Needle. Thread."

Embracing the doll, she pokes her nose deeply into its curls. After a few seconds, she snaps her head upright. Laying the clown beside her, she darts her hand back into her bag, unzips an interior pocket, emits a 'whoosh' when she finds it.

Cracks crisscross the faded photo in her hand. She maps a twisted finger down one worn crack.

"Hello, James. Violet."

A young man, young woman and little girl grin back. The man is tan, athletic, clean-cut. He sits on a doorstep, the child on his lap. The girl, a round-faced toddler with an Annie-like mop of curls, clutches a clown doll.

The smiling mother leans into her husband, arms wrapped around his arm. Her husband and daughter wear shorts and T-shirts. This younger Rose wears a nurse's uniform.

Rose kisses the photo, flattens it, re-zips it in the pocket. As she is about to pick up the clown again a needle-sharp scream blasts her eardrum. In her confusion she drops her bag. She bends to reclaim it, coming face to face with a tear-stained little boy who's clutching at her skirt with one hand and fighting the pull of a huge paw with the other. She forgets her bag.

"No," the child wails.

The paw belongs to a beefy, hard-faced man in a black leather jacket. A child's Superman backpack flops off his shoulder.

"Don't cry," she whispers to the boy. She guesses he can't be more than two or three.

"Mommy," the boy cries, "Mommy says don't."

But it is not just his tears that disturb her. Below his blond curls, one of his cheeks wears an angry, pus-encrusted sore.

The child's sobbing slows, softens, but he doesn't loosen his clutch on her skirt.

"Let go, Bobby. We haven't got time for this," the man says. Ashen-faced, he wrestles the child's grip from the little woman's skirt. The child now in his arms, sobbing into his neck, he stoops to pick up her bag, his face even chalkier as he stuffs the newspaper back inside, snaps the bag shut, hands it to her.

"Thanks."

The man sets the boy down again, takes his hand. Before she or the man can react, the little boy's other hand darts, lightning fast, grabs her clown.

She snatches it back, stuffs it in her bag, snaps it closed.

The little boy sticks his thumb in his mouth.

She scoops up a handful of snow, offers it. "Might help," she says, shifting her glance from the man's face to the boy's cheek.

"What?" For the first time the man looks at her. His eyes roam her face, her worn clothes, stop at her scarred hands.

"Bobby's cheek," she says, still holding out the snow.

His jaw tenses. "Mind your own damn business."

She looks down at her hand and blushes; the melting snow dribbles to the ground.

He gathers up the boy, rushes down Derby Street, turns onto Pickering Way.

The last thing she sees are the boy's eyes peeking back at her. And something lying in the snow, a small, blue Spiderman mitten.

She swoops it up and hurries after them, finds the man carrying the boy up a stairway in a back alley.

He sees her, grimaces, growls, "Get away."

Rose backs away, shaking her head and muttering. She returns to Derby Street and her granite perch and settles the carpetbag once again on her lap.

She looks at the small mitten, drops it into the bag before taking out her own mittens. A gull squawks overhead and she watches it circle for a moment. Then she bolts upright, raps the side of her head, reopens her bag and pulls out the newspaper.

It's right there on the front page, "Boy Kidnapped, Mother Frantic." She searches the article, hopes for a photo of the missing child. No photo.

Rising to her feet, she concentrates on the Derby Street, Pickering Way corner, suspicion nibbling the edges of her mind.

Bobby kidnapped? Bobbie's cheek? Cigarette burn? Worse than her suspicion is her certainty that even if she's right nobody would listen to her, believe her.

A booming voice bursts through her musing.

"Got us some lunch money." Flo waves as she steps off the curb, her wide, gap-toothed grin proclaiming victory.

"Not Bobby," Rose tells herself, stuffs the newspaper back into her bag, stands.

Flo strides up beside her. "Ya stayed put. Good girl. Took so long 'cuz that cop took his time jawing with the counter guy." She waves a fistful of dollar bills. "We made ten bucks and some change." She stuffs the crumpled bills back into her jeans pocket. "Ready for Dunkin' Donuts?"

"Ready."

"Good. An' I bet ya forgot what night it is and who's rustling up supper at the soup kitchen."

The little woman squints at the ground confused.

"It's Tuesday, Rosie."

"Tuesday? Tuesday. Forgot."

"Well, don't forget the nice warm beds Sister Anne promised us once we get ourselves full of Harry's famous chicken soup." Flo raises her hand in a half high-five.

Rose returns the gesture, feigns a smile. But as they leave, she can't stop herself from a backward glance at Pickering Way.

□ □ □

Night envelops the communal bedroom. Rose surrenders to sleep and soon she's gasping and flailing at a gray veil separating her from the screaming child. She calls to the child. "Violet? Mommy's coming!"

Through misted vision she sees the little girl reaching out to her, hands aflame.

"Mommee!"

Rose's panic rises. She rips off the veil. But it's too late. Violet's face melts into a wall of flames, replaced by the face of a little boy. A little boy with a pulsing blister scarring his cheek. The blister grows, obliterates the boy as he too melts into the flames.

Rose covers her face but not before seeing a leering, life-sized clown replace the howling boy, lurch in her direction.

The boy's wails echo in her ears.

"Wake up," she tells herself. Her eyes feel glued shut. She marshals her will, forces them open.

"Not real," she whispers and relief floods through her. Pulling a Kleenex from under her pillow, she sops sweat from her face and neck. She looks around, dazed, finds she's safely tucked in her bed at St. Clare's shelter though she hears no bed-rumbling snores from Flo. Then she remembers pleading a headache, going to bed earlier than the others.

Below her, the low hum of the TV competes with Flo's booming voice. "C'mon Sturm." Must be after eleven if Mike Lynch is reporting on the Bruins game.

Rose's legs twitch.

She reaches under the bed for her carpetbag, creeps over to a window, looks out onto the street. A bright half moon waxes above, lights the bag.

She removes the clown and studies the newly mended arm. Seconds later she returns it to her bag, takes out the Spiderman mitten, puts it back.

More hoots from the TV room. Usually Flo's enthusiastic cheering for the Boston team of the moment, the Bruins or the Patriots or the Red Sox, comforts her, but tonight she can't stifle the memory of the insistent nightmare or the image of a little boy, cheek marred by a cigarette. "Is he alright?" she murmurs.

Her gaze shifts to the street below. A few quarter-sized snowflakes drift by, and she longs for their cooling touch. If she hurries, she might be able to slip out the side door that's left open for smokers. But at 11:30 the alarm is set for the night.

She gets up and paces. "Almost 11:30," she tells herself.

The voices below quiet. It's now or not at all. She hurries over to her bed, plumps her pillow and blanket under the coverlet. Noiselessly she covers her flannel pajamas with a sweater and her windbreaker. She gathers up her bag and galoshes, tiptoes down the stairs to the hallway below, sneaks to the side door. Sweat trickles down her back as she inches the door open.

Once outside she slips away from the porch light, presses herself against the house next door. A lock clicks in place.

The falling snowflakes cool her cheeks as she pulls on her galoshes, adjusts her hat and scarf, glides forward to the icy sidewalk. Thicker clouds move in, covering the moon. The muffled moan of a distant foghorn blares.

Head down, she slogs forward. A dark car sends a spray of wet snow across her galoshes. She keeps slogging until she stands in front of a street sign. Pickering Way.

She turns the corner, scuffs along, stops in front of the alley where she last saw Bobby and the man. She approaches the stairway and is about to climb when a bare bulb clicks above. The bulb brightens the second-story doorway, illuminates the man. Her heartbeat thrums louder and louder inside her head as she watches him scowling into the night sky; she balls herself further into the shadows.

He spits, retreats inside, clicks off the light.

She spots a park bench resting against a building across from the alleyway. She scrambles to it, clears a spot, sits. The horizon gleams with reflected light from the illuminated clipper ship floating on Derby Wharf. She removes the Spiderman mitten from her bag, debates whether to leave or climb the stairs and drop the mitten by the door.

Undecided, she waits. Five minutes. Ten. Her spine softens into the bench, her head tips forward, weariness overtakes her.

A sudden, disorienting odor jolts her awake. Gasoline? She straightens, rubs her eyes. Nightmare? Real?

"What do you think you're doing?" a deep, masculine voice growls amid scuffling sounds from above.

She stands, squints upwards, sees two dark figures wrestling back and forth along the apartment wall.

She slings the handle of her bag over an arm, hunches forward into a crouch, and scuttles to the foot of the long, rickety stairway.

"Give me that."

A cigarette lighter flares above, turns her to stone. She aches to run. Run to safety. Run back to the shelter, to the warm bed, to her sleeping friends. Run.

But she can't—not with Bobby up there. The memory of his teary face grips her, vise-like.

She hurtles up the stairs. As she reaches the top, a figure flies past, missing her by inches. Harsh light etches the grimacing face of the man. He bangs against the iron railing, slams his head, slumps back.

A sharp movement from the other end of the porch catches her attention. A second figure pours something from a large square can, pours along the base of the apartment wall. Rose's stomach sickens.

She was right about the stench. Gasoline.

A scream sticks in her throat. She pivots toward the stairs, flaps her arms, again longs to run. But memory chains her.

Memory of a younger self, bare fists pounding a smoke-framed door. Shrieking for James. Shrieking for Violet. Begging them to answer her. The image morphs into yellow-slickered men. Dragging her away. Nothing she can do, nothing anyone can do.

A snowflake tickles her forehead, brings her back, back to this second-story porch, back to this awful smell. And she knows that right here, right now, she's found another chance.

Behind her the downed man groans.

She ignores him, focuses on the deadly liquid cascade, swoops at the can, swirls her carpetbag with memory-fueled might. The bag connects, delivers a satisfying thump.

She raises it for another strike.

A cackle of ugly laughter erupts as the dark figure lurches, rears above her.

Rose flinches. For a moment the laugh confuses her.

"Get out of my way, you piece of shit."

Rose gapes.

A ferocious, blonde Valkyrie of a woman flies at her, teeth bared, eyes bulging. She snatches Rose's bag, splats the little woman to the ground, hurls the bag at her.

Rose ducks as the bag whizzes past, hears it slam into the wall. She covers her head, cowers. When she doesn't feel a second blow she uncovers, sees the woman's found a different target. Now she's looming over the dazed man.

"Told you I'd do it, Georgie. Told you I'd kill him if you ever tried to leave me. Kill you both." She holds up a lighter, giggles girlishly, flicks.

The man never takes his eyes off the lighter. "Don't, Monica. I'll do anything—"

"Too late, Georgie-Porgie. Till death do us part." The blonde squeals and leans the flame into a nearby pile of gasoline-soaked rags.

As the flame leaps, so does the man. He throws himself at the woman. They grapple.

Rose forgets them both. She sees nothing, nothing but flames climbing, smoke swirling.

Her lungs fill. She coughs, pulls herself up, concentrates. Striping off her jacket, she raises it above her head, brings it down. Thwack. Thwack. Thwack. Up, down, up, down. Gradually she begins to make headway. The flames sputter, flare anew, sputter.

As she pauses for a breath, a steel trap encircles her throat. With a desperate twist she turns. The blonde balls her fists.

Before either woman can move the man lunges. Bangs into the blonde, pulls her away. Rose shudders, returns to her task. Bending forward, she scoops little handfuls of dirty snow onto the hissing refuse. Finally she stands, surveys the smoldering, stinking mess at her feet. Choking spasms rack her body, wear themselves out. Her gasps for air slow. Her rasping breath quiets.

Quiets, then once again sharpens when a horrible, echoing scream flails the air behind her. Squinting into the dimness, she sees the man, now down on all fours, calling down the stairs, "No. Monica. No."

Rose rushes to him, follows his gaze. Her stomach lurches. The strange angle of the blonde's arms, legs, neck, deliver the final verdict.

Beside her the man's shoulders shake in wild, convulsive quakes. Rose darts a hand to his arm, pulls it back, returns it.

"She tried to kill us. She—" Tears arc down his craggy face.

"Bobby hurt?"

"Bobby? No. Thank God. He's sleeping." He grabs Rose's hand. "Had to get him away. She burned him. To get back at me. My fault. I— Let's go. Inside." He drags himself up, slogs to the door. "I need to check him, call the cops." He stops. "You're shivering. C'mon inside." He steps aside, waits. "My name's George. What's yours?"

Rose seizes her carpetbag, her charred jacket, follows.

George nods Rose over to a chair by a small Formica table. "Be right back. First I've got to check Bobby." He disappears down a small hallway.

As she waits an idea takes hold. She retrieves her clown, checks it, finds it unharmed.

George returns and stumbles over to the sink. He runs the faucet, splashes water over his face, says, "Bobby's still sleeping. Slept right through all the racket. I don't even want to think about what would've happened if—"

She thrusts the clown into his hands. "For Bobby. When he wakes. Please." She watches his face.

His features soften as his eyes flow over the gift. He carefully sets it on top of the small refrigerator. "Thanks," he says, "Bobby really took a liking to it, didn't he? To you too. By the way, what did you say your name was?"

Rose traces and retraces the hem of her sweater.

"Your teeth are chattering." He sweeps her ruined windbreaker off the chair back, throws it into a wastebasket. Then he reaches up to a hook by the door and removes his well-worn leather jacket. He drapes it around her shoulders. "It's yours. Least I can do."

"Oh," she says, flushing. "So soft." She runs a scarred hand over the plush lining. He helps her jam her trembling arms into the sleeves. Despite the trembles, she manages to zip up the jacket, not caring that the sleeves drip past her fingertips.

"Got to call the police," he says, reaching into the Superman backpack hanging on another hook.

"P-p-police?"

"Don't worry. The cops know about Monica, know she wanted to kill us, never mind her con job on the reporters."

He lifts a cell phone, presses buttons. "Damn, I need to recharge."

"Gotta go," she whispers.

He puts the cell phone on the table, points down the hallway. "Regular one in the bedroom. Be right back."

Out the window Rose sees the night surrendering to a pinkish dawn. If she hurries she can be at the shelter by the time the smoker's door reopens. Quickly she removes the Spiderman mitten from her bag, lays it on the kitchen counter. Slip-sliding out the door, she mouths an inaudible goodbye.

She inches down the steps and tries to pass the dead woman, can't, stops.

"Sad," she whispers, removes a dingy washcloth from her bag, covers the woman's face. "Sad and stupid," she says, crosses herself, straightens, hustles away.

She flits from side street to side street, serenaded by fading siren wails.

Finally she reaches the shelter, peeks up the driveway, waits. Within minutes the side door opens. Several women jostle out, light cigarettes, stamp their feet. She steals forward, hoping to slip inside unnoticed.

A rough hand grabs her arm.

"Where ya been, Rosie? Been worried sick you was in trouble." Flo grumbles, "Ya look like hell and ya smell like it too. Better get yourself into a hot shower, quick." Before Rose can respond, Flo looks down at the leather sleeve in her hand. "Where'd you get the nifty jacket?"

"Couldn't sleep. Needed air."

"And?"

"Met a man."

"Met a man?"

"Traded clown for jacket."

"Traded? Hot damn! How'd you pull it off?"

"Shush. Need a shower."

"Yeah. Later," Flo mouths.

"Thanks," Rose replies.

Flo motions a pretend-zipper across her lips, opens the door for her friend.

As she squeezes past Flo, Rose pictures a little boy hugging a clown. A butterfly-smile flits from her mouth to her eyes as she enters the warm hallway. She's looking forward to the coming day, even more to the night. Tonight, for the first time in a very long time, she knows she'll sail her dreams to smoke-free shores.

Don't Call Me Simon

Alan McWhirter

I have this fantasy where I get stuck in an elevator with the most gorgeous girl in the world. It might have happened that day in the Ebony if Plain Jane hadn't beaten Gorgeous to the lift. The fates weren't with me or with Gorgeous. On a good day fantasies come true. On a bad day they end in murder.

☐ ☐ ☐

Five minutes ahead of my four o'clock chat with Mortenson I dropped into the lobby of Waterbury's Ebony Hotel and waited for the lone elevator to make a labored descent. The Ebony was once the crown jewel of early twentieth-century Waterbury, the brass capital of the world. A smattering of the rich and famous once spent the night at the Ebony. JFK once spoke from the balcony on election eve. Now the lobby is decaying badly and a lot of John Smiths register at the Ebony.

The hotel's not all that's changed since the mills closed when I was ten and my parents moved to New Haven. Once upon a better time I was a New Haven cop. Then Internal Affairs threw me off the force. Now I'm back where I began.

☐ ☐ ☐

The elevator arrived empty and Plain Jane followed me aboard. She was in her forties, a bit heavy, a bit boxy. Not the fuel of fantasies. Her hair was cut short and ragged. She had a flesh-colored bandage across the middle of her left cheek. Her clothes were retreads, poor-ly fitting second-hand jeans and a scruffy I Luv Waterbury sweat-shirt left over from a ten-year-old promotion, both standard issue at the St. Vincent DePaul shelter. She would have passed for a local except for the Gucci handbag and the Christian Dior lashes.

"What floor, sweetheart?" I asked.

She gave me a piercing look. "Four."

I pushed her button, then mine.

As the curtain closed on another lost fantasy, Gorgeous, a tall, thin, angular blonde in her early twenties, wearing tight jeans and a tighter blouse, made a run for the closing door. Jane gave Gorgeous the glare teenage girls dish out when the school tramp parades by, diverts the eyes of boys at the lunch table, and sucks the air out of civil conversation.

I tried to save her, Gorgeous, I mean. But I couldn't remember if the rescue button, the one with the arrows pointing in the opposite directions, is on the left or the right. Jane was close enough to jam the door. She didn't try. I guess she had her own fantasies. Plain Jane bailed at the fourth floor and I rode the grinding lift to the penthouse on the sixth.

□ □ □

When I came down an hour later a uniformed officer, barely old enough to shave, stood scribbling important things in his important notebook.

"Excuse me, sir." Rookie cop. Way too polite. "But did you hap-pen to see a young blonde woman in the hotel this afternoon?"

"Not as well as I wanted to," I said.

Rookie stopped writing important things in his important note-book. "Sir, you may have been one of the last people to see the young woman. I'm sorry but I'll have to ask you to come with me to the basement."

Damn near apologetic. He'd learn, or find himself writing parking tickets instead of homicide notes.

"The basement?" I asked.

"To meet with the detectives."

□ □ □

The Ebony was built in 1905 before the need of parking, except for horses. The basement doesn't lead to an underground parking garage. The basement leads to damp basement storage, the boiler room and a dead end. One stop down the elevator pried itself open. Fresh blood drenched the time-creviced concrete landing. Crimson ooze seeped into the nether world below the cracks.

"Shit!"

Gorgeous lay in a heap, her left cheek flush against the cold gray concrete. Gorgeous wasn't gorgeous anymore. There was a scarlet crease on the right side of her forehead. What I could see of her face was caved in. More than one blow. More than several. A lot of blood splatter. Someone sure got messy about their messy business.

The paramedics were done. Forensics was about to begin.

Gooch, Detective Brad Gooch, growled as I stepped into the middle of his untidy crime scene. "Christ Almighty! If it isn't the Saint himself."

Gooch wasn't referring to my morals. The old New Haven police chief had been a fan of Simon Templar when Roger Moore played him on TV and hung the nickname on me. At one time I was okay with the nickname. Now it's a bitter reminder of my past failures. The label reached Waterbury when Gooch checked me out a while back. Maybe Gooch meant well. Maybe not.

"Glad to see you too, Gooch," I said. "Starting in the basement again?"

It was a sore point with Gooch. He'd risen to sergeant only to be busted to "start" for some indecent indiscretion. But he was stubborn and persistent and worked his way back to sergeant and then lieutenant. Some make it back. Maybe me. Maybe someday.

Rookie burst my reckless thoughts. "Lieutenant Gooch, this gentleman may have been the last person to see the lady alive."

"What did you use this time, Simon, the butt of your pistol or a wine bottle?"

I'd used both—when necessary—and Gooch knew it. Wise-ass teenagers these days. They think you're easy pickings just because you're walking home from a bar and over fifty.

Gooch waved the back of his hand at Rookie. "Upstairs and see what other horse shit you can turn up." Then Gooch turned to me. "What can you tell me about her?"

"Nothing," I said. "Honest." Usually when someone starts with honest, it's a sure sign they're not. I was. This time.

"Then why are you here?"

I mentioned Rookie's polite invitation. Gooch frowned. Gooch always frowns. Never saw him smile. I nodded at the blonde corpse. "Who is she?"

"Angel Carlson, new girl working the hotel circuit. Busted once. Got accelerated rehab. Didn't take, I guess. She went back to the same line of work."

One step away from an elevator ride with a Waterbury angel, and then . . .

"Got her wings clipped," Gooch said on cue.

"Yeah."

"Okay, Simon." Gooch was overdoing it. "Tell what little you do know."

I explained how I left Gorgeous in the lobby when I went upstairs for my meeting.

"With who?" Gooch asked.

"She was alone."

"I mean you, wise ass. Who were you meeting?"

"Divorce lawyer. Mortenson," I said.

"About whose divorce?"

"Mine."

"Again?"

I shrugged my shoulders. For some, the third time's the charm. For me, it was just another failure.

"That's it?" Gooch asked.

"All of it," I replied.

"Run along."

I did, to Murphy's, the pub across from the bronze stallion atop the granite fountain at the east end of the city green. A Piece of Old Waterbury the pub claims. If there's a new Waterbury I can't find where they put it.

By the way, my given name's Joe Chandler.

□ □ □

The next morning, Gorgeous made page one. The Waterbury *Republican American*, a family paper, spared its sensitive readers the whole truth and referred to her as a local girl, from Prospect, single mother of two, working her way through college.

That might have been the end of things if it hadn't been for Doonesbury.

Living in New Haven, you read Doonesbury. It's a civic duty. The conservative *Republican* doesn't carry Doonesbury. My generous neighbor, who grew up outside of Norwalk, still gets the *Stamford Advocate*, which does. When her dogs are done with it and when she remembers, she leaves me her abused copy.

Rummaging through the remnants, looking for the comics, I stumbled on her picture. Her hair was shoulder length and pre-arranged. But it was her, still plain, definitely Jane. There was a mole or birthmark where I'd seen the bandage the day before.

Plain Jane turned out to be Elizabeth Longley, thirty-nine if you believed the pitch, a Greenwich native, former southpaw batting champion on the high school softball team, a recent widow, her husband lost in a boating accident six months past.

I should have felt better knowing the identity of the one person besides Mortenson who could give me an alibi if Gooch couldn't come up with a better suspect. But there was a hitch. The photo of Plain Jane was attached to her obit. She'd died in a "fiery car crash" four days earlier.

I rescued the leftovers of the three-day old *Advocate* from the recycling pile. A page-four story detailed the death of Elizabeth Longley. Her charred remains were found behind the wheel of a tree-hugging Porsche, ten miles north of Greenwich, across the Westchester line on a remote stretch of roadway, at three in the morning.

The obit mentioned no surviving kin. The wake was scheduled for that evening at the Throckmorton Funeral Salon in Greenwich, near the New York border.

□ □ □

I'm allergic to wakes and funerals. When I go, my wake will be across from the horse at Murphy's. It's where all my friends hang out. The whole city can come if they like. Drinks are on me till the money runs dry. Have a good time. Enjoy life.

It's fifty miles from blue-collar Waterbury, the ex-brass capital of the world, to white-collar Greenwich, the unofficial capital of Fairfield County, Connecticut's gold coast and one of the five richest counties in America. It's a lifetime's journey if you're headed uphill. If you're headed the other way, you can make it in an hour. I considered inviting Gooch. But the lieutenant specializes in deaths, not resurrections.

The gold coast funeral salon was like funeral homes elsewhere, too quiet, too formal, too dead. I expected a closed casket. They're always shuttered for burn victims. Instead there was a plugged urn. I would have paid to watch mourners pay their last respects to a jar full of ashes, but there were only four visitors and no mourners. When you fall from grace in Greenwich you fall fast.

Two short, chubby, middle-aged women with Hispanic accents speculated whether they would get paid for last month's work; the cleaning ladies. An old woman dressed in black draperies mumbled something unintelligible. I asked if she was all right, hoping to unravel her connection to Jane. The Grim Reaper's girlfriend had no connection, just lived across the street and routinely spent her evenings praying over whoever was destined for glory on any given day.

And there was the fat guy—one of Big Nose Sammy's muscle men. I recognized him from my time on the force when I worked an organized crime surveillance. The fat guy didn't belong there. He probably figured the same about me.

I checked the sign-in book and took down the names of the cleaning ladies. Sammy's guy didn't sign in; neither did I.

At nine time expired on the ashes. Given the few who showed for the wake and the price of real estate in Greenwich, I figured the salon wouldn't bother with a proper burial; just dump the ashes in the public rose garden in the morning.

□ □ □

I made the free fall back to Waterbury, googled "Trevor Longley" and located the *Advocate*'s story of his disappearance six months earlier. The small-town midwest native and owner of the less-than-seaworthy *Weekend Mistress* was presumed drowned in a "tragic mishap" midway between New London and Montauk Point.

Longley had been a financial whiz. He'd risen from obscurity, made his fortune, and lost it several times, directing private hedge funds. The accompanying photo revealed a sharply dressed man with a full head of hair, thick eyebrows and a bewitching twisted smile that fell off the left side of his face. He could have done a lot better than Plain Jane, but maybe she came with her own treasury or at least the right connections.

□ □ □

The next afternoon I dropped in on Pete Riccio, clerk at the Ebony, one of the friends I'll invite to my wake. It only took ten bills to remind him what good friends we were and get me a look at the registration book. The day of the murder there had been four guests on the fourth floor. Plain Jane wasn't one of them.

Mr. & Mrs. Henry Doolittle occupied 401. Mahogony had 404.

"Just . . . Mahogany?" I asked.

"Yup."

"What sex?"

"Hard to know," Pete replied.

Mr. Smith was registered in 406.

"Original," I noted. "A regular?"

"Came in six months ago. Never left."

"Mr. Smith pay by credit card?" I asked. Pete gave me a worried look. Maybe he thought I was slipping. Maybe I was. Nobody named Smith pays with a credit card.

"He still here?" I asked.

"Yup."

"Is he in?"

"Yup."

I started for the elevator.

"No tip?" Pete inquired.

"See you at my wake," I replied. "Drinks are on me."

□   □   □

My gut feelings have been wrong before. Maybe that's why I've been married and divorced three times. But deaths and resurrections don't usually happen in the same place at the same time without a connection. I couldn't shake the feeling that Plain Jane and Gorgeous were tied together.

I took the Willy Wonka Express to the fourth floor, unaccompanied by the plain or the gorgeous. Four-O-Six is at the end of the hall opposite the stairwell. Along the way I avoided the dark brown spot on the vomit green carpet. God knows who or what put it there or how long it's been putrefying. I knocked on 406. No one responded. I knocked again—louder.

"Who is it and what do you want?" A male voice. Hard to tell the age.

"Hotel security," I said. "We've had thefts from several rooms recently. Just checking to make sure we haven't missed any."

"Everything's fine. Now, goodbye."

"Well, if you find anything missing, let the front desk know, will ya?"

"Goodbye."

"And if you see a woman in her forties with a bandage on her cheek will you let me know? We think—"

The door opened a crack and I got an eyeball. "What?"

I told him again. "Kinda plain looking woman. She's not one of the staff and we think— You haven't seen her, have you?"

"No, I haven't."

The door was now open half way. The toupee was gone. But the eyebrows were still thick and the smile still fell off the side of his face.

Two were still dead. Gorgeous was dead and the anonymous someone in Plain Jane's urn. Murder was contagious. So were resurrections. Trevor Longley was alive and hanging out at the Ebony.

□   □   □

The next afternoon, Saturday, I dropped Elizabeth Longley's obit in front of Pete.

"Seen this one?"

"Maybe," he said.

"Just maybe?"

"Just ten?" he asked.

I dropped five on the counter. "That's my supper money." Pete didn't seem concerned. He pocketed the bonus.

"Looks like one been coming and going on occasion the last couple of months."

"Bandage on the left cheek?"

"Yup. Recently."

"Visiting the fourth floor?" I asked.

"Visiting Smith," he replied. "Just like the blonde that got herself killed."

For once I got my money's worth.

Ten seconds later, the elevator landed. The deceased Trevor Longley stepped off and passed fifteen feet behind me on his way to somewhere. By the time I got to the front door he'd vanished. The resurrected are pretty slippery.

There's a couch in the far corner of the lobby behind a phony philodendron. The stuffing is leaking out—leaking from the couch, not the potted plastic pretender. I glanced at Pete and nodded at the comfy corner. "Mind if I sit a while?"

"Nope."

Aaah, Pete. A man of few words and you pay well for them.

"When's the wake?" he asked.

I settled into the stuffing, one eye open, one closed. I trade off. Each gets a little shut-eye.

□ □ □

Just before six, Plain Jane slipped in, alone. She had on a new pair of old jeans and a different color sweatshirt still proclaiming I Luv Waterbury. This time I didn't buy it. I opened both lids and hustled to catch the same freight. She hit four.

"Good evening," I said. "I'm surprised to see you again."

No response.

"I'd thought you'd left us." I tried.

No reaction. We passed the second floor.

"Nice evening isn't it, Mrs. Longley?"

"What did you say?"

"I said it's a nice evening, isn't it?"

"After that?" she said. "Who did you call me?"

"Elizabeth Longley. That is your name."

Plain Jane offered no denial. The tortured elevator struggled to a fourth floor berth.

"Who are you?" she demanded.

"Private investigator," I said. "Ralph W. Emerson." I like his work. "Shall we talk here or in your room?"

She had a key. Number 406 is one of the Ebony's traditional extended-stay suites. Across the room, opposite the door, at eye level, was a large ornate brass-edged mirror. Just below the glass a single brass candlestick languished on the mantel of a once working fireplace. She slammed the door.

"Who hired you?" she demanded. I didn't say.

I walked over to the mantel, took down the candlestick, gave it close inspection and put it back. Brass candlesticks always come in pairs.

"New jeans, Mrs. Longley? New sweatshirt? By the way, who was hiding in your urn?"

She couldn't know for sure what I knew, which was next to nothing, but she must have figured I knew more than she wanted me to. She dropped to the closest chair and began to bawl.

I've been burned playing a sucker for the helpless female. This time I wasn't. But I went along for the ride. I handed her a box of tissues, one of the few conveniences the Ebony provides free of extra charge. I figured she'd need a minute to recover her senses. She overplayed her hand and took two.

"It wasn't my fault," she said between the sobs. "My husband dreamed up the whole thing."

She balked at more. I primed the pump. "Your husband faked his own death. Then what?"

The tears dried up. She tried a new approach. "If you'll forget what you know, I'll make it worth your while." Given her looks I figured she was talking money. She was. "Whatever they're paying you, I'll pay double."

Coming from someone hanging out in the Ebony the offer seemed an idle threat. Besides, Gorgeous hadn't given me a penny. I wasn't interested in doubling the fee.

"You must have something you can do with a bit of cash," she said. "Say ten grand. Tonight?"

"I can't be bought," I claimed. That isn't true. Ten grand would buy one hell of a wake. But I like trying on dishonest virtue from time to time. "Now, do you want to talk to me or should I give Lieutenant Gooch on East Main a call?"

"You mean that nosy police officer who was asking questions the other day?"

Gooch did have a Roman nose that got in the way of his seeing clearly from time to time.

□ □ □

It took an hour, another box of tissues and a second fondling of the brass candlestick.

Seven months ago Trevor Longley bet the financial crisis of the century was a hoax. Along with his own small stake and the life savings of a number of hard-working honest folk, Longley lost a big play from a capo connected to Federal Hill in the eastern province of Rhode Island.

Greed and survival being the better parts of valor, Longley cashed in, committed his records to the Atlantic along with his identity, and ran with the proceeds. He left his wife behind to collect the real payoff, a life insurance payout of $800,000.

The insurance company bought the lost sailor routine. The mob connection was less gullible and kept a thoughtful watch on the hardly-grieving widow. She'd been looking over both shoulders for months. Two weeks ago Elizabeth got the insurance payout, her cue to be terminated along with the good captain. I was willing to bet, when she dearly departed, she didn't leave the insurance payout to charity.

Jane claimed she followed husband's orders the night of her own death. Said she left her rented Porsche in the driveway as directed and hung out three days in Yonkers until she got word to meet her husband. Swore she didn't know the details of her demise until she read them in the paper. She stayed one night at the Ebony, hated it, and moved to the Sheraton five blocks away.

"Once a week, for six months, I've come to this godforsaken place dressed like a common street urchin," she said. "Look at me!"

I did. Nothing impressed me, except that she wasn't wearing the jeans and sweatshirt she had on the other day.

She went on. "And then last week I saw that blonde coming from his room."

How ungrateful. Her dead husband carried on an affair with Gorgeous while poor Elizabeth waited for the insurance company to pay up. That explained the look she gave Gorgeous when we left the truly deceased in the lobby.

"All this time my husband's screwing some Tin-Town whore!"

I guess Jane hadn't heard of the Brass City.

The Ebony's one elevator is the slowest ever built and an ex-softball star can move quickly. Jane must have ducked into 406, returned to catch the elevator on its return voyage after I got off at the penthouse, pushed 1 and B for basement and picked up an unsuspecting Angel Carlson at the lobby. Then she gave Gorgeous a one-way ride below ground and rendered the unsuspecting lift an unwitting accessory to murder. Jane probably took the stairs back to the fourth floor.

A batting champ could wield a mean candlestick. If the missing twin was used to kill Gorgeous it was long gone along with the clothes Jane wore that day.

I was certain Jane killed Gorgeous and maybe whoever drove Jane's Porsche to glory. But it would be hard to prove. Her husband would appear an equal or better suspect. And Jane wasn't above blaming him.

She upped the ante. "I could come up with twenty grand in an hour."

Jane had the money. Trevor Longley didn't.

"I'll think about it," I said.

Now that I'd spooked her, Jane would run, with her deceased husband or without him. I left Jane a second box of tissues, returned to the lobby and renewed an acquaintance with the leaking couch.

□ □ □

Jane fled minutes later and I followed her the five blocks to the Sheraton while she chatted on her cell. Ten minutes later I tracked her back to the Ebony. She was carrying a good-sized gym bag and tilted badly to the right. Money can be a heavy burden, especially if there's a lot and it's weighted with guilt. When she took the lift, I checked with Pete.

Trevor Longley had returned minutes after we left. If I dropped in on the postmortem pair and pointed out Jane's offers and accusations, I might get Trevor to roll over. I don't have to worry about reading the rights. I'm not a cop anymore.

I told Pete to call Gooch if I wasn't back in ten. He asked if I was packing.

"Of course not!"

□ □ □

The guilt-ridden elevator ached with a remorse Plain Jane couldn't muster. A familiar rush of adrenalin swept me up in past times. Except this round I had no backup. I got off and faced right. A familiar figure disappeared down the stairwell at the end of the hall, wearing gloves and carrying a gym bag. Never looked back.

I put my ear to 406. No sound. Death has its own kind of quiet.

I knocked. No answer. I knocked again. A moan, and then a scream. Old instincts. I pulled the piece I told Pete I didn't have and kicked in the door.

Jane was on both knees, woozy, a bloody five-inch kitchen knife secured in her right hand.

"Put the knife on the floor and back away!"

There was a commotion in the doorway behind me, but I didn't look back.

"Put the knife down and back up!"

Jane finally complied.

A woman's voice. "Oh my God, Henry! Look!" Henry, I assumed, managed a grunt.

Then a third oddly pitched voice. "Someone call the police!"

Good idea. Two feet from Plain Jane, Trevor Longley lay lifeless. The left side of his forehead bore evidence of a blow from the brass candlestick lying beside him. The one blow wouldn't have killed him. The multiple stab wounds on the left side of his chest did.

□ □ □

The locals took ten. Gooch arrived soon after.

"You again?" he asked.

"Not this time," I said.

Henry and Mrs. Doolittle reported what they'd seen. Mahogany gave a more detailed account. I explained to Gooch that the corpse and the lady were both formerly dead.

The scam would unravel. But Jane would blame the gold coast gambit, the Porsche tragedy and the death of Gorgeous on her husband. Trevor Longley was no longer around to contest the accusations. Still there was the small matter of his corpse. Jane must have finally realized the implications.

"I didn't do it! I didn't do it!" They all say that, even the innocent. "I didn't do it!" Jane kept repeating this to anyone who would listen. "When I came in the room, Trevor was sitting on the couch.

A man grabbed me from behind and smothered me until I passed out. But I saw him in the mirror. The fat man, I saw him."

She pointed at the ornate mirror at the far end of the room. We all looked. The only reflection was Jane's pointing an accusing finger back at herself.

"There was a man—a fat man. He stole my money! He stole my money—and he killed my husband." Spousal concern seemed an afterthought. "I didn't do it!" Jane was sounding desperate. "The fat man!"

She thought it was all about her. But what about the woman whose fried remains were served to the ravenous roses in the park in Greenwich? And Gorgeous? What about Gorgeous? And her two kids left without a mother?

Plain Jane had been willing to part with twenty grand. Three days before, when I couldn't locate the left button with the right arrows, Gorgeous had paid with her life. Plain Jane's story about a mysterious fat man and a gym bag? Who'd believe her? Not a jury. Not without corroboration.

Jane filed a final appeal to my better conscience. "The fat man? You must have seen the fat man!" She demanded confirmation.

Gooch took stock of the gathering. Mr. and Mrs. Doolittle shook their heads. So did Mahogany. Gooch looked to me.

I believe in the Waterbury Fair Play Doctrine. Maybe that's why I never fit New Haven. If the bad guys play fair so will I. If they don't, then the rules of fair play don't apply. That's the way it works in Waterbury. Always has. I shook my head and made the verdict unanimous.

Gooch cuffed Elizabeth Longley, charged her with killing her formerly dead husband and read her the rights.

◻ ◻ ◻

They're all gone now—American Brass, Chase Brass, Century Brass, Scovills. The mills are gone. The workers are gone. The mill families are gone. All that's left are some brass candlesticks, and a few of us with brass balls and a Brass City sense of fair play.

I gave Plain Jane a wink, told Gooch I'd give him a statement in the morning and escaped the Ebony for the familiar lonely Waterbury night.

I crossed West Main and focused through the fog on the traffic light at the east end of the green. Then I navigated the Saturday night shroud to Murphy's, across from the horse, where prewake festivities were under way—and nobody calls me Simon.

The Right and Left of Maintenance

Susan Oleksiw

The departing figure left the office as though gliding on glass, her silk sari shimmering rather than swaying. For a moment, Anita Ray felt a pang of envy for the silent beauty embodied in Sushira Panaik, but then sighed and pulled out the desk chair. Anita had long ago come to grips with her height and a walk that was graceful but not entirely Indian. Her American genes showed up in the oddest ways—Indian features and an American lope.

"Let me see those, Sushira," a man's voice said. A moment later, he continued, "Really, Sushira, your friends are pathetic. You can see it in every snap. Come on. I'm hungry."

Out of the corner of her eye Anita watched Sushira and her husband pass in front of the registration desk and out the front door. With the downturn in the economy, fewer and fewer foreigners were booking rooms, which meant Hotel Delite had been forced to lower its prices to attract more custom. The result was more families who let their children get into all sorts of mischief and who treated the hotel staff as personal servants, watching over them while they worked and correcting their every move. Professor Panaik, as he insisted on being addressed, was the worst of the bunch, in Anita's opinion—he bullied his wife, ignored his mother, and mocked his younger sister, a sad little creature who hobbled about on a crutch.

□ □ □

At six o'clock in the evening Anita closed up her photography gallery and headed back to Hotel Delite. Tourists were strolling along the boardwalk, the women selling fruit had packed up and gone, and only a stray dog wandered across the sand. The restaurants were ready for the evening meal, and Anita glanced at the seafood offerings laid out on tables in front of each restaurant. The shrimp looked especially inviting tonight, and she let herself wonder what the cook would have available for her and her aunt.

"How about some shrimp tonight?" Anita said as she came up to the registration desk. Her auntie Meena gently laid down the telephone. Anita gasped at the look on her aunt's face—ashen, lips trembling, eyes round and tearing up. "Oh, Auntie! What is it?"

"It is Professor Panaik! He has fallen off a cliff! Oh, Anita! All through the brush—a hundred feet or more!"

Anita winced. She shut her eyes against the image of a torn and battered body coming to rest at the foot of a cliff. "What about Sushira? Is she all right? Was anyone else hurt?"

Meena shook her head. "No, she and her mother-in-law and sister-in-law were farther back when the ground gave way. They have gone to hospital, but they will return here. I have sent the car to be ready."

Anita nodded. Yes, that's exactly what she would have expected. If any trouble befell a guest, Auntie Meena immediately began to treat them as relatives who needed special care and attention. Sushira and her family would be tenderly looked after until they felt ready to leave.

□ □ □

In the morning Anita sent out for additional newspapers—she wanted to learn as much as she could about Professor Panaik before the police arrived for their obligatory questioning. The three Panaik women had returned late the night before, exhausted and grieving, and would probably sleep in at least until eight or nine o'clock.

"How can you be so studious at this hour after all that has happened?" Auntie Meena lowered herself into the chair opposite Anita at the small table near the window. The two women rarely joined the guests at the large dining table, both relishing the quiet early hours, with the sound of the Muslim call to prayer in the distance, along with the music from the Hindu temple and the occasional hymn sung by a worker on her way to church. The early morning was a cacophony of worship. Meena glared at the newspaper when Anita failed to answer. Then, in frustration, she grabbed the top of the page and shook it.

Anita apologized and offered a cheery good morning. "It's the obituaries. I had no idea Professor Panaik was so famous."

"He was?" Meena began to look worried. Had she really overlooked someone famous? Was it possible?

"Don't worry, Auntie. He wasn't famous for anything we consider important now."

"Oh, that's a relief." Meena smiled and flicked open a cloth napkin, laying it across her lap. She waved to Moonu hovering in the doorway and ordered coffee and idlies, then began her usual inspection of the dining room without leaving her seat, twisting about to make sure the main table was fully set, the sideboard properly laid out, the chairs suitably arranged. "Ah, so what was the poor man famous for?"

"Research on the Hindu law of maintenance."

"Good heavens," Meena said, her eyes rising involuntarily to the ceiling.

Anita smothered a laugh. "No, Auntie. Not buildings. Relatives."

Anita lowered the newspaper and grinned. Meena glared at her. "I'm sorry, but it is funny. He hardly seemed the type to consider anything so pedestrian." Anita struggled to compose herself.

"Anyway, he lectured and published on Hindu law, especially the law of maintenance."

"Ah, a scholar, a Sanskritist." Meena relaxed in her chair, a smug smile warming her face as Moonu placed a small pot of coffee in front of her. "Yes, he would select us as the most suitable hotel. We are very traditional. And this maintenance. He said many wonderful things about it? Yes?" She paused. "Er, what is it?"

"It's the old Hindu law that the head of the household is responsible for maintaining the weakest, including a discarded wife and other poor relations. It's more complicated than that, but that's basically it. And Congress included it in The Hindu Adoptions and Maintenance Act in 1956."

"Ah, of course. Family is so important." She poured cream into her coffee. "And he said many wonderful things about this law? Always a great man would appreciate this."

Anita picked up the newspaper again. "He argued it all hinges on what kind of estate a man had and . . ." Anita began to read silently. "Frankly, Auntie, I don't get it."

"Well, he was a scholar, isn't it? We are not expected to understand such things. That's why we have lawyers and courts, isn't it?" Meena wouldn't admit it, but she disliked anyone who made her feel inferior. She pulled her coffee cup toward her and a little wave splashed over the side.

"It does make you wonder, doesn't it?" Anita said, once again lowering the newspaper. "I mean, his choice of a subject for his research. Just think of it. He supports his young wife, his mother, and his unmarried sister, who is unlikely to marry. Plus his mother is relatively young and could live quite a long time."

"I see nothing strange in this. It is the proper way, isn't it?" Now that she was no longer warmed by the idea of associating with a great scholar, she was motivated to give a critical eye to everything in her path—especially the idlies placed in front of her. She turned them around and upside down with her fork before giving a reluctant nod of approval to Moonu.

❑ ❑ ❑

The CID officer looked about as uncomfortable as any man Anita had ever seen in the hotel. He gazed upon the three Panaik women seated in a row of chairs in the hotel office and then glanced at the door, as though this might be his last opportunity to make his escape. Anita made herself useful and unimportant by hovering nearby with bottles of water and tissues; in this role she became invisible. But it did her little good—no one had anything revealing to say.

"We are looking over the spot where this most unfortunate event is happening," the officer said, swinging his head back and forth as he spoke, like a metronome beating out each syllable. "Yes, he is having a most long descent to the foot of the cliff."

Sushira winced and looked down at her hands clasped in her lap; her sari pallu was pulled over her head and draped over her shoulder, making her the image of the modest wife, now widow. Her mother-in-law kept her eyes on the officer but reached out her hand and rested it on Sushira's. The sister, Padma, seemed like a feral cat, watching, still, tensed and ready. Her crutch lay on the floor beside her.

"I am apologizing for saying these things." The officer smiled and abruptly turned to Padma. "You are finding this excursion successful? You are not falling in the sand?" His eyes flickered over the crutch as he waited for her reply.

"I am having no difficulties," Padma said, doing her best to straighten her shoulders though they had never been straight. "I am accustomed to walking in difficult places with my crutch. It is no matter."

"Hmm." The officer smiled approvingly, then grew serious. "And you are all living together?"

"Yes, together," the old woman answered. She had the quiet

voice of a caged lion, and Anita had the feeling she would be fierce if the world ever set her free. She reached out her left hand this time and squeezed her daughter's wrist.

"Yes, most appropriate." The officer closed his eyes and nodded in approval. But as Anita looked over the trio she felt anything but the warm glow of a cozy family.

□ □ □

Auntie Meena was in her glory fussing over Sushira, a new widow, and the other bereft women, so she didn't notice Anita slip through the doorway and clamber into an autorickshaw. The ride was bumpy all the way to the small Shiva temple perched high on a bluff overlooking the ocean. Below was a wide beach that stretched to the south as far as the eye could see; to the north lay headlands and hotels, and beyond them the city of Trivandrum. The temple was empty in the early afternoon, not even a caretaker hovering around the gates. Anita climbed out and looked around.

For as long as Anita could remember she had sent tourists up to this spot to enjoy the view, watch birds diving among the tree branches, and walk through the groves cleansed by ocean breezes. The small temple, busy at dawn and dusk, sometimes remained open an hour or so after puja was completed to let tourists enter and view the sculptures and bas reliefs. The temple was modest and small, but authentic, and the priests receptive to those who seemed interested in learning about their faith, Hinduism. But the temple was closed when the Panaik family visited the area, and no other tourists had been about.

Anita crossed the sandy parking area and approached the edge of the bluff. The fall looked almost mild, but on closer inspection anyone could tell that it wasn't—the bushes would cut a body to ribbons, the boulders and rocks along the way would smash bones and tear flesh, the sand would choke and blind. Anita stepped gingerly along the edge until she spotted what she was looking for—the path through the brush Professor Panaik's body had taken. She lay down and reached over as far as possible. About two feet below the edge a root from a nearby tree stuck out, its sheath torn away. Anita felt along the sandy face and found the other half of the torn root. She pushed herself away from the edge and sat against a tree, drawing up her knees and wrapping her arms around them.

The police had been very clear that the professor had fallen to his death, down through the brush to the beach below. They had found blood on the boulders he had hit on his way down, shrubs and saplings torn and crushed. And yet, when he had fallen, he had been facing toward the cliff and able to grab hold of a root in an attempt to halt his fall. Could he have felt the ground giving way, turned, and slid downward, grabbing at the root as he started to fall? Could he have fallen, reached out and grabbed the root but been unable to stop himself? Had someone else fallen and torn the root as they fell?

Anita began to crawl along the ground on hands and knees about three feet from the edge, running her fingers gently over the sand. She had come out to this area numerous times but had never paid much attention to what she walked on, just stepping carefully toward the edge so as not to slide or fall. Now, she wondered just how loose the ground really was. She crawled sideways pressing her fingers here and there closer to the edge, and then she felt something. Along the edge was a hole about two inches deep and two inches in circumference. She went along further, and came to another spot with such a hole. Anita continued on in this way until she had counted over twenty such holes.

Far below on the beach a shout went up and Anita looked out to see a fishing boat coming in to land. Half a dozen fishermen ran forward to ready themselves to help and haul on the net. They moved quickly and efficiently, each one knowing his job and where his compatriots would be as they all worked together. They had learned to move together as a single unit from the very beginning, and each new fisherman moved into his place already understanding from watching as a child how to be part of the greater whole. Anita knew they couldn't see what had happened up here, and probably didn't care.

Once again she thought about how we live our lives among so many people, but when it comes down to it we are truly alone. The fishermen have their own cares and labors, and though she could see them work and struggle, she could do nothing about it; it was their work, their struggle, just as she had her own. Her empathy made her feel she was part of the group below, but in a moment a breeze ruffled her dupatta and she caught it flying off her shoulder. She was once again standing outside a closed temple, wondering at the emptiness of it all.

□   □   □

The sound of crying floated on the late afternoon air. There was no one else around to hear it, as Anita leaned out the dining room window and listened. This was the hour when the hotel was usually empty, the time between the late afternoon nap and the rush to enjoy the remaining time of the day, before it was time to prepare for dinner. Anita was pretty sure what she was hearing was one—or all three—of the Panaik women sinking into grief.

The sobbing was interrupted by a soft voice, murmurings, shuffling furniture, and then a door closing. Whoever it was had left the little balcony, gone into the room, and shut the door. Anita grimaced. Really, she thought to herself, did she think Sushira or even Padma was going to begin confessing to murder on the balcony? And why did she always have to think every unexpected death was a murder?

"I won't answer that," Anita said as she pushed herself away from the window.

"You won't answer what?" Auntie Meena breezed into the room carrying a stack of sheets in her outstretched arms.

"The questions you want to ask but won't." Anita smiled. Meena gasped.

"Oh, you wicked girl! I have no such thought." Her aunt blushed and looked around for somewhere to lay down the linens. She slid them onto the dining table, and then pulled a letter from her sari blouse. "I am returning this to the Panaiks. It fell into their trash."

"Hmm. What else do you have hidden in your choli?" Anita said as she took the letter.

"Wicked girl," Aunt Meena said, but Anita noticed that the words carried no passion.

Anita opened the letter and scanned the contents. "Maybe she meant to throw it away, Auntie." Anita didn't comment on the care Meena had taken to tape the pieces together again. She turned it over and noted it was addressed to Sushira Panaik.

"Certainly not. Would you throw away a letter from a lawyer? And he is an important one, a famous vakeel. I was . . ." Meena looked about for help in her now shamefully helpless state. "What do you accuse me of? It was in the litter basket. Am I to waste paper now too?" And with her recovery, she grabbed the pile of sheets and stalked out of the dining room.

Anita found it easier to go along with her aunt's excuse that she had really salvaged the torn pages from the litter basket and taped them together. Auntie Meena, despite her shrewd management of Hotel Delite, always believed she was daily on the verge of catastrophe—bankruptcy, unknown creditors banging down her doors, strange relatives showing up and demanding care and support. Life held many terrors for Meena Nayar, and almost all of them figments of her imagination. But Auntie Meena was also just as curious as Anita sometimes.

The letter was short and cryptic. After rereading the letter and discarding the opening and closing paragraphs as nothing more than courtesies, Anita concluded that the core point seemed to be one sentence, in the middle paragraph: "Pursuant to your query of the 15th instant, such is indeed the situation. Steps have been taken in light of professor's premises." What on earth did that mean?

□ □ □

Anita walked up the hill past the line of autorickshaws, chatting with the occasional driver waiting hopefully in the back seat for a customer at this evening hour. Few tourists went anywhere at night that required an auto, and most drivers left the resort at dusk. Anita got the name she was looking for, climbed into an auto, and headed off.

Ten minutes later Anita leaned out of the auto and studied a cream-colored taxi parked just inside a broad metal gate. She crossed the yard to the front door, pressed the bell and waited. A young boy, perhaps seven or eight years old, peeked out from behind the worn red curtain covering the open doorway. Anita asked for his father, the driver.

"Yes, it is my taxi." The man gazed suspiciously at her. It was clear he had retired for the day, and was now relaxing in front of the television, where the voices of his children competed with those on the screen. He fussed with his lungi, pulling it higher over his undershirt. "Yes, I am taking this family to the temple on the cliff. Yes, they are paying me." He lowered his chin. "I am receiving no tip."

Anita walked over to the taxi, out of earshot of the rest of the family. The man followed her slowly, still suspicious.

"They are staying at our hotel, Hotel Delite."

The driver said he knew this.

"And it just seemed to me that on top of everything that happened, the younger sister, Padma, seems extremely unwell." Anita paused. This had to be a good lie to get the information she wanted, but she tried not to give in to the quick ripple of pleasure she felt every time she came up with what she considered a really good lie. "I am thinking that perhaps she wore herself out, or perhaps came in contact with something that gave her some rash or allergy. Did you notice this?"

"Not possible." The driver was adamant and repeated this opinion several times.

"Yes, but, she could have encountered lots of things—a snake, a rat, some plant."

"No, no, not possible. She is the crippled one, yes?" He shook his head again. "She is not leaving the taxi. She is not feeling strong, and she is remaining sitting in the back seat."

"But—" Anita stopped herself. She had seen marks along the cliff that she had taken to be the foot of the crutch, but if Padma never left the taxi, then the small pockets came from something else or . . . "The mother is most agile, isn't she? Not like one would expect from her age. But she can always lean on her daughter-in-law."

The taxi driver dropped his chin and glared at her, and Anita had the sinking feeling he knew exactly what she was looking for. She leaned back against the taxi, folded her arms, and waited. He pulled out a white handkerchief from the fold of the lungi wrapped around his stout waist and shook it open, then walked to the front of the car and snapped it against the hood, displacing the few specks of dust that had landed there.

"And you? Did you help the mother and daughter-in-law?" Anita asked.

His head popped up and he stared at her. "Me? No, no, not me. I am driver. I am parking at the near side of the temple, not on the cliff side."

"So, you didn't actually see anyone walk as far as the cliff," Anita said.

"Exactly so." He waggled his head, a man completely innocent. "I am helping the old woman and the younger one to find the path around the temple, and the young sister, Padma, she is staying in the car." He folded his handkerchief and slipped it back into his waistband. "But she is giving her crutch to her mother, to help steady her." He sighed and said, "The girl is kind."

□ □ □

Anita liked to see things for herself. As a result, twenty minutes later, she found herself at the foot of a steep cliff.

"That way," the driver said, pointing northward. She began walking, stopping every now and then to pull apart the shrubbery, until she came to the spot where the professor had landed. She rummaged through the shrubbery, the broken branches, and followed sandy footprints, but in the end she was frustrated.

"Who found him?" she asked the driver. "Do you know?"

In another five minutes, the auto pulled up in front of a small house on a paved road, three lanes inland from the beach. The house was quiet, with only the occasional voice and burst of laughter breaking the evening rest. Anita pressed the bell.

"It is my younger daughter who is first there," an old woman said. She stood as straight as a banana tree, her arms akimbo, suspicion in every fiber. After a moment, she relented and called her daughter.

"He is lying on the ground. He is not even moaning. He is dead, I am certain." The daughter was about twenty, already married with a small child and another on the way. She glanced at her mother after every sentence, though it didn't seem to Anita as though she were seeking approval.

"Can you just point to the spot?" Anita asked. She shushed the driver before he could interrupt and drew the woman away from the house. "I am thinking that there might be something to find at the site." The woman paled, and Anita pressed home her advantage. "The police will want to know, but they appreciate honest help."

The woman resisted, but in the end Anita's nudging was too much. As the sun fell into the sea, its sudden disappearance without fanfare or beauty, a single light over the door picked out the sparkling gold in the woman's palm, a small earring of conservative design.

□ □ □

"Are the Panaiks still here?" Anita asked as soon as she returned to the hotel. Her aunt nodded yes, but before she could say anything, Anita hurried from the room. "I'll be upstairs if you need me, talking to Sushira." Auntie Meena barely had time to protest before Anita's sandals were slapping on the stone stairs.

Anita was all apologies when Sushira opened the door. Behind her Padma and her mother were sorting clothing strewn about the bed, suitcases open on the floor. "I so want to talk to you before you leave." Anita pushed her way into the room and sat down on the edge of the bed.

"We are preparing to leave," Sushira said. "We are taking the midnight train north. This has been a difficult time for us, as you can imagine."

"Far better than you may realize," Anita said, and was gratified to see Padma's head jerk back. Anita let the silence lengthen—she never felt uncomfortable in this kind of situation—and then smiled. It was time to get to it.

The old woman raised her hand as Anita began to speak and turned to find a chair. She sat down heavily, her feet flat on the floor, her hands resting on her knees. "You have something to say, yes?"

Anita nodded, wondering at the old woman's apparent resignation. "I went out to the temple this afternoon and walked along the edge. It's quite desolate during the day—no one else is out there. Just the birds. And of course the fishermen far below." She paused recalling the scene. "The sand along the cliff edge is quite soft, as I discovered. I think you discovered that too."

"That is why my son fell to his death."

"True, in part."

Sushira looked from one to the other but didn't speak; instead, she moved closer to Padma, and rested her hand on her sister-in-law's shoulder.

"But I noticed that he must have fallen backward."

"I'm sure he tried to save himself," the dead man's mother said. She spoke without emotion, without feeling, tonelessly, sending a shudder through Anita.

"Yes, by grabbing hold of a root." Again Anita paused. "And of course falling just at the spot where the ground was ready to give way—not everyone would have noticed that." Anita caught Sushira glancing at Padma, but the widow quickly composed herself.

"He went too close to the edge, the ground gave way, he fell." The old woman lifted her chin. "There is nothing more to it than that."

Anita looked at Sushira, ever the modest widow. "You wear the pallu pulled over your head so modestly even here, in your own room, among women only."

"I have lived a long time in the North."

"You can abandon the habit today, your last day here. Yes?"

Sushira drew her hand away from her sister-in-law and pulled on the edge of the pallu, drawing it closer around her head. Her eyes were steady, but pained, not the eyes of a cold-blooded killer, and not the eyes of a grieving widow. Her pain seemed to be deeper, an ache that swept up from a life gone wrong, that strangled hope and compassion.

"We are leaving soon. Why are you troubling us?" the old woman asked.

Anita turned to the dead man's mother. "That's a fair question, Mrs. Panaik. I suppose I'm here because I have something of a compulsion when it comes to death. I'm curious and nosey. People do such odd things to each other, and I just have to figure it out."

"The police have completed their investigation. He fell. It was an accident." Sushira spoke softly, but her voice was not tender or grieving.

"And in some ways I suppose it was," Anita said. "After you got him to walk along the edge, and gave him a little push to throw him off balance, and he grabbed for something, anything to hold onto, including your sari. He got a piece of it, I suppose, but mostly he got this." She uncoiled her fingers, and the single earring glistened in her palm. Padma gasped. "Your ear is bloody and you cannot let anyone see it—hence the pallu over your head. He must have ripped off the ear lobe."

"I perhaps lost the earring in the confusion," Sushira said, her eyebrows lifting. This time when she laid her hand on Padma's shoulder, she seemed to be steadying herself rather than comforting the other.

"I went to the library this evening and read the professor's most recent publication on the Hindu Law of Maintenance." Anita stood up and pulled a sheet of paper from her pocket. "You've probably seen this already, but I found it surprising, confusing, and very alien-ating. He didn't believe in the law of maintenance, but he seems to have spent a large part of his career on this topic." Anita turned to Padma.

"He studied many subjects within Hindu Law," the old woman said.

"But none so thoroughly, and with such passion," Anita said. "Since you stayed in the car, Padma, I'm thinking you are the main reason for your brother's death. Your mother and Sushira both have their own money from marriage—they could have survived—but you don't have anything. Your brother was rearranging his estate to leave you out—to make sure you would be sent to an ashram as a charity case unless someone else took you in." Padma pulled away from Sushira's hand, and started to rise.

"Go get me a bottle of water, Padma," her mother said. "Go," she repeated and waited as the girl limped from the room. Sushira shut and locked the door behind her.

"I am giving no remorse," the mother said. "He was my son, but what he meant to do was cruel—it would have been the death of my daughter, turned into a beggar on the streets. I cannot protect her if I am not here, and I will not live forever."

"He taunted us with it," Sushira said as she came to the bed and sat down. She let her pallu fall across her back, but one part snagged on the bandage wrapped around her ear before falling onto her shoulder. "He was a great scholar of the old laws and he despised so many of them."

"He wanted to overturn the old laws," his mother said, "and while it was all scholarship, articles for learned journals, it did not matter. But then he wanted to put his views into practice."

"We had to take action while we still could," Sushira said.

"He terrorized my Padma," the mother said. "So I did this thing." She squeezed her eyes shut, gave her head a shake. "I acted for my daughter."

"And I too." Sushira nodded and smiled gently at her mother-in-law.

◻ ◻ ◻

At breakfast the next morning, Anita pulled out her chair to sit down but before she could do so she was caught by her aunt's smug look.

"What are you up to, Auntie?"

Auntie Meena picked up her coffee cup and took a sip, holding the saucer in front of her chest. "Nothing. Nothing at all."

"Well, something is making you look like the cat that swallowed the canary." Anita sat down and reached for the coffee pot. "I'll find out somehow, so you might as well tell me."

"The Panaiks are gone. They have loaded their luggage and are driving to the station. All three are together in the seat. I have seen them. I have waved to them." She paused, cocked her head to one side, and smiled. "Up the road they have gone, onto the station."

"That's nice." Anita took a sip of her coffee. Nice and strong.

"Yes, and not a single arrest." Meena lowered her cup and saucer. "A death and not a single hint of suspicion." She looked inordinately pleased.

"Who said so? Just because I never said anything to you doesn't mean what you think it means."

"Eh?" Meena looked ashen. "What do you mean?"

"Do you like this earring, Auntie?" Anita laid a delicate gold earring of traditional workmanship on the table. She believed the mother would confess if necessary, part of her determination to protect her vulnerable daughter from poverty and degradation, and Sushira would admit to helping her, but it didn't matter. No one could prove anything—the police had been completely satisfied and there was not enough evidence to rebut their decision. Anita accepted this, but she had decided to keep the earring as a reminder of just how hard it was to know right from wrong.

Ivory

Nancy Means Wright

It was small, as baby grands go, a baby-baby grand, built by German craftsmen, Indian rosewood veneer. Florence worried about the rosewood: it was getting to be extinct—what would they say at customs? (She'd had trouble with dictatorial customs officials before—almost struck one, but managed to keep her temper in check.) By then of course—too late to save the tree! But the finish was exquisite, polished to a rich rosy patina, the instrument a century old perhaps, and still capable of perfect tune.

She knew. She was one of those blessed with perfect pitch. At school, in chorus, the director had only to say, "Florence, give us an A," and she'd give it, unfailing as dawn.

So naturally she pursued a career in music—what else? Not singing, no, for perfect pitch didn't make a soloist: she never had the diaphragm, the vibrato a singer needed. But piano! Her mother was a piano teacher (never a performer); she saw that her daughter, an only child, got an early start. From the time she could reach the pedals of her mother's old upright she was at it: two hours a day, and then three, and four as she labored into her teens. At nineteen she won a contest; at twenty-two performed with the local symphony.

And was stuck! She couldn't seem to move beyond, though she auditioned and auditioned. She was almost relieved when her mother died—could never bear the grim V of her mother's pale brows when she had to admit a rejection. And yet afterward, alone in the old Vermont farmhouse, it was almost as though that obsessive spirit breathed into her; she was suddenly crazy to succeed! She'd practice up to ten hours a day: sonatas, serenades, Beethoven, Mozart, Vivaldi, Chopin. A cellist from the Vermont Symphony wanted to marry her; she refused. She imagined him playing the cello while she cooked his dinner. No, music and marriage wouldn't mix.

She got so she lost breath when she stepped outside her mother's house she'd inherited; was disoriented, fearful that someone would assault her, run her over with a motorcycle, a fast Porsche, damage her hands. She wouldn't even open a can. She ate mostly frozen stuff, out of cartons. But she'd be a celebrity one day, wouldn't she, when she was ready?

And then, when she was thirty-one, and beginning to see her youth shrink away, realizing she'd rarely been out of Vermont, much less abroad, she was invited to a competition in Germany. Berlin! It was the cellist who wangled it for her. "Time you let down your hair, Rapunzel," he said, and after two glasses of red wine, with Ted looming over her (he was a tall, big-boned man, too tall really for her pear-shaped five-foot-three), she made arrangements. He drove her himself, to the Burlington airport. Without him she might not have gotten on the plane.

She took a first-floor room in a Victorian house on the outskirts of Berlin. It wasn't easy getting around: she didn't speak German (her grandfather was killed by a German sniper in World War Two and her mother made her learn French). But with the help of the landlady, she bought a piano. The competition was two weeks away; she had to practice. The landlady, a big breasted, pink-cheeked woman who always dressed in purple, was delighted; she "luffed moosik," she said.

The four sweaty men who carried it into the room (first they had to move out a huge mahogany wardrobe) admired the finish, the delicate floral design on the rosewood, but exclaimed loudest over the keys. "Such beau-tee-ful i-fory!" the one who spoke English said. "Must off been a beeg heliphant." And Florence laughed; it was hard to connect an elephant with the finely carved ivory keys that seemed to glow in that dark room draped in purple brocade. The landlady rushed out and back again with an ivory carving, a naked lady, to place triumphantly on the piano. "Dey match," she exulted, and Florence clapped her hands.

"Vil play a be-au-tee-ful tune," the workman who spoke English persisted, and feeling euphoric, the landlady begging her on, Florence sat down to play a Beethoven sonata in E flat major.

"Allegro molto e vivace," she announced to her audience. She found herself gazing between chords into the English-speaking workman's eyes—he was a poet, he'd said, trying to feed his muse.

They were all silent a moment afterward, while she caught her breath, felt the blood thump in her veins; and then ten sweaty hands burst into applause and she realized she had never played so passionately.

She had inspired a poem the poet-workman told her as he left; he would hurry home to write it. "Ja!" he shouted, "be-au-tee-ful poem!" and she felt herself to be that beautiful poem, a thing her glass never told her, and later in the room, ran her fingers over the naked ivory carving.

But it was the ivory keys, she decided, that made the difference. Her fingers literally flowed through the sonatas. Watching in the mirror opposite, she saw herself a princess-turned-white-duck, skimming the surface of a pond, then up, up into the bluest of skies, racing the shredded clouds. Heading east into purple hibiscus—and ah! she was a woman again, skin like fine bone china, like ivory, running into the arms of her poet-lover.

She spent the whole day, every day, practicing, lost nine pounds—though the landlady brought her treats: rich buttery pastries filled with chocolate, and chatted of tourist sights she must see. But after a polite nibble, Florence would say, "After the competition I'll eat you out of house and home. I promise! I'll creep through the art galleries, walk that broken wall." For the Berlin Wall had just fallen, that very year of 1989.

And the practicing paid off. She didn't win the competition, but for the first time in her life she was a finalist! A marvel, really, considering the dozens of competitors from all over the world. The applause went on and on; people rushed up after she played the Beethoven to congratulate her in a babel of languages. And it was all because of the rosewood piano with the ivory keys. Though she'd had to use the institute's piano for the competition, she told her Vermont cellist afterward on the phone. "Yes, of course the keys were ivory, Ted, but not like my baby grand. If I'd had it, and more time for practice, I'd have won, I just know it!"

She heard him chuckling. He was a rational, sequential person; he called her a random abstract (she didn't always like that). But he had her interests at heart. "Auditions coming up next month— Boston," he told her. "We'll go together, shall we? I'll get us a room." (He hadn't given up on marrying her.) All right then, she would put Berlin behind her, have the piano shipped home, sell her mother's old upright, and set her sights on Boston. One could manage in life knowing that Something Waited Around The Corner, couldn't one? She had never felt so optimistic, the air was never so full of light. She might even marry Ted; they could move to Boston, take an apartment—just so it was filled with sunlight, no smog.

□   □   □

The day of her departure she hailed a taxi; there was the sweet expectant smell of a foreign morning. Already they'd come for the baby grand—expensive, oh terribly. She'd had to wire her home bank for money, dip into her savings. But never mind. Her poet-mover had it crated, the precious keys done up in the thickest of wraps. It would fly air freight, the day after her passenger plane left; they promised the utmost care—Germany loved its music. She was wearing a black gaberdine suit, white silk blouse and sheer black stockings: she was a musician, she had a master piano, she would dress to meet its expectations. Besides, it was November—who knew what turn the weather would take? Ted had said it was snowing in Vermont: she imagined the thick flakes falling past the Middlebury College museum windows, illuming the treasures there.

"Careful now, that's a magic piano," she told the poet-mover, and he laughed and said he remembered the keys. "King of jungle, Lord of helephants," he bellowed; and though she didn't like to be reminded about the poor elephants, poached for their ivory, she laughed, and said, "Ja, ja! But it's the craftsman who shaped and polished those keys whom we want to applaud."

"Da helephant—he iss da true craftsman," the poet insisted, and pocketed his tip (smaller than she wanted to give him, but she'd spent a fortune already in shipping fees). She kissed his hairy cheek (there was his reward! both of them laughing) and off she drove to the airport.

Before checking in, she went to the air freight building; she would see to the piano personally. They didn't want to let her in, but she persevered, offered what was left of her German marks to the man at the gate, was finally ushered inside. And there, with the other outsized boxes, was her crated piano. A big-bellied man stood by it; he wore an orange necktie, a dour expression, appeared more official than the others in their drab green uniforms with BERLIN on the back. He was "Zoll-Beamt—Customs Officer," he said; he spoke a heavily accented English. He didn't look at her, just nodded at one of the uniformed men, pointed a thick finger and said, "Open."

"Open? Open what? You can't open my crate!" she squealed— then thinking of the rosewood, sucked in her breath. Surely they wouldn't—

"Fraulein, iss Klavier—piano, no?" said the official. "Got keys, ifory keys?"

Ivory! The word shocked. She curled her fists into her palms. "But all good pianos have ivory keys!" And then when she saw the official give the worker a nod: "Well, these keys might be plastic, I do think so. Look, I spent hundreds having it properly crated, you have no right—it's old—worth thousands of dollars. An antique. It's invaluable!"

"Antique? Den iss ifory, ja," the man said, the words coming out like flat stones scaled into a river. "Old days, who had plastic?"

"But this is German customs!" she argued. "You have no right. This piano is going to the United States!"

The man made a sound that was half-laugh, half-disgust. "States dey nefer let ifory through. Nefer. Nefer! Iss new regulation, joost this year. Germany iss cooperating now—cifilized country. You buy Klavier in India—den dey let you pass. Tird world," he said, and spit on the concrete floor.

She recalled a defense class she had taken. "Be firm," the instructor had warned. "Don't give in—unless all else fails, your life at stake. Only then, give in." And her mother: "Curb that temper now, Florence. It's gotten you into trouble before. Calm down."

She drew in a breath. "It's an antique," she repeated. "Surely the new regulation does not apply to an antique."

That stopped the fellow for a moment. Then he said, "You haf proof? You haf document?"

Document? She had no document. She'd bought the piano from a private citizen who spoke little English. She hadn't thought of papers—it wasn't a pampered canine, for God's sake, going into a dog show. "You cannot do this," she said, the anger grinding up into her throat. "That is my piano. I'm a concert pianist. That elephant died over a century ago. What can you do with that ivory now?" She heard her voice crescendo, a high C.

"We won't take Klavier," the official said. "Only keys. No ifory will leaf Chermany!" He spread his legs squarely on the floor. He was a tyrant. He was the man who killed her grandfather. She wanted to retaliate. She bared her teeth at him but his expression didn't alter.

"Why, you might as well take my fingers!" she cried. She wiggled them: they were live birds, flying away from the crouching tiger.

Already they were closing in on the piano: men with sharp tools, wrenching, twisting off the crate—then the ivory from the keys—she could hear it squeal. Like nails scraping a blackboard—a personal assault! Her flesh trembled, her bowels threatened to give way. She flung herself on the men; her hands fought, her nails attacked.

She was yanked back, her stockings ripped. "Iss new regulation! Law!" the official bellowed. The silk of her sleeve gave way. "You got Klavier," he cried, "in States you put ifory if you can find. Not from Chermany! Iss illegal I'm telling you. Illegal!" He dismissed her pleas with a downward slash of his hand and stomped out of the room.

If all fails, give in; the defense instructor's words came back. "Calm yourself," her mother hissed in her ear. She leaned against a counter. They were up to B sharp already, stripping the wooden keys. "Wait, stop!" she cried. "One more time at least. Let me play."

The workmen glanced at one another; one of them smiled. "Mein dochter haf klavier," he said. He made a welcoming gesture with his arm, pulled up a crate for her to sit on. She chose Beethoven, the sonata in A flat major she'd played at the competition. The third movement, a funeral march. "Sulla morte d'un Eroe," she announced. It was all that came to mind now. It was heavy, sonorous, and grim. The splintery wood of the ripped-up bass keys added a macabre undertone to the piece. The men listened respectfully; the man with the daughter took his cap off. Afterward, no one clapped—do you applaud the dead? Slowly the men went back to work, pulling off the remaining ivory—carefully, like compassionate dentists.

When they were done, the ivory dropped into a box like dead jagged teeth, the official came back in. "Fraulein. Gif you new crate," he said. He shouted orders at the workmen, who followed him out of the area—all except for one elderly man, who was left to sweep up the debris into a trash can. A wall clock said it was 4:14—her plane was due to depart in thirty minutes.

Something snapped then in her brain, as though an elephant had thundered up to confront her. My ivory, she thought, I am not leaving without my ivory. The old man had his back to her, he was bent over his dustpan and broom. The box of her stripped ivory was still on the counter. Her ivory. The ivory from her king elephant. Quickly she stuffed it into her pockets, her purse, unbuttoned her blouse to drop a few strips into her bra. She reached into the box for the last tendrils—and felt a hand clap her shoulder. "Nein, nein!" the old man grunted, and snatched at her right hand to pull away the ivory.

"Ja!" she screeched and shoved him, hard, with her shoulder. He was slight of stature, a bag of brittle bones. But he was resilient; he came back at her. "Nein!" And tried to force open her fingers—she felt a bone bruise, a vein swell. Filled with fury she grabbed his neck with her free hand and squeezed; she heard him gag, then a crash as he fell against the metal trash can. But she couldn't stop to look, to consider; it was late. She raced, crazy-legged, for the door before he could rise to summon others. Then out through the gate with her precious ivory and up the walkway to the US Air Departures building.

There, she slowed to a walk; checked in, showed her passport, and moved like a sheep through security. She heard the loudspeaker: "Flight 2087, boarding now."

She was still dazed as she settled into her seat on the plane; tried to block out what had happened—the old man would be all right, wouldn't he? Her fingers were strong from playing but not strong enough to kill, were they? No. She paid for a glass of whiskey, though she didn't usually drink hard liquor. She pushed away the sausage supper the stewardess thrust under her nose. The ivory lay cradled between her breasts like the child she'd never thought to have. She tried to pull words together to describe her exhilaration at rescuing the ivory, but couldn't summon them. There was no one at home she'd be able to talk to—Ted would never wholly understand.

"But why didn't you let them keep the piano?" she could hear him say. "You know you could get ivory over here—on the black market at the very least."

And how could she explain, rationally, why it would not be the same? Why it had to be this ivory, this magic ivory, from the King of Elephants! So. She would have the baby grand repaired and polished, the ivory matched and glued back onto the hardwood keys. She would have two full weeks to practise before the Boston audition. The one she was going to win. Yes, win!

She put her head back against the seat as the plane flew toward home and envisioned an elephant, a magnificent beast with fiery gold eyes. She was riding on his smooth, magical tusks. They were soaring through the ether, up into a pure blue light. Beethoven rang in their ears; the elephant chanted a poem, a breathless tale of a wild duck that turned into a princess.

When the stewardess came for her empty glass, she murmured "Thank you," and nodded a regal head.

□ □ □

Back at Logan Airport she handed in her customs slip. She had painstakingly described her purchases: the low-necked, ivory-colored silk gown she'd bought for the competition, the shiny new black pumps, the blue-and-white striped tie for Ted.

"Passport, please? We must see your passport." The customs official was tired; you could see the irritation in the red flush of his cheeks, in the narrowed, red-rimmed eyes. She was suddenly exhausted herself; her watch read 11:50—but in Berlin, it was already morning.

"Passport, madam! Show it. Now." Ah. She opened her purse. But in her scurry to reach the baggage area, her passport had some- how gotten stuck under the little pile of ivory. She tipped the purse and shook it; reached in to tug out the document—and the shiny black bag slipped from her weakened hands.

It was like slow motion then: the ivory falling bit by strip out of the purse, herself dropping to her knees to gather it; the customs man following with his eyes—she heard him say "ivory," and whistle. The man holding out his hand for the purse, then grunting into his radio; a second official running up, and a third—the three men sur- rounding her; the airport police dragging her by the arm to a private room.

They hurled questions at her. Had she come from Berlin? Did she have a piano crated? Did it have ivory keys? Illegal ivory that had disappeared, they'd been informed. There was a witness in intensive care with a head injury. Did she know something about that? "I'm afraid we'll have to search you, madam. It's illegal now, to bring in ivory."

She nodded, she knew. She was done in; she could only hang her head.

And after the search—by a woman whose fat fingers probed pockets, purse, bra, even panties for every shiny bit of her precious ivory—there was Ted, altogether shocked, yes, at what she'd done.

Yet the next day he brought in a lawyer. They would not prose- cute her, the lawyer decreed—though there was the matter of the old man she had injured—perhaps killed—but with breath enough to identify her.

For now, the lawyer said, she was free to return to Vermont.

But without the ivory.

□　□　□

Home alone in Middlebury, waiting to hear from the lawyer if the workman had lived or died (already the Germans had appropriated her rosewood baby grand), she covered the old upright with a purple cloth and piled books, photos, and vases of silk flowers on top. She brewed a cup of hot chamomile tea and sipped it slowly, gazing out her picture window. It had snowed the night before; the landscape was filled with bizarre shapes and surprises; the sky was a Ferris wheel of swiftly moving clouds (very like an elephant)—but inside the house there was an awful quiet.

When she held up a hand, she felt she could see not only her career but her entire life flowing out through her fingers—like bubbles of ivory.

P to Q

Nancy Brewka Clark

You want to lose some of that extra poundage there, Jody, or you're going to end up sticking yourself with little needles all day long to see how much sugar you've got."

I look down at my midriff. It's terraced in fat, like some kind of Chinese mountainside. I love Chinese food, so I don't think the connection's so bad. But Maisie's looking at me like I'm on the planet just so she can have a cause.

"You keep putting on weight," she says, "and you're going to die young."

I put my hands on the fat. It's warm through my jersey, almost as if it has its own heating system, sort of like a human Florida room. It's not squishy either. It's good hard American fat, earned the honest way, by eating. I eat in front of the tube, I eat in the car, I eat at my desk and I eat at the table. I even eat in bed. Fact is, I love to eat. Yum-yum!

"You should eat to live, not live to eat," Maisie says. "That's what my granddad Horace always used to say. And he lived to be ninety-nine. Expected to make a hundred, but he laughed too hard at Leno."

"I don't care for late-night TV." I try to pick up a bunch of files but she puts her scrawny, little chicken claw on them. The nails are heart-red and they come out of her fingertips like saw blades.

"They have places you can go, you know," she says. "You could go to one of those fat farms, Jody."

"I'm not rich and I'm not famous."

"What's that got to do with your health?" She drums those brutal nails on my filing like she's getting fed up with me.

"Folks who go to those places have plenty of money and nothing better to do," I say. "Besides, I'm not that fat."

"The heck you aren't." She squints at me. "What are you, a size 16? 18?"

"I go by the letters, not the numbers."

She stares at me. I can see the contact lenses resting on the bulge of her eyeballs. "Well, then, what letter are you? L? Or are you maybe two letters, say, XL?"

"Sometimes I'm an M." I feel good inside saying that, because it's the truth. Last week I bought myself a sweatshirt in Wal-Mart and it's a Medium. I think it might have come from the men's section, but it was right there on the Misses' rack.

"More like a Q," she says, looking at my middle again.

"I don't wear pantyhose."

"If you wore a dress once in a while you'd wear them," Maisie says.

I think of giving her some lip, something like, "So, if you don't like the way I dress, fire me," but I don't want to get fired. Despite working for Maisie, I like it here. I could do a lot worse than eleven bucks an hour. Besides, it's work you don't have to think about very much, just entering claims in the computer and seeing they're filed right after they're printed out. So instead I say, "You can wear dresses, Maisie. They look good on you."

"They'd look good on you, too, if you'd only get rid of some of that fat." She steps away from me and puts her hand to her chin, like she's some kind of artist studying her subject and wondering where to go from here. "Why don't you want to? You just tell me that. Why does a pretty girl like you want to carry around that extra flesh?"

"Maisie," I say slowly, "why are you ragging on me? Why do you care whether I weigh a hundred or two hundred?"

She looks taken aback, like I said something too personal to her. "Well," she says, "it just makes me, you know, sad to see a young woman not take care of herself. You know, once you lose your youth, you can't get it back."

I figure Maisie's fifty or thereabouts. I feel a nip of pity, even if she does wear P. "You look great, Maisie."

She smiles and runs both hands with those red, red nails along her size 4 hip bones. "Well, I try." She wipes the smile off her face. "And you should try, too. You owe it to yourself."

There isn't much I can say to that, so I just sit back down at my computer. She takes this as a sign that I'm done listening, so she goes off saying, "I like you, Jody, and I'm going to help you."

Next day, darned if that woman doesn't come in with a newspaper clipping. I find it on my desk, after break. "CHANGE YOUR LIFE BY CHANGING YOU!" it screams at me. "AN HOUR WITH RAY RENDLE WILL CHANGE YOUR LIFE! ARE YOU READY TO CHANGE? BECAUSE RAY'S READY TO CHANGE Y-O-U!"

"Seems the gist of it is, he wants to change me," I say when she comes by my desk. "Guess he can try."

"So, you're interested?"

Maisie sounds as if she's won some kind of battle. "Sure. What's an hour?" I keep my tone casual but deep down inside I'm feeling this little squiggle of excitement. Spring's just around the corner. Maybe by July I can fit into the bathing suit I'd kept from high school. It's a good one, a Jantzen.

Her nail taps another line of print. "Sixty dollars. Got that?"

I try not to show that I'm insulted. "Of course I do." I think about what I'm saying. "I can put it on plastic, right?"

"I'll call," she says, "and tell them to hold two seats."

"You're going too?" I'm confused. "Why do you want to go to

a fat seminar?"

She hits the clipping again with her nail. "Oh, it's not just for fat. It's for other things, too."

"Like what?" I lean closer to the newspaper ad. I never looked beyond the headline.

"It's to improve yourself," Maisie says, "all over, inside and out." She laughs, showing those kind of thick, pushed-together, even teeth that you know are caps, especially when you see the person's gums. "Guess I could use some of that, too." She holds out her hand. "Give me your card. No point in getting them all confused by using two."

Remembering how Maisie's tighter than a tick with her own money, I'm a little slow to undo the clasp of my pocketbook. "Don't tell me you have credit troubles." She sighs. She doesn't have to say it, but I hear "too" just as plain as if she'd yelled it in my ear.

"No, course not." Feeling the heat rise in my face, I open my wallet.

"That's good." She snaps the card from my fingers. "Those interest rates are murder."

On the big night I pick Maisie up at twenty to seven. "Cutting it close," she complains. She pulls off her glove, one of those little stretchy things they sell in Kmart for a buck a pair, and wipes the seat with her palm before sitting, like she thinks there might be greasy crumbs on the upholstery, but I've already used my Dirt Devil.

"We have reservations," I point out and cruise down Elm to Canal past the old brick mills, all fancy condos now, with Maisie chatting in my ear about what she'd nuked for dinner, a cheapo Weight Watchers type shrimp platter the local Shop 'n' Bag puts out, 410 calories. "Not counting the cardboard," I say, but she doesn't crack a smile, just checks her watch.

It's ten to seven when I turn into the armory parking lot. They still have all kinds of tanks parked on view there but they aren't taking up any spaces, being behind a metal fence. Lumps of dirty snow press up against the chain links like a litter of abandoned puppies at the pound, and I feel a kind of chill come over me, the kind that a hot chocolate with plenty of whipped cream would cure in an instant.

"Not as many cars here as I would have thought," Maisie says as she slides out. "What's the matter with people, anyway? Everybody can improve themselves if they just get off their butts."

I lean over and lock her door, which she has neglected to do, and then get out myself. "I'm lighter already," I say, "a hundred and twenty bucks lighter," but I laugh to show her I'm just joking. All things considered, I'm in a pretty good mood. After all, she can't stiff me forever and besides, maybe this Ray guy would find some knob or something in my brain he could twist a little, adjust, so to speak, so that I'd take a carrot over a Ring-Ding every time.

The armory's about one-quarter full. We check off our names at the door and then Maisie asks the girl where our seats are. She doesn't like it when the girl says we can sit anywhere, expecting to have her own chair for the money, but I just walk on in.

People have left the first five rows of set-up chairs empty, probably being afraid that if they sit too close they'll be called up on stage and forced to do something stupid, like pretend to be a chicken, although this guy isn't a hypnotist that I know of. The audience is mostly women, but there are a few men scattered here and there. One, a little skinny guy with less hair than an organic mushroom, is sitting by himself in an aisle seat muttering into his BlueTooth. When he starts pecking away at the laptop balanced on his knees, I whisper to Maisie, "Bet I know what he's going to change." She gives me this quizzical look and I wink. "His batteries."

The lights are brighter than natural sunlight, so everybody looks even more yellowish than they normally do at the end of winter. I can hear a bunch of people coughing and clearing their throats and I hope they'll all take a Sucret before this Ray guy starts his talk. "Let's sit here," I say, and start to unwrap my scarf, but Maisie shakes her head.

"Let's get closer," she says. "Look at all the empty seats up front."

I don't want to cause trouble, but I don't want to be right up there in front either. "Too close. You have to look up. Strains your neck."

She thinks about this. "Okay." She dumps her coat over the back of the chair. "You win." I start to say we don't have to stay here if she's going to get all bent out of shape about it but she's looking over my shoulder at the stage. "Sit."

Ray Rendle turns out to be a guy about forty with a graying flat-top, V-neck gray plaid vest, gray flannel pants and gray Hush Puppies that make him look like something from an old 1950s Sears catalog. We'd found a bunch of them cleaning out my grandmother's house and I couldn't get over what women did to themselves back then to look stylish, from the shellacked hairdos to their teensy little waists. And the shoes—you'd think they'd all have died from broken necks just navigating their Hoovers in those foolish high heels.

Anyway, when he leans toward the microphone with this big grin and kind of croons, "Tonight your lives are going to change and change in a way you never expected, trust me," I wish I had my money back and a plate of rocky road fudge. But then he starts talking and before I know it, I'm nodding along with everybody else as he touches on points familiar to us, boredom, loneliness, lack of opportunity, how we're starved for love and affection, in short, the works.

"He's good, isn't he?" Maisie asks me, smug as if she'd given birth to him.

"So far," I say, not willing to give in too soon, "so good."

"Now," Ray's saying, holding on to the edges of the podium and speaking right into the microphone, "guess what I'm going to do."

"Drop dead!" comes a woman's voice from way in the back.

The whole auditorium creaks as everybody swivels around.

"Who is that?" Ray holds his hand up to his forehead like a visor. "Ma'am, do you have something to say?"

This average-size woman in mauve sweats lets out a screech—"Who're you calling ma'am?"—and keeps on screaming as she runs towards the stage in the empty space between the last chair and the wall. ". . . tracked you down . . ."

Because the ceiling is high and the hall is three-quarters empty, her voice isn't anywhere near as powerful as she must have thought it would be. ". . . the kids still think you're . . ." Instead, it's like a weak, little stream of sound unspooling out behind her as she barrels past our row. ". . . just like these morons."

Maisie turns to me. "Huh. Must be his wife." From the disgust in her voice, you'd have thought she expected to have a crack at him herself, maybe throw her panties up on stage or something.

"Poor guy," I say and get to my feet with everybody else so I can see better.

The woman stops right at the edge of the stage. Even with her back to us, I can see she's breathing hard. "You're not God, Ray Rendle," she calls out like she's in a play and up comes her right arm.

"No!" Maisie digs her nails so deep into my arm I think she's going to hit an artery. She's clinging to me like a cat to a curtain when I pull us both down onto the floor, knocking the folding chairs every which way.

You know how they always say, "The shot rang out!" Well, it's more like *Saving Private Ryan* without the popcorn. First comes a sharp crack and this loud ping and then a boom goes rolling around

the old auditorium so much like thunder that I'm not even particularly surprised when it starts to rain.

"Got her," somebody shouts just as the sound system announces
in Ray Rendle's voice, "Lady, you need help."

Maisie moans, "Oh, Lordy, Lordy, I'm covered in blood."

I dare to lift my chin from Maisie's hair as everybody around me
begins to pick themselves up off the floor and squawk about the
downpour coming from the sprinkling system. "It's okay, Maisie.
It's only water. She shot a pipe."

I drag us both to our feet. The guy with the laptop is straddling
the woman right there on the floor, twisting her arm back with one
hand and holding her gun with the other. He looks dazed but happy
and I wonder if he's got a stomach for violence or is just overjoyed
at the human contact.

Maisie says in this little trembly voice, "Listen, honey, I'm sorry
I dragged you into this. Let's get our money back and then go for hot
fudge sundaes, my treat." She shakes a drop of water off the tip of
her nose. "Where's Ray Rendle?"

The stage is empty.

"Money back, heck." I start to chuckle. "You know something,
Maisie?" Now I can barely speak I'm laughing so hard, laughing
like I haven't laughed since I was in high school and wore a B cup.
"I couldn't eat a thing."

Jimmy Says

Kate Flora

I've just undressed and turned off the light when I hear the voice from Jimmy's side of the bed. Just a quiet voice in the dark, a little twangy, a little tired, a little bit Southern, and raspy, the way it got sometimes, like someone had sanded his throat. "Gun show," he says. "Cops aren't getting anywhere and they're not going to. You've got to go to a gun show."

I feel a shiver. It's been a while since Jimmy and I talked. I only wished he'd choose another topic. Going to a gun show is the last thing I want to do. I've always been scared of guns, and after what's happened, it's gotten a hundred times worse. I've had to stop watching the TV—not just the news but most of the programs—and any kind of loud noises make me flinch. But he was right. Cops weren't getting anywhere, and Jimmy never was one to sit around and wait.

"How will I know what to do?" I say, pulling back the covers and sliding in. "I can't talk gun. They'll spot me as a fake a mile away."

"Loreena, darlin', they don't care if you're a hairy ape or a moron. They just want to sell guns."

I don't much like the hairy ape remark. It's true I've let myself go a little, not shaving my legs or doing that damned waxing that hurts like hell and costs the earth. Being a dark-haired woman's not easy. Jimmy never did understand that—how much work I put in to

160

look good to him. For him, 'cuz Jimmy liked to show me off. He must of read my mind, because the next thing he says is, "Honey, I wasn't talking about you. You know that to me you're the most beautiful girl in the world. I was talking about them."

That makes me feel better. It also makes me feel like hell. Because Jimmy, for all that he's here in the dark, in the bed, talkin' to me, is dead. And that's why he wants me to go to this gun show. Because he wants to get the gun dealer who sold that handgun to the stupid little piece of shit who shot him. Jimmy knows the little POS isn't the real bad guy. The real bad guy is the one who sells guns to morons and hairy apes and drunken little can't-hold-a-job wimps like the one who tried to rob him at an ATM.

I say "tried" to rob because the little jerk was so shocked when Jimmy said no that his gun went off, and when he saw that he'd actually shot someone, he wet his pants and ran off blubbering. The camera in the ATM booth recorded all that—little POS was too stupid to wear a hat or a hoody, like all the real criminals know to do. I guess that was one kind of break, because when you're talkin' stupid, how stupid is it that the people who install these security cameras always have 'em pointing down and all the bad guys know that?

"Heaven to Loreena, come in, please," Jimmy says. He used to say "Earth to Loreena" but he's not on the earth no more, and I guess he must be in heaven 'cuz why else would he say that? Anyway, he's always teased me about my attention span, and now here he is doing it again and the guy is for gosh sake's dead.

"All right, Jimmy." I say it with a sigh, because I don't want to, but I never could say no to Jimmy. "I'll go to a gun show, but you've got to come with me." I wriggle down into the blankets and close my eyes. He usually doesn't stay around for long. I don't know if that's heaven's rules or what. "I miss you," I say.

"It's nothing to how I miss you," he says. "I'd give anything to—"

"Don't!" I say, probably too loud and probably Missus Nosy

Parker Jones, who's just on the other side of the wall, has got her ear to the plaster and is wondering what's going on over here. I wonder if she can hear Jimmy, or if that's just me. "Don't say you miss me, or how you'd like to touch me, or any of that, Jimmy. Please. It gives me such an ache inside."

All I get from his side of the bed is a sigh. Just a whisper in the dark and then, though of course he makes no sound when he leaves, I just know he's gone. The room feels horribly empty and I pull his pillow over my face—the pillow that still smells faintly of him—and cry until I fall asleep.

The next morning, from my desk at work, I make a beauty appointment. I shouldn't of let down like I did, like I've got no self-respect unless Jimmy's around. My boss, whose name is Clyde, is a bear all day, which is how he gets whenever his wife's got her period and she won't sleep with him. They talk about women getting PMS, but never about how that makes guys PITAs. And I've got no sympathy, because my husband's dead and won't sleep with me, which, if you ask, is a hell of a lot worse than Clyde's got it. Not that I'd ever tell him that. He thinks I'm a sweet little bunny and dumb as they come, never mind that I can keep his calendar straight when he can't, keep the books of this business straight, and correct the spelling in his letters.

At lunch time, I'm about to go for a salad when that detective comes in. The one who investigated Jimmy's case. He hasn't got a whole lot more upstairs than Clyde does, from what I've seen, but he's trying. I mean, he could just give up—he's got the guy who did it—but like Jimmy and me, he thinks the real bad guy is the one who sold the gun to a kid with a record who shouldn't of been allowed to buy one at all. Like Jimmy says—they'll sell to anyone. So he comes by, this detective, whose name is Killeen, that's his last name, his first name is Liam, to tell me how he's making no progress finding this gun dealer.

Killeen has these odd light eyes, like one of those Alaskan dogs, only his are greenish not blue, and rusty hair and rusty spots on his skin. His skin is pale and dry and he has a thousand wrinkles around his eyes. He's tall and has big hands and he takes a lot of notes. Sometimes, when Killeen is around, I can feel Jimmy's there, too. What I can't tell is whether Jimmy's there because Killeen is another guy hanging around me, or because he wants to tell the detective something. He's around right now, Jimmy is, so I excuse myself and go to the ladies, because if no one is in there, Jimmy may talk to me.

"Tell him you want to meet with the guy who shot me," Jimmy says.

This idea shocks me so I'm almost sick, but Jimmy won't back down. "You've got to see this guy and ask him what the gun dealer looks like. We can't find him, else, Loreena, and I know the kid will talk to you. He feels awful guilty."

"You can't ask me to do this," I say, and my voice is all shaky and weird because I'm upset. "I don't want to see him, Jimmy."

"Oh, darlin'," Jimmy's voice has that sex-in-the-dark rasp he knows I can't resist. "You know I wouldn't ask if it weren't so important. But I've been talking to him—"

"You've what?" My voice is real loud, and I clap my hand over my mouth to hush it. "I thought you only talked to me."

"He doesn't know it's me, Loreena. I'm just playing games with his mind, see, letting him know that if he doesn't help us find this guy, he's gonna be haunted forever."

That's Jimmy. He sure loved messing with people. His momma says he was like that even as a kid. Which makes me ask, "You visit your momma, Jimmy? You talk to her?" I would have been pissed if he did, since Jimmy doesn't like his momma.

"Oh, Loreena, get serious. Will you go see him?"

"You think Killeen will let me?"

"Honeybunch." There was that rasp again. I could feel it like a tongue all over my body, going all light-headed in a stupid office restroom. Jimmy's always been able to do that to me. "He'll do whatever you want if he thinks it'll help him nail this guy. And he's not so dumb as you think."

I hoped Jimmy was right. "Okay," I say. "Anything for you, Jimmy."

I look in the mirror and think, oh hell. Loreena crying again. People in the office must get so sick of me. I soak a paper towel in cold water, press it against my eyes, and go back to Killeen. He's sitting just like I left him, the most patient man in the world. I grab my purse from the back of my chair. "Let's go get some lunch," I say, and head for the door.

He doesn't eat enough to keep a bird alive, just a bowl of soup and some crackers. No wonder he's so thin and dry. It makes me want to cook for him, but even as I have the thought, I know it's not about him but about me. How much I hate the empty condo, my pathetic little meals for one. Jimmy loved eating, so cooking for him was fun. Now food is just a lonely thing I make myself do. Maybe Killeen's like that, too. Maybe he eats soup because he's lost the ability to think beyond necessity.

Jimmy's rasping tongue has made me ravenous. I'm having a burger with bacon, cheese and onions. Now I cut off about a third of it, put it on my bread plate, and pass it to Killeen. "I want to see Dombrowski . . . that guy who shot Jimmy. Can you set that up?"

He studies me with those odd eyes like he's trying to read something through murky water. I just let him look, and while he looks, he eats the burger. Finally he says, "Why would you want to do that?"

I could of lied but I'm a bad liar. Most of the time, anyways. So I just tell the truth. "I want to know about that gun dealer. I want to know what he looks like. I don't want anyone else to go through what I'm going through just because some sleaze wants to make a buck." I give it a beat, watch him look sadly at the empty plate, wondering where the burger went, then I say, "Can you get me in to see him?"

"I can try."

□ □ □

Jesse Dombrowski looks unfinished, like God started to make a good-looking man and got distracted. He's got nice dark eyes and a decent nose, but his mouth is little and pouty and his chin kind of blends into his neck. His body is made funny, too, which I see when he comes through the door and walks up to the window. He's got good shoulders and then his stomach kind of pouches out and his legs are short and bowed. His nails are chewed to the quick and he looks like if you yelled "Boo!" he'd fall over dead.

I've dressed carefully for this. I'm waxed and my hair is done in layers of dark, fluffy curls, the way Jimmy likes it. I'm wearing black, which is what Jimmy said I should do, a modest V-neck which hugs my curves but shows no cleavage and a pencil skirt that comes below my knees. Heels, of course, and sheer black stockings. I know I look good because the guard stumbled over his own feet bringing me in here.

Dombrowski picks up his phone so we can talk, but he puts it down again and lowers his head, like he's praying. Then he puts both hands up against the glass and presses his nose to it, like he can see me better that way. It reminds me of a dog I had once that hated it when I'd go to school. He'd press his paws against the glass and whine. At least Dombrowski isn't whining.

I point to his phone and he picks it up again.

"I'm sorry," he says.

"I know you are."

He looks hopeful, like maybe I really do understand. "The gun just went off," he says. "It just went off. I only meant to scare him."

Like that matters. Jimmy's just as dead. "Tell me about the guy you bought the gun from," I say.

He shrugs. He only wants to talk about himself, about his guilt, about how he didn't mean to. Like he's my sister's seven-year-old and not a grown man who's killed somebody. But I arrange my face into a sympathetic look. "He's the real bad guy here," I say. "He's the one who's responsible." I give him the full benefit of my blue eyes. Jimmy says I have the most innocent eyes in the world. Sweet eyes, he calls them.

But this guy is resisting my sweet eyes. "You've got to believe me," he says. "I didn't mean to hurt him."

"The gun was defective," I say, agreeing with him. "That's why it went off and shot Jimmy." Like his finger wasn't on the trigger. Like he hadn't robbed people before, though he'd used a knife then. His dark eyes are looking like my dog again, kind of pathetic and grateful. I half expect his tongue to loll out. Next he'll roll over so I can scratch his belly. The thought makes my stomach turn. I don't want that showing in my face, so I lower my eyes and search through my bag. I've got a real handkerchief. White with lots of lace. I take it out and dab at my eyes. "I would be so grateful if you could tell me anything that might help me find that dealer."

He's never said anything to the police, and they've asked him a zillion times. Early on, when he was still wet from peeing his pants, he said he got it at a gun show. He's never said another word. Makes me wonder if the sleaze-ball who sold him the gun has connections inside and they're pressuring Dombrowski to keep quiet. "I don't know why you'd want to take the fall for this alone, and leave him free to get a lot more people killed."

I dab at my eyes again, but I don't have to fake it. I'm thinking about other women in my situation, women who just love their husbands so much and then one day get a phone call that slams them into black hell. I'm thinking about what this little POS did and why he's protecting someone. Why he'd ever want it to happen again. So

I ask him. "I loved my husband Jimmy," I say, and the tears just well up. I can feel their hot trails down my face. "Every day I hope it will stop hurting so much and it just never does. The empty bed hurts and the empty house and his empty chair there across the table from me."

It feels like my throat is gonna close. I try to blink away the tears. I try to swallow, but when I talk, it's just a kind of whisper. "Why would you ever want this to happen to another person? Which it will, for sure, if that man's not stopped."

The guard is coming over to see if I'm okay. I wave him off, thinking I'm about to get somewhere. Dombrowski blinks, like he's about to cry, too. "He was fat," he says. "Really fat and he had a beard." The hand that isn't holding the phone mimics bushy. For a minute he's silent, like that's as far as he's going to go. I hold my breath, keeping my eyes on his face. My sweet eyes. "Glasses," he says, "thick like bottles, with dark rims and tape on one corner."

Another silence. Come on, I silently coax him. Come on, Jesse, you can do this. You want to do this. Do this and you can stop hearing Jimmy's voice in your head. Just give it up. "I don't know," he says. "I just don't know."

I look at him and shake my head. "Jesse, why would you want to protect him? He's ruined my life. He's ruined your life and . . ." I pause here so I can shift my voice into a softer register. He can't see how I'm mad at him. He has to think we're in this together. "He's broken your mother's heart. You know, Jesse, I think she would be proud to hear that you've stepped up to protect other people, that you're doing the right thing, don't you?" Killeen has told me about Dombrowski breaking his mother's heart. She still comes to see him, though, all the time. That's what love is like.

He hauls in a breath that makes him shudder, his weak chin trembling, and I know he's going to give it up. "His name was Roger something," he says, "came from somewhere up in Maine, some little town, said he runs a gun shop there. He specialized in cheap handguns." Then his faces goes all white, serious, this-man-is-sick kind of white, and the hand that's holding the phone starts to shake. "And oh . . . my . . . God . . ." he says, "now he is gonna know that I talked and someone's gonna kill me."

I guess I'm supposed to care, but I don't. I do tell him that I'm proud of him, and that he's doing the right thing. And that he should tell the people at the jail so they can be sure he's safe. I say all the right sympathetic things. And I don't give a rat's ass if someone sticks a knife between his ribs and kills the little POS. Only not until I've found that dealer and he's gone down. They'll need Jesse for the ID, so I guess I'd better tell Killeen what I've heard.

When I'm back in my car, I call Killeen. "We need to talk," I say, and he wants to meet me for lunch, which is okay. This time, I'll do the ordering. Get him that burger whether he thinks he wants it or not. He sounds excited, if I can read excitement from the slight change in his low affect. Honestly, the man is such a stiff.

I'm threading through a tangle of traffic, feeling totally exhausted from having to do all that acting, when Jimmy says, "You were great, Reen," and I almost go off the road.

"Hey," I say. "You nearly killed me. Can't you rustle or something, instead of just talkin' like that?"

"Sorry," he says, not sounding sorry at all. "I'm dead, honey. This is just how it is."

I wonder if this is how it's gonna be forever. If Jimmy's just going to keep appearing in my life, a sudden voice out of nowhere. I've got no plans, but someday, when we're a ways down the road and I'm done with this scum of a gun dealer, I might want to have a life again. Will there be three of us in the bed? And will the guy be able to hear Jimmy, too, or just me? I mean, he says that POS Jesse can hear him. It's kind of a creepy idea.

As usual, Jimmy's read my mind. He always could do that, even when he wasn't dead. "Relax, Loreena. You think I like this?

Coming back here to see you, when I can't even touch your lovely body, which, by the way, I'm happy to see you got waxed. I just want revenge, darlin', and I cannot do that without you."

"Revenge, you mean, getting this guy arrested, Jimmy?"

"Oh, no, darlin'," he says. "I've got something more interesting in mind."

□ □ □

Killeen doesn't think I should go to the gun show, but I've told him that it's just something I've got to do. "For closure," I say, which is what Jimmy told me to say, and it must mean something to Killeen, because he stops giving me such a hard time and says he'll go along with me. I don't know how Jimmy feels about this, he's been pretty quiet, except for this morning, when he was there in the bedroom, telling me how to dress.

"Tight black pants," he said. "And a low-cut top. And your black leather jacket. The short one with zippers on the sleeves. Yes. Oh, yes, Loreena, just like that." Curling his tongue around the yes like a cat licking cream. "And the lace-up black boots. Oh, yes. You look good enough to eat."

"Or sell a gun to," I say. "Am I supposed to buy a gun or just try one out?"

"We'll cross that bridge when we come to it," he says. There's a knock on the door. Killeen has come to pick me up. He's not the kind who'll sit out there and honk. He'll get out of the car. "Nice guy," Jimmy says. "He's got real manners. So let's go, honey. You got money?"

"I've got money." We go downstairs together, I know 'cuz I can feel him there, and then I kind of can feel him in the car. I think.

□ □ □

The gun show is kind of disappointing. In appearance, I mean—just a big armory full of brown tables, like a tag sale, only the tables are laid out with knives and swords and every kind of gun imaginable.

Not that I've ever tried to imagine guns. Quite the reverse. The crowd is heavily male—no surprise—and most of them are engaged in ardent conversations about the wares being displayed. Men pick guns up, hefting them like they're trying to guess the weight. Snug them into their shoulders and site down the barrels. Occasionally one caresses an especially fine wood stock like guys at the race track touch horses.

It's a great big, macho, killing-machine love fest. And I'm afraid, once again, that I'm going to be sick. I will it away and walk the room with Killeen. Today's he's wearing jeans and a gray UMass sweatshirt and he hasn't shaved, so his pale face is furred with reddish stubble. He stops now and then to check something out. I'm surprised at how he smiles when he holds a handgun. Killeen isn't much of a smiler. Unlike me, he seems right at home. But the guys aren't checking out his ass, are they, while I feel like I'm wearing a neon bra that glows right through my top.

We've gone all the way around the outer ring of tables, and are walking slowly down the next row, when I see him. I try not to do one of those cartoon stops where my feet would squeak on the hardwood floor, but it's hard. I have to force myself to look normal. Jimmy doesn't help. He's whispering in my ear, so loud you'd think other people could hear him. "Do you see him, Reen? Jesus, what a freakin' hog."

Jimmy's right. The guy who sold the gun that killed him is fatter even than I'd imagined from Dombrowski's description. A kind of walking mountain that jiggles all over as he moves. Unlike some of the other tables, where things are arranged with care, he presides over a jumble of cheap, tired, rusty looking guns, many of which look like they probably don't work at all. I'm thinking it when Jimmy says, "No wonder that POS's gun went off. Look at this crap."

Killeen has walked right by. I don't know if this is because he didn't notice the man or so the man won't notice him. But I'm not walking by. I go right up to the table and start picking things up. It feels, crazily, like some lady at the grocery trying to find a good melon. I'm shifting guns this way and that, ignoring the fact that my gut is doing the hula, looking for one that feels good in my small hand. Man Mountain doesn't say anything. He just watches me, his wheezy little fat-man's breaths his only sound. I would of thought he'd be eager to sell me a gun.

Then I find it, half buried under some bigger, heavier guns. A cute little palm-sized revolver. It has a lovely mother-of-pearl handle and it's small enough to fit in my pocket. I pick it up, examine it, enjoy its feel.

"This shoots .22s?" I ask the man.

He nods. "Not much of a gun, lady."

I make my blue eyes big. "You mean it couldn't hurt somebody?"

"Could kill somebody." He breathes, taking the gun and examining it, checking the squeeze of the trigger and how it loads. He has one of those small, high voices so surprising in a big man. "You get close enough."

"How much?"

He names a price. I'm about to agree but Jimmy's there in my ear. "Haggle," he says sharply. "Bat your blues and bargain with the man."

I get it for a good price, I guess. I know nothing about gun prices. Shoes, yes. But I've never wanted to know about guns. There is no paperwork. Nothing with my name on it, only a scribbled sales slip with nothing but a price and a serial number. At least there is this—they've got the gun that killed Jimmy, so they can trace that number if this man keeps his sales slips. I decide to check. I flap the yellow slip at him and say, "You keep these things?"

His eyes narrow, like he's wondering am I a cop. Then he grins, a loose-lipped grin that shows too many yellowed teeth. "What do you think, girlie?"

Girlie thinks he does keep them. That they're somewhere in a grubby box in an attic or a basement. That he goes over them sometimes, on winter nights, the way a miser counts his gold. Beneath the mountainous flesh, something evil lurks, something that takes a pleasure in selling weapons others will use to destroy each other. He confirms it when he hands me my gun, which I tuck away in my purse. "Boyfriend problems?"

"Husband," I say.

He nods.

I barely make it to the ladies before I get sick. After, I am a trembling wreck as I take out the gun and examine it. "There's no time like the present," Jimmy says.

I'm alone in the room, so I say, "Jimmy, I don't think I can do this."

"You saw him, Loreena," Jimmy says. "His face. He wants people to kill each other. That big fat blob gets off on it. I'll bet he picks up the paper every morning, hoping someone has used one of his guns. Don't you want to stop this?"

"I don't want to go to jail, Jimmy."

"Trust me, Loreena, you'll be okay."

I try to tell him I don't think so. I'm here with a cop, aren't I? Killeen is bound to try and stop me. Or shoot me. And then I wonder, is this what Jimmy wants? For me to be dead, too, so we can be together in heaven? It doesn't sound like Jimmy, though. And as if he's read my mind, which I think maybe he can, he says, "Reen. Reen. Reen. Don't even think it." His voice in that low register again, running over me. And he tells me what to do.

I wait while the dealer makes another sale, to a creature so shifty, so obviously bad that it strengthens my resolve. I slip through the gap between his table and the next, and hold out my gun, giving him the sweet, blue-eyed look. "Could you . . . I mean . . . would you mind . . . just showing me how to load this?" I offer the gun and some bullets.

"I don't—" he begins, but his evil side is caught. He wants me to use this gun on somebody. Wants it enough to break his own rules. He shows me how to load it, letting me watch as he slips in the bullets. Then he demonstrates how to hold it. How to squeeze the trigger. "Squeeze," he says. "Nice and slow and steady."

I take the gun and try to imitate what he has just done. I do it badly. He reaches out to correct me and somehow, the gun swings toward him as I steady it and slowly squeeze.

The look of surprise on his face is wonderful as he falls backward, gun in hand, his dirty gray Moosehead Lake sweatshirt blooming with three dark red rosettes.

Killeen bursts through the crowd. Screaming, I throw myself into his arms, pitching a full-blown, hysterical fit. "He was just showing me how it . . . and suddenly there was . . . and OH MY GOD! Is he okay?"

"Well done, Reen," Jimmy whispers. "You're the best girl in the world."

This time, I hear him go. A whoosh like a passing truck. And I think maybe he's gone for good now. At peace, isn't that what they say?

The Greatest Criminal Mind Ever

Frank Cook

With a final, friendly wave to the bookstore owner, author J. Nathaniel Coldridge stepped into the cold night air, turning the collar up on his heavy black coat and pulling his dark gray homburg down close over his eyes.

"Another successful reading!" he cheered himself. "My fans adore me."

The line had stretched out the door. It took almost thirty minutes to finish autographing all the copies of his newest mystery, *The Silly Secret Serviceman*, and he could feel in his bones it would be another bestseller. Hollywood would be calling.

He could almost smell the money. The thought warmed him against the Boston cold.

By nature and by practice, Coldridge was an arrogant man. By size, he was somewhat tall but intimidatingly wide—looking all the more so with the added weight of his long black coat. Still, he had managed to set a brisk pace back to his apartment overlooking the Bay when the desperate plea caught him from behind.

"Monsieur!" It came again. "Un moment of your time, s'il vous plait!"

Coldridge turned and waited for the stranger, a Frenchman he presumed, noticing before all else the book the latecomer held tight to his chest as he hurried toward him.

"My good friend." Coldridge gave a hearty greeting. "I'm afraid you've missed my reading. But I always have time for another autograph."

"Ah, merci," the man said, catching his breath.

Coldridge reached into his suit coat and withdrew a blue (never black!) ink pen that he always carried for just such occasions. "And to whom shall I make it out, hmmm?"

The Frenchman smiled brightly. "Ah, to me, of course," he said, his lyrical accent lifting each word. "To Jean-Claude." He touched his hand to his chest. "C'est moi."

With a practiced flair, Coldridge moved the pen across the title page, admired his own signature just a moment, and then handed the book back to his devotee. "I hope you enjoy it," he said confidently.

"Ah, I'm sure I will, monsieur. Merci beaucoup. You are one of the world's greatest criminal minds."

"Well, thank you," acknowledged Coldridge with feigned modesty.

Done with his admirer, he turned and took a step away, but then stopped and turned back around.

"Oui, monsieur?" the Frenchman said in surprise.

"Actually, nothing really," Coldridge replied. "Well, just a small matter."

The Frenchman cocked his head to one side, waiting to be of service.

"You called me one of the world's greatest criminal minds. Actually, even the harshest of literary critics have called me the greatest criminal mind of all time."

A bright smile exploded across the simple Frenchman's face and he nodded enthusiastically. "Ah oui, monsieur! You are among the best ever!"

Coldridge's smile remained fixed on his face. The Frenchman

hadn't quite gotten the point. "Well, actually, my reviewers would suggest that I am the best ever," he emphasized. "Not just among the best ever."

The small man took a moment to comprehend what he was being told and his smile slowly dissolved.

"Mais oui, if you say so, sir. But surely there are others."

Coldridge suddenly lost patience with this bore. He really didn't enjoy bantering with his readers, despite what it said in his press releases.

"Yes, yes, of course," he snapped, "there are many others who call themselves mystery writers. But I think if you check your sources you will find that none have exceeded me. Dashiell Hammett, Agatha Christie. Even Sir Arthur Conan Doyle himself. All very fine. But I think my numbers speak for themselves. In all humility, I think you will find that I am the best. Not one of the best. But the best."

Satisfied that he had enlightened the man, Coldridge turned again and began walking, but succeeded in only three strides.

"Mais, monsieur," the Frenchman called again. "Surely there are others. How you say in your Wild West? There is always someone faster. Non?"

Irritated, but forcing a patient smile, Coldridge again faced the man. "Well, perhaps in the Wild West, as you say, there was always someone faster. But in the literary world, I think, in all modesty, you will find no one ahead of me. I know I can't think of anyone. Can you?"

The question was intended to be both rhetorical and final. Instead, the Frenchman took it as an invitation. "Well," he drew out the word. "I myself sometimes," he began, reaching inside his suit coat pocket as if to take something out.

Instantly Coldridge sized up the man again and concluded his generous patience had been misplaced.

"Ah, a fellow author." Coldridge bristled, his warm breath fogging the space between them and freezing the Frenchman's hand inside his coat. "And I suppose you happen to have a manuscript with you, and if I could possibly take a look at it, and perhaps recommend it to my publisher, you would be ever so grateful, is that it?"

Coldridge waited barely a beat before answering his own accusation.

"Well, I shan't!" His temper flared. "My good man, this is no way to secure a foothold in the publishing business. You cannot accost a famous author on the street, tell him he's second rate and then ask for a favor. I won't do it. Now leave me alone!"

The smaller man recoiled at the indictment and instantly took his empty hand out of his coat.

"Non, non, Monsieur Coldridge," he defended. "I only meant that—"

"Well, what are you then?" Coldridge challenged. "A playwright, perhaps? A biographer? Short stories?" Then added with extra venom, "comic books?"

Coldridge had intended to verbally strip the man naked, yet the Frenchman seemed resistant to insult.

He answered, "I am a puzzler, sir. That is all. Like your Larance. I like to figure out questions."

Coldridge stood back and composed himself again. At least this stranger knew the hero of his novels, the handsome, rugged Private Eye Lawrence Matador.

"You mean you're an 'investigator,' " Coldridge corrected. "A sleuth. You investigate crimes. Amateur, I gather," he said, looking the man over. "Well, whatever you are, and whatever you've written, I don't have time. Good evening."

"Of course," the man said sheepishly. "I am sorry to have bothered you. I only sought to entertain you with a trick riddle. Mais non, you are busy. Truly you are the best. As you say in American, 'Ne-veer-mind.' "

Frustrated, Coldridge knew he should walk away, yet this little man was obviously baiting him and no doubt would snicker behind his back that he had bested the great author if Coldridge didn't respond to the contest.

"All right, Mr. Puzzler," Coldridge said impatiently. "What is this riddle? Hurry up."

The Frenchman's face turned up in a sly grin. "Can you answer thees one?" he said. "Two chimney sweeps go down a chimney. When they reach the bottom, one washes his face and the other doesn't. Which one washes? The first who went down or the second? Could your La-rance answer this, eh?"

Coldridge's sneer turned into an incredulous smile. "My God, man, what kind of question is that? Every schoolchild knows the answer. The first man down will have a dirty face, but look at the second man, who has a clean face, and believe his face also is clean. The second man, however, will look at the first man down, see his face is dirty, and will assume his face also is dirty, and will go wash. It's quite obvious!"

The Frenchman's grin melted, hearing the riddle so easily answered and delivered with an insult attached.

"My friend," Coldridge condescended, "if you can't do any better than that, then you simply have no place as a mystery writer."

Feeling he had thoroughly vanquished his foe, Coldridge turned and again began walking away—fully expecting he would not be rid of the little Frenchman quite so easily. And sure enough, the call quickly came from behind.

"Ah monsieur, monsieur. Another one, s'il vous plait. Please. Another chance to stump the great La-rance Matador. Please."

Coldridge stopped and rolled his eyes. He turned back to the Frenchman. "All right, one more—then I absolutely must be going."

The Frenchman beamed once again and Coldridge could see he was thinking hard. "Ah ha!" he said after a few moments. "This one, please: A dog is tied to a ten-foot rope, but his food dish is fifteen feet away. Yet, he is able to eat from the dish. How is this possible?"

Coldridge looked down at the man and almost screamed. "You are pathetic," he cried. "Again, every schoolchild knows that the other end of the rope isn't tied to anything, thus allowing the dog to go anywhere it wants! Truly, sir, you have no business attempting mystery stories. Detective Matador would laugh in your face!"

Coldridge felt he had not only defeated the Frenchman but had destroyed the man's dignity as well. He was pleased by both.

□ □ □

"You really have to stop these people in their tracks," Coldridge emphasized into the phone a short time later, peering out the window of his condo at the twinkling boat lights in the Bay below. "Otherwise, they take advantage of your celebrity. They want to be like you, but they never will be and it's really kinder that they learn their place sooner rather than later. As Matador always says, 'These people get what they deserve.' "

"So then what happened?" said Kendra Sithcow, editor, friend and occasional muse to the author.

"Well, he became quite enraged," Coldridge explained, sipping a sherry. "He said I had dishonored him—actually he dishonored himself—and demanded retribution! Can you imagine? He wants to ask me another question. Bet me a thousand dollars I couldn't answer it! Took his wallet out right there on the sidewalk and thumbed through a number of bills—I have no idea how much was there."

"My God, Nathan, you should have called a cop."

"Oh, he was harmless enough," Coldridge dismissed. "Little man. More a danger to himself than to others, I suspect."

"So what did you tell him?"

"I laughed in his face, of course." Coldridge chuckled. "But he kept yelling, 'At the scene of T*he Potty Policeman*. Twelve o'clock noon! Where La-rance'—he kept calling him 'La-rance' instead of 'Lawrence,' kind of a gallant ring to it actually—anyhow, he kept saying 'Where La-rance rescued l'gendarme!' And, of course, he told me to bring my money. Really, quite the crackpot."

The line was silent for a moment before Kendra spoke. "You mean he wants to meet you in front of L'Espalier?"

The author should have been complimented that Kendra remembered the details of *The Potty Policeman* (a beat cop taken hostage while his pants were around his ankles in the restroom) but it never occurred to Coldridge to be grateful. "He wants to meet me where Matador cracked his first case and humiliated the police, all without missing his reservation."

"Sounds like a wacko."

"But literary."

"You're not meeting him, are you?" said Kendra.

There was too long a pause before Coldridge answered, "Of course not."

□ □ □

It was a few minutes after noon when Coldridge stepped from a cab on Boylston near the entrance of L'Espalier. He had no intention of being early for such a ludicrous appointment, and told himself there would be no waiting for his inquisitor, should he be late. He doubted the Frenchman would show up, but if he did, Coldridge was confident he would destroy him again. Either way, just as the famous Matador had done, he would blithely keep his reservation inside.

He had barely finished his obligatory scolding of the cab driver, however, when he heard the happy words, "Bonjour, monsieur!" from behind him.

In the bright light of the cold afternoon, Coldridge reconsidered the man he had met on the dark sidewalk the night before. The

Frenchman looked somewhat older than Coldridge imagined. And perhaps a bit more shabby. Thinner. He wore a fedora, and brown tweed jacket over a worn dark red sweater. No overcoat.

"Are you ready?" the Frenchman said.

Coldridge shrugged, supposing that he might as well go ahead with this silly exercise.

"Did you bring your money?" the Frenchman said, then pulled his own wallet out without waiting for the author's reply. "I have mine. You see? Oui? Yes?"

"Yes, of course," Coldridge said, putting his hand up as if the sight of the Frenchman's wallet made him nauseated. "Please, mister—" Coldridge stopped, having forgotten the man's name.

"Jean-Henri," the Frenchman promptly filled in.

Coldridge frowned for just a moment as if something was out of place. But it eluded him.

"Yes, well, Jean-Henri, is this really necessary? You know, that thousand dollars of yours is really quite a lot of money. I realize it probably all looks like funny pieces of paper to someone from France. But really, you could probably just pay an agent to read your story for that. No need to further embarrass yourself."

The Frenchman snapped his wallet closed and held it in his hands. His face reflected the atrocity of the remark. "I know what I am doing, mon ami."

Coldridge looked deeply into the man's eyes, confident the Frenchman really had no idea what he was doing.

"All right, let's get this over with. Your riddle?"

"Mais oui," the man said. "It goes like this: Les police are called to a house. When they arrive, they must break in through la porte— ah, the door. In the middle of the room they find a man hanging from a rafter, his feet off the floor. There is no furniture in the room, nothing at all, and all les doors and windows are locked from the inside. What was le dead man's occupation?"

A confident smile spread across the Frenchman's face, certain he had redeemed himself from the night before.

Coldridge looked at the man only briefly, then up Boylston toward the library where he had lectured so often, and then back down toward Fenway where he refused to go since that other author started camping out there.

Then he turned back to the Frenchman standing anxiously before him. "Obviously," he said. "The poor tormented soul was an ice man. He threw the rope over the rafter and then stood on a block of ice until it melted away and hung him. Terrible way to go."

The Frenchman was stunned.

□   □   □

"You're an idiot, you know that?" Kendra said that night.

"These people get what they deserve!" Coldridge laughingly defended. "He almost threw the money at me. Then he practically fled toward the T. Really, its serves him right. He's the one being foolish."

Kendra caught the change to present tense. "He is the one being foolish? What do you mean by that, Nathan. You're done with this fellow, aren't you?"

"Well," Coldridge said, the mirth showing in his voice. "He did rave something about ten thousand dollars and *The Doughnut D.A.*"

"*The Doughnut D.A.*?" Kendra repeated. "Where Matador foils the bank robbery while the D.A. is standing in line with a box of doughnuts?"

"And eating one! Powdered sugar, if you recall," Coldridge chimed in. "I loved writing that."

"Yeah, but the real D.A. thought you were making fun of his office."

"I'm sure he's gotten over it by now."

"Ten thousand dollars? Cash? Nathan, promise me you won't meet this man. This is crazy."

There was a long pause. "Good night, Kendra." He hung up, and leaned back on his couch to admire the view.

□ □ □

Even as Coldridge walked down Arlington Street toward Sovereign Bank—the setting where Matador had vanquished the robber—he could see the Frenchman pacing back and forth on the sidewalk with a large white Macy's shopping bag in his hand. It was another sunny morning and less cold. The slight rise in temperature seemed to bring out more people. The street was bustling with activity, men in suits dodging around construction workers in jeans who, in turn, were watching young secretaries in short coats (and short skirts) making their way into the surrounding buildings.

As the author approached, he almost felt sorry for the Frenchman—almost. Coldridge believed, however, he was doing this for the benefit of the literary world, to separate the truly gifted from the pretenders.

The Frenchman's voice was flat, his disposition neither sunny nor friendly. "Bonjour," he said. "Here is my money."

The man quickly opened the shopping bag and Coldridge looked in, seeing a jumbled collection of twenties, fifties, some tens and possibly a few fives.

"Do you want to count it," he said coldly.

"I do not," Coldridge said diffidently. "And here is mine."

Coldridge opened his suit coat enough to reveal a white envelop.

"That's it?" The Frenchman was surprised.

"One hundred one-hundred-dollar bills," Coldridge assured. "That much money. You'd think it would be more than a half-inch thick. But it's not. Your riddle?"

Coldridge's confidence was mirrored against the Frenchman's nervousness. The author detected more than a hint of fear. Still the smaller man stood up straight and squared his shoulders as if girding for battle. He began:

"Le world's smallest dwarf worked in the world's largest circus. Because he was so small, he was le most famous dwarf ever—tout la monde. However, he was blind. Nevertheless, les autre dwarfs were jealous of him. They hated him. Le dwarf went to bed in his circus trailer one night but didn't answer his call the next morning. When les police arrived, they found him dead, with an empty bottle of sleeping pills by his bedside and wood shavings on le floor. Les police ruled it a suicide. What would Detective Matador say?"

Coldridge gazed up the street toward the Boston Public Garden. His eyes then swept the busy street scene, briefly resting on a man with a coffee-and-bagel cart and a line of people waiting patiently for a fix of caffeine and cream cheese. Somewhere down the street, a construction worker started in with a jackhammer.

He absent-mindedly fingered the envelope in his pocket, then shrugged.

"Detective Matador would agree that the dwarf killed himself," Coldridge said. "But he would call it murder—not suicide. Clearly, one of the dwarf's enemies snuck into his trailer during the night and whittled off the bottom of the blind man's cane. When the dwarf awoke the next morning and stood up, he had to reach his cane down further for it to touch the floor. The poor dwarf assumed that he had grown during the night, which would mean that he was no longer the world's smallest dwarf. Believing his days of fame were over, he killed himself with the sleeping pills."

□ □ □

"And did he give you the bag?" Kendra said over the phone.

"Hmmm, more or less." Coldridge giddily recalled the sight. "He dropped it, right there on the sidewalk. He didn't throw it down. He just dropped it, like he had been struck by lightning. I truly believe the man was dumbfounded. He's obviously misjudged who he's up against."

Again the tense change to the present caught Kendra's ear. "Nathan, I beg you, please tell me this game is over."

After a moment, Coldridge responded with a chuckle. "Yes, I believe it almost is. Tomorrow. I surely won't go any further and I'm sure he couldn't afford to."

"And what are we playing?" she said.

"One of my favorites. Where Lawrence Matador saves the day and makes fools out of the entire FBI at the same time."

"*The Insipid Special Agent*?"

"Indeed! I must say this Frenchman is a student of my work." Coldridge sounded pleased.

There was a long pause on the other end of the line. "How much money?" Kendra asked.

Coldridge only laughed into the phone. "Sleep well, my dear. I'll call you late tomorrow."

Coldridge stood and swirled a glass of port as he looked out onto the Bay below. On the coffee table behind him was the Frenchman's shopping bag, its contents spilled across the table and onto the floor.

Ten thousand dollars to the penny.

In the morning he would stop by his bank and withdraw ninety thousand more.

□ □ □

The day should have been busy. Coldridge should have been writing at his computer, but he found it difficult to concentrate. He mowed through several Sudoku puzzles—he found the logic of the quizzes helped him think—and then tried reading, but found other authors tiresome. Whenever interviewers would ask, "Who is your favorite writer?" Coldridge would always quip, "Rachel Ray."

Most of the afternoon was spent on the phone with his publicist discussing *The Silly Secret Serviceman*. "Yes," to "Regis and Kelly." "Of course," to "Oprah." "No, I don't think so," to "The View," and "Oh, she's always fun," to "Ellen."

And the West Coast autograph tour? "I'm looking forward to it," he lied, wondering again whether people in California could even read.

At 2:00 P.M. he went to the bank with a briefcase. He told the young female teller he needed to withdraw ninety thousand dollars and received a slow, uncertain, "I see," in response. "Just a moment, please."

As he fully expected, a few moments later he was whisked into a private room where he was seated with a branch executive. After rigorous identification was provided, and casual but impertinent questions were deflected, the executive was left with no choice but to provide the cash.

Forms were filled out and signed. Coldridge had expected the bureaucracy, but all in all, it had gone rather smoothly.

"No, I don't need an escort," he assured the branch executive. "This isn't New York. What harm could come to me?" He laughed.

Still, he hurried directly back to his apartment with his briefcase and refused to make eye contact with anyone on the street.

□ □ □

At 10:00 P.M., Coldridge looked out his window and decided that it was time to go. "How appropriate," he thought to himself. A wet fog was beginning to settle in. Perfect for a mystery writer, but lousy for getting a cab. He'd have to walk.

He already had put the Frenchman's ten thousand back into the Macy's bag, then moved his own ninety thousand into the bag as well. On his way down in the elevator he wondered if he could somehow mold the events of the last few days into another Lawrence Matador novel.

"Perhaps not," he lamented, for the prey had been too easy to catch. "Perhaps if I add a girl?"

Coldridge quickly made his way back to the bookstore where he had first encountered the Frenchman, but when he arrived he did not enter the store.

The climax of *The Insipid Special Agent* had been set in the dark alley behind the store. Coldridge recited the lines of his own book as he walked around the corner to the back.

". . . In the blackness of the night, only a single dim bulb hanging over the back entrance showed Matador the path to where the trio of hooligans held the pretty, young and frightened FBI agent." He pictured Anne Hathaway in the role.

But there would be no trio of hooligans out tonight, Coldridge happily concluded, only one lonely Frenchman who was about to lose everything he had.

At the mouth of the alley, however, things were wrong. Coldridge only saw gaping blackness before him, the bulb over the bookstore's rear entrance apparently either broken or burned out. Still he took a few hesitant steps. "Jean . . . ah . . ." he called, once more having forgotten the Frenchman's name. "Jean . . . ?"

"Paul, monsieur. Jean-Paul. I am here," the Frenchman said, striking a match so that Coldridge could see him standing against the wall on the left. "Matador's light! It is broken, non? I can hardly see back here."

Whatever reluctance Coldridge had about entering the alley disappeared at the sound of the Frenchman's voice. "Ah, well, when you've been a mystery writer as long as I have, you get use to walking down dark alleys," he bluffed. "This is all very dramatic. But perhaps we should move out a little closer to the street so we can see each other."

"Certainement," the Frenchman agreed cheerily, "lead the way."

Coldridge was surprised to find his opponent in such a good mood, which in turn put him on guard. Perhaps an extraordinarily difficult riddle was upcoming. Coldridge had never considered the possibility he could lose.

"Very well then," he said, once they had moved to the edge of the alley. "Your riddle, please?"

"It is very easy, monsieur, I am afraid Detective Matador would have no problem with this one."

Coldridge watched the Frenchman dig through his coat pocket, much as he had the first night they met.

"But before the riddle, a question, monsieur. How do you say in American? 'Your money or your life'?"

The Frenchman pulled a gun from his coat.

In his years as an author, Coldridge had written this scene dozens of times, but nothing compared to the reality of a handgun being pointed at his chest.

"A robbery?" Coldridge was incredulous. "You're robbing me!" he restated the obvious. "Jean . . . Jean . . . whoever you are . . . this isn't fair at all!" he began scolding, but the Frenchman simply lifted the gun higher so that it was pointed directly at his face.

He repeated calmly, "Your money or your life, monsieur. Or, if you prefer the classic, 'Stand and deliver!' "

The absurdity of Lawrence Matador's fictional skills swept over Coldridge. Matador would go for the gun and twist it out of the attacker's hand, then give the hapless predator a karate chop.

In this real back alley, however, Coldridge realized he'd be dead before he took a step. He dropped the Macy's bag at his side and stepped back.

"This has all been a setup," he realized out loud.

"Oui, monsieur."

"Your manuscript?"

"I am not a writer, monsieur," the Frenchman apologized.

"But the riddles?"

"You said it yourself, every child knows the answers."

Coldridge had been had.

"You'll never get away with this," he growled. "You'll be in jail before the night's over."

With his free hand, the Frenchman retrieved the bag and stepped away from his victim.

"Non, monsieur." He shook his head. "I will not be in jail before the night is over. This crime will ne-ver even be reported."

Coldridge's eyes went wide with fear. "You intend to kill me? You're going to gun me down like an animal?"

The Frenchman took another step back, holding the gun steady. "Oh Monsieur Coldridge, you haven't asked me for my final riddle?"

He waited just a moment, disappointed, as Coldridge stood mute. "Ah, I see," he said. "Don't want to play anymore, eh? Well, here it is anyway:

"Le world's greatest mystery writer walks into a dark alley with a shopping bag full of money. He is a best-selling author, mais he has embarrassed many law enforcement agencies by writing books like *The Potty Policeman, The Doughnut D.A., The Insipid Special Agent* and many more. While the author is in the alley he is, unfortunately, robbed. Now the riddle is: Who does the author tell? Does he call les police, so they can laugh that le great creator of La-rance Matador has been conned? Does he complain to the District Attorney, who would delight in calling les media for what would be a very entertaining news conference? Or perhaps would he call the FBI, so agents all across the country could mock the idea that the wealthy author had lost a few dollars to a humble Frenchman whose name he can't even remember? Imagine what delight that would bring to the authorities, and ridicule to the author? Imagine l'embarrassment! The laughter! And, sadly, imagine what it would do to future sales if your readers learned Monsieur La-rance was so très gullible?"

The Frenchman moved back another step and returned the gun to his coat. "Non, monsieur. I will not kill you. I don't think this crime will ever be reported."

Coldridge felt his anger deflate, and he was left to only stare at the man. As his senses returned, he realized his hands were in air, and he slowly put them down.

"Truly, monsieur, I am an admirer," the Frenchman said quietly.

"You are the world's greatest criminal mind. But alas, I am the world's greatest criminal. As La-rance always says, 'People, they get what they deserve,' non?"

The Frenchman tipped his fedora to the author, then turned and quickly walked away with the bag

A moment later Coldridge heard his name spoken somewhere on the street behind him. "Nathan?" The woman's voice came again. "Are you okay?"

The thoroughly ruffled Coldridge quickly put his arms at rest and turned to face the woman walking toward him.

"Why, Kendra, what are you doing here?" he said, smoothing out his coat.

"I was worried about you," she said, tentatively lowering her can of pepper spray. "I heard voices but—"

"And what did you hear?" Coldridge insisted.

"Well, nothing, really," Kendra sounded perplexed. "That was him, wasn't it? The Frenchman? It sounded like he was complimenting you."

Coldridge turned in the direction she was looking. The man was gone. "Why yes, you just missed him. Charming fellow, really. Quite bright, as it turns out. Quite bright."

"Does that mean you lost?"

Coldridge curled his hand around the woman's arm, and together they walked out of the alley. "Oh, I lost a few dollars," he said. "But Kendra, I've come up with a dandy story."

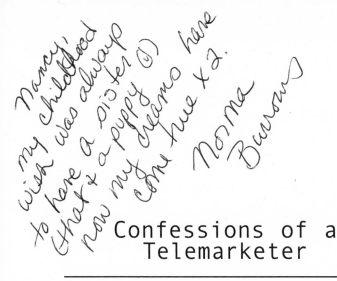

Confessions of a Telemarketer

Norma Burrows

No one in their right mind would give a postal worker a hard time. Their tendency to go "postal" is well documented. However, it is socially acceptable to harass and be rude to telemarketers over the phone. I am here as a telemarketer to ask you, Do you have a death wish? Do you have any idea what the rejection level is like in this field? Depending on what you are peddling it can be as much as 98.6 percent. Can you begin to imagine the long-term effect your comments have? Not unlike water on a stone I can feel myself morph. Being treated as if I am not even human, eventually I begin to forget the social graces. You do realize that when the dialer pulls up your number, this is why you hear nothing when you first pick up your phone; my computer screen is propagated with all of your personal information. I can see your name, address, phone number, etc., all the while you are chewing me a new one. Now I ask you, is that really a good idea?

I know I sound a little wounded. I feel it too. The good news is my boss has approved my two-week vacation to start next Monday. When I come back from these "getaways," I am refreshed and renewed. The tension is gone. I think of it as a retreat— there is after all a spiritual component. I am soon to meet the Johnson family from

Newark, NJ. It never ceases to amaze me how charming these folks can be in person.

Bad Trip

Judy Copek

The stragglers waited for the last airport bus to their motel. Kevin had left his cell phone in the seat pocket and had to race back onto the plane to get it. The guy with the screaming baby ran back, too, looking for a missing pacifier. The girl in the halter top and the dude with a ponytail had stopped to have a smoke. The old couple had tottered through the terminal propping each other up. It was 1:00 A.M. and the air felt sultry, with that torpid southern heat that made you feel limp as a possum. The street in front of the terminal had a wet oily sheen, and puddles lingered on the sidewalk and by the curb.

Returning from Grandpa's funeral, they were delayed by weather across the Eastern Seaboard. His wife, Jeanine, yawned and leaned against him. He took her hand. In the glare of the lights outside the terminal, her eyes looked tired and hollow.

"In the morning, babe," he said, "we'll get home in the morning."

Everything felt damp—the air, his white shirt, even the suitcases. He sensed the presence of the massive river, surging to the Gulf. A mini-bus pulled up, and a sweating driver grimaced as he loaded the luggage into the back. Kevin waited until he saw their bags safely stowed. Like cattle moving into a car, he trudged behind Jeanine as she edged to the backseats. Nobody spoke, except for the baby, who let out intermittent sobs and hiccups.

They passed through dark neighborhoods and along rain-soaked streets. Kevin woke up with a start when the bus stopped in front of the Southern Comfort Motel. He still held Jeanine's hand.

In the glare of the street light, the one-story motel needed paint or maybe a charge of dynamite. The phrase "Southern Discomfort" popped into his head. For Jeanine's sake, he hoped the room would be clean.

The driver got out and began unloading the luggage. "Be here at the curb tomorrow morning at 6:30 A.M.," he said, "sharp."

In the lobby, the odor of burning plastic with hints of ammonia and the whiff of disinfectant assailed him. Maybe a trace of urine. Disgusting. There was no furniture to conceal the stained linoleum floor, and he noticed no breakfast room, just a dented old vending machine. The desk clerk, a woman with a truculent face, sat behind a scratched panel of Plexiglas with small openings at mouth height and at the bottom for paper or financial transactions.

The guy with the ponytail raised his eyebrows. "Not exactly the Ritz," he said under his breath. "I hope to hell the AC works."

They let the old couple register first. Jeanine smiled at the baby, who was looking around wide-eyed over his dad's shoulder. The dad looked young, little more than a teenager.

"How old is the baby?" asked Jeanine.

"Six months tomorrow."

"Hard to travel alone with a little one."

"You got that right." He paused and looked at the baby and then at Jeanine. "I'm kind of new at this, and I'm out of diapers and for-mula. I never thought about the plane being so late and not getting home tonight."

"Oh, God, what are you going to do?" asked Jeanine.

He gave a hopeless shrug. "Do you think I could put some orange soda in his bottle?" He pointed to the vending machine.

Jeanine frowned and said she didn't know, but Kevin could see she was dubious about the orange soda idea.

"He's a cute little dude," said Kevin. The baby smiled at him.

When it was their turn to register, Kevin asked where he could find an all night drug store. Jeanine gave him the look.

The clerk said there was an Eckerd's maybe a mile away.

Kevin asked the clerk to call a cab. "We've got a baby who's running low on food and diapers," he said.

The clerk gave the registration form a brusque push through the Plexiglas. "Cabs don't ordinarily come here at night."

"Well, that's reassuring," Jeanine spoke up.

"Call the dispatcher," said Kevin. "Tell him it's the law." He squinted at the clerk, who wouldn't meet his gaze.

They walked down the shadowy hall. From one of the rooms a television blasted the hall with bombastic music and sirens and squealing tires. The smell grew worse. Kevin felt the crunch of broken glass and other unidentifiable crud under his feet. God, what kind of a place was this?

The kid with the baby was fiddling with the door of the room next to them. "It's unlocked," he said. "Do you think it's okay to go in?" The baby let out an outraged howl.

"I guess," said Kevin. "Turn on the room light." He cleared his throat. "Listen, if I can find a ride, I'll make a trip to Eckerd's for whatever you need. Just give me a list."

"That would save my life. And Stewie's here."

Jeanine was giving him an incredulous bug-eyed look. "Are you out of your mind?" she whispered.

"Somebody's gotta do it."

"Why does it have to be you?" She glared at him. "I don't want to stay in this dump by myself. Not for one stinking minute."

Kevin's thoughts flashed to Grandpa, a sturdy farmer with a crosshatched neck from seasons in the sun. Friends and relatives had crowded the church to overflowing. The preacher had mentioned Grandpa's solid work ethic and his sense of rectitude. Grandpa always did the right thing. Many people remarked that Kevin, the oldest grandchild, was the spitting image of Grandpa as a young man.

He patted Jeanine's shoulder. "I won't leave you alone, babe. I promise."

It was stifling inside the room. No AC. Smelly, too. What was that odor? The light switch by the door didn't work, but the bathroom light turned on. He saw Jeanine blanch as she examined the bathroom. Broken sink and filthy tub. The towels looked grimy, even used.

The bedside lamp had no shade, and Jeanine let out a squeaky scream when a cockroach skittered behind the headboard.

"I won't sleep a wink," she said.

Kevin tried to open the curtain which fell off the rod into his hands. The glass in the sliding door had a zigzag fracture, and Kevin noticed it wasn't even locked. Probably because this lock didn't work. Outside, the water in a small swimming pool looked murky. When he looked again, he saw two guys sprawled in the lounge chairs by the pool. They were smoking little glass cylinders, not cigarettes or weed. Were those crack pipes? With a pounding heart, he jerry-rigged the curtain to cover the window again.

"This is the worst dump I've ever seen," Jeanine said through clenched teeth. "What's the matter with that airline?"

"Babe, I think they put us up in a crack house. Can you believe it?"

"I can believe it!"

The bed, covered by a stained brown spread, had been made in a hurry by someone who didn't make beds for a living. Kevin laid his suitcase on the bed and took out cargo shorts, a T-shirt, and his sandals. While Jeanine frowned at him, he changed clothes. Next door, the baby was wailing.

"You don't run around a tough neighborhood in dress clothes. Makes you look like a mark."

"You shouldn't run around a tough neighborhood period." She plopped onto the bed and put her head in her hands.

There was a knock on the door and they both jumped.

"Yeah?" said Kevin.

"It's Stewie's dad," a nervous voice said.

Kevin opened the door. The guy looked rumpled and red-eyed, like he had had a long day. "I'm Mark," he said, and reached around the baby to put out his hand.

Mark gave Kevin a list and thirty dollars. "Formula, diapers, applesauce and rice cereal if they have it. And some wipes. If there's change, grab me a Snickers Bar, and you get something for you and your wife too." He nodded toward Jeanine.

Kevin nodded. "I want you and the little dude to stay with Jeanine. When I get back, I'll knock on the door."

Watching him remove the gold watch that had belonged to his Grandpa, Jeanine was staring at him as if he was someone she didn't know. He tucked the watch into a corner of his suitcase. He thought a moment, then grabbed his driver's license and a twenty out of his wallet, and slipped them into his pants. He slipped the wallet into the suitcase with the watch.

Jeanine hugged him with a surprising fierceness and whispered to get back soon. Like he was planning to dawdle. Mark sat with the baby in a chair by the window.

On the way to the front desk, Kevin passed a man shambling down the hall, singing to himself.

Please, God, see me through this ordeal.

"Did you call my cab?" he asked the desk clerk. With her big shoulders, squat body and thick wrists, she could double for a female bouncer.

"They won't come," she said in a brusque voice.

"They won't come if you don't insist. I need to get to the drug-store."

Her shrug said, "Not my problem."

A girl with café au lait skin and dark shoulder-length hair pushed open the door and ran up to the counter. She didn't look like a denizen of the Southern Comfort.

"Was a man here asking for me?" she asked in a breathless voice that sounded like honey.

"Yeah. Some guy called," said the clerk. "Asked if the chick with the odd name, Lantana or something like that, was in room 206?"

"He knew my room number?" Her eyes were as big and worried as Jeanine's had been.

The clerk nodded, showing minute signs of animation.

"Then I have to check out right away. Here's the key. Credit my card." She glanced over her shoulder. "Can you hurry?"

As he walked by, Kevin admired the girl's tight denim mini-skirt and cleavage-baring top. Heels a mile high. Sexy, but classy. What would a girl like that be doing here?

He went to the door, still hoping against hope for the cab, but the only car was a gleaming black Mercedes with the engine running. When he stepped outside, the muggy air and the reek from the big river hit him with a one-two punch.

The girl dashed out of the lobby and opened the door to the Mercedes.

"Any chance you could give me a ride to Eckerd's?" asked Kevin, moving toward the car. "We have a baby who needs food and diapers." He pointed to his list, knowing he sounded incredibly lame.

The girl seemed surprised, and looked at him from his buzz cut hair to his brown Teva sandals. "Sure. Ya'all get in. But I'm in kind of a hurry." Sweet, soft southern drawl.

The Mercedes' interior smelled of leather and perfume and cigarette smoke. Music with a reggae beat poured out of the speakers. The girl grabbed a cell phone from a big silver handbag and tossed the bag into the back seat.

Too late Kevin remembered his phone was in Jeanine's purse where he had stuck it after he got off the plane. He knew this girl wouldn't wait for him to run back to his room.

Cursing his forgetfulness, Kevin leaned his head back and took a deep breath.

The girl pulled into the street and zoomed through the sullen night, handling the car with relaxed assurance, glancing between the street and the cell phone in her left hand.

"I'm Kevin," he said. "I sure do appreciate the lift."

"Lantana."

"Pretty name. I've never been in a Mercedes. Great ride, so smooth. How's it handle?"

"It's cool. My . . . boyfriend's car. We . . . share it." She smiled, not at Kevin, but at some thought.

The empty street was lined with derelict buildings, a junkyard, a boarded up pizza place, and a nail salon. Kevin noticed the street sign read "Third Avenue." Finally he saw the drugstore up ahead on the corner.

"This late, they'll have to ring you in," said the girl.

"Thanks again for the ride."

"No trouble," she said, stopping in front of the door.

She hadn't asked why a white man staying in a crack house was looking for baby food in the middle of the night. He had been too nervous to inquire about the man who knew her room number and what she was doing at the seedy motel.

Tires squealed as she took off. Grandpa would have said "like a scalded dog."

□   □   □

When he unloaded the basket full of baby supplies onto the counter, Kevin asked about a cab. The cashier said he could call one, but don't expect it to show up. Kevin rolled his eyes and added two hefty Snickers Bars to the order. For Mark and Jeanine. He wasn't hungry. The tab came to $29.43. He hadn't realized how expensive a baby could be.

"Is it safe to walk back to my motel?" he asked the cashier.

"Whereabouts is the motel?"

"Third Avenue. About a mile down the street." He didn't want to say "Southern Comfort Motel." Might as well have asked if it was safe to walk to the crack house.

The cashier seemed evasive, saying, "I always drive home." He handed Kevin a plastic bag that didn't quite accommodate the long package of diapers and another with the formula and the rest of the purchases.

"Have a nice day."

Kevin wanted to reply with an expletive. Instead, he pushed open the door and stepped outside. Who would bother a guy lugging bags of baby supplies?

A black kid lounged against the plate glass window. In the glare of the overhead light, Kevin noticed his psychedelic T-shirt, dark sunglasses, and cornrows. He appeared to be text messaging, and he glanced in Kevin's direction.

"Yo!" he said.

This guy with his loud T-shirt didn't seem threatening, and he was even friendly.

"Hi!" said Kevin. "I see the rain finally stopped."

The kid put his phone in his pants pocket and continued to stare at Kevin. He flicked his lighter open and lit two cigarettes. Beckoning to Kevin, he asked, "Smoke?"

Kevin shifted the plastic bag with the formula to his left hand

and took the offered cigarette. "Thanks." He had never smoked.

"Alvis," the kid said.

"Elvis?"

"Alvis. With an 'A.' Also knowd as Trick Magnet."

Kevin didn't think he could ever address anyone as Trick Magnet.

"Oh, sorry, Alvis. I'm Kevin." He wasn't sure what to do with the cigarette or if he should shake hands.

"You owes me some money, Kevin." Alvis's smile looked frosty, but Kevin couldn't tell for sure without seeing his eyes.

He hoped his mugging, if that's what would happen, might be quick and not too painful and that he would be able to reach the night bell and then the cops could come take him back to the motel.

"Why do I owe you money, Alvis?" he asked, surprised to hear his voice, steady and reasonable as if he had just asked, "Any good barbecue joints around here?"

"You spend time with that slut in the Mercedes. You owes me money."

"Hey man, she just gave me a ride." Was this guy her . . . pimp? Who assumed that Kevin had—the thought was too bizarre.

"How dumb you think I be?"

"She only gave me a lift from the motel down the street. So I could buy formula and diapers for the baby." He jiggled the drugstore bags up and down, and felt beads of sweat on his brow.

"Southern Comfort?"

"That's the place. Where the airline put us up for the night." Kevin didn't want to utter "crack house" or "bad neighborhood" or anything that might smack of disrespect.

Alvis laughed. "You're shittin' me."

"No, there's a big group of us staying there."

Alvis laughed again. "Now I heard everything. You kin apprise me of the necessary information while we stroll back that way."

Alvis pointed to the street. He seemed almost jolly.

Kevin put the cigarette in the direction of his mouth, and then tossed it down. He wished Alvis would take his dark glasses off. He wiped his moist forehead, and felt more sweat oozing down his back.

They began walking up Third Street toward the motel. Alvis kept Kevin between him and a chain link fence. The humidity must have been ninety-nine percent. Most of the street lights were off and it looked like they were walking toward a black hole. Somewhere a dog barked, a menacing sound. Kevin's heart throttled his chest. Maybe he should mention the baby again.

"I be in marketing, you might say," said Alvis, taking out his phone again and flipping it open.

"I'm a help desk technician."

Alvis considered that for a moment. "Then we both be in the helping professions."

"I guess," said Kevin.

"Now you be helping me. With the information." Alvis pushed a number and put the phone to his ear for a moment, then he flipped the phone shut.

"What information do you want?" asked Kevin.

"The bitch in the Mercedes. The information is where you found her, what she say, where she was going, all those details of the situation."

Kevin told him about Lantana's conversation with the desk clerk and how he had asked for a lift to the store. That they had talked about the Mercedes. What a fine car it was. That it belonged to "her boyfriend."

Alvis muttered, "Yo, yo, yo," to every fact Kevin provided.

"It sure was nice of her to help me out with a ride to get the baby's stuff. The poor kid hasn't had any food since this afternoon," said Kevin, playing the daddy card. "He's really hungry." He jiggled the plastic bag again.

"Lantana's profession is be nice for money. Otherwise, she's disrespecting me." The low voice was cold.

Kevin was silent.

"She high?" asked Alvis.

Kevin turned and stared at him.

"Mr. Help Desk, be bounteous with some answers."

"She wasn't high," said Kevin. The girl had seemed edgy, but normal. Alvis was the unpredictable one.

They crossed an intersection, where a street light cast shadows on the puddles in the road. Kevin glanced at his companion. Slim, well-muscled, nobody he could outrun. New Air Jordan sneakers on his feet. Not as young as Kevin had assumed. Nice looking guy, actually. Kevin had never met a pimp or prostitute or spent the night in a crack house. If he could only keep Alvis walking and talking, maybe he could work this thing out. In the distance, Kevin thought he could see the green neon sign of the Southern Comfort Motel.

Alvis lit another cigarette, but didn't offer Kevin one.

"He's a cute little dude, the baby," said Kevin.

"I be three times a daddy," said Alvis, with no particular pride.

"Boys or girls?" asked Kevin.

"All three boys," said Alvis.

"Cool," said Kevin. "Pretty soon you'll have a basketball team." He didn't ask if Lantana was the mother.

Alvis stopped in front of a boarded-up quick-mart. "Now let's address that money you owes."

Kevin wished he hadn't cleaned out his wallet. Maybe Alvis would have been satisfied with two or three twenties.

"Sorry, Alvis. I spent my cash on the baby."

"Clean out your pockets." The blade of a knife gleamed in the dark. Kevin dropped the bag with the formula and heard the baby food jars crack on the cement sidewalk. With a trembling hand, he turned one empty pocket out and was getting his twenty and the pitiful bit of change from the other pocket when a car pulled up next to them.

Lantana in the black Mercedes.

The window on the driver's side slid down. "Alvis, honey, I been looking for you. Hey, Kevin!" She smiled at him.

"You wait right there, white boy, like you have Gorilla Glue on those pitiful shoes." Alvis turned away and snapped his knife shut. He walked with a weird swaggering limp at he approached the Mercedes. Kevin noticed the elaborate embroidery on Alvis's back pockets and down the legs of his jeans. Expensive. Alvis cuffed Lantana across the face through the open window.

"How many times I say you call me Trick Magnet? And don't look me in the eye like that!"

Lantana rubbed her hand across her face and muttered something Kevin couldn't hear.

He wanted to take off and race back to the motel, which now seemed a place of safety, but he didn't think his Jell-O-like legs could run. He waited while Lantana spoke to Alvis in a soft, reasonable voice. Alvis brushed his hand across her face and deposited a kiss on her cheek. Kevin wondered if Alvis was apologizing. He couldn't imagine Alvis apologizing to anyone.

Alvis turned and beckoned to Kevin in a lordly way. Kevin picked up the dropped bag and approached the Mercedes, feeling ready to beg, like a supplicant. Lantana watched him with emotionless eyes.

"The information is determined by me to be basically correct," said Alvis in an imperious voice. He removed his dark glasses and looked at Kevin. "Lantana's client didn't follow the proper protocols, and she freaked." He paused. "The people helping professions can be a pain in the ass." He polished his shades with the hem of his shirt.

"That's for sure," said Kevin. He wondered if he was free to leave or if Alvis would threaten him again with the knife. He could have wrung the sweat out of his shirt.

"Drive Kevin Help-Desk back to the motel," Alvis told the girl. "You check into a room, and we proceeds from there."

"Aren't you coming?" asked Lantana.

"Business situation in the neighborhood requires my attentions," said Alvis. "I be by later."

Still shaking and weak with relief, Kevin climbed into the front seat and Lantana drove off. The AC felt cold on his wet shirt. Neither of them spoke. Lantana checked her cell phone as she drove. Kevin wanted to tell her he was sorry if he got her into trouble, that he was sorry Alvis slapped her, that he was sorry that she had to have sex with strangers.

"Really sultry tonight. Is it always this hot around here?"

"Summertime." She continued to watch the tiny screen on the phone. "Alvis bark is worse than Alvis bite."

A good thing, thought Kevin, as Lantana pulled into the Southern Comfort lot. He said, "Well, here we are."

She didn't park, and left the motor running.

"Listen, thanks for everything. I . . . I . . . "

"No problem." Her eyes were locked onto the cell phone.

Clutching his shopping bags, he opened the door, and turned back. He wouldn't wish her a nice evening like the stupid clerk at the drugstore, or follow his impulse to tell her to drive the Mercedes to Key West or Nevada, somewhere far away, and get a "real" job.

She didn't look up from the cell phone. Did she have a text message from Alvis changing the plan? She pulled away and drove off into the night, leaving Kevin with his questions and two white plastic bags.

He rang the bell to get into the motel. The clerk acknowledged him with a surly nod. The lobby still reeked of burning plastic, ammonia and disinfectant. Weird stuff crunched under his feet again as he walked down the hall to the room. Nothing had changed. He could hear the baby fussing. He knocked softly and called, "Jeanine?"

She opened the door right away, as if she had been waiting on the other side.

"Oh Kev, I've been crazy with worry about you." She threw her arms around him.

"Babe."

"Thank God you're back."

Mark, who held the baby in the chair by the window, stood up. Kevin put the shopping bags on the bed. "I dropped a bag and I think the applesauce broke. Hope it's not too big of a mess. Can you manage all right?"

Mark nodded. Kevin found a Snickers Bar and gave it to Jeanine. Then he handed the bags to Mark.

"See you in the morning," Kevin said. "Hope the little dude will be all right."

Mark thanked Kevin as fervently as Kevin had thanked Lantana. Kevin closed and locked the door.

Jeanine flung her arms around him again, and rested her head against his chest. "I'm so glad you're back."

"That makes two of us."

"You didn't have any trouble, did you?" she asked, hugging him tighter.

"I got a ride both ways."

He would tell her in the morning. When they were out of this place. When they were safe in the air on their way home. He would tell her then.

The Devil's Dumping Ground

Joseph Souza

Father Tommy Doyle hit a low fade down the center of the eleventh fairway. I took a few practice swings, teed up after him, and then drove one down the left-hand side that landed in the rough fescue. Towing carts behind us, we reminisced about the time we spent here before it became a golf course. The Quincy Quarries was what this godforsaken pit was called when we were kids. What was once our playground was now filled with the refuse from Boston's biggest public works project. The Big Dig.

I hadn't seen Tommy in over fifteen years. He'd been assigned out of the Boston Diocese in the late nineties. A few days ago he called me out of the blue, said he was in town and would like to see me. I'd been a close friend of his brother, and the three of us had grown up on the same street in South Boston. There was much to catch up on.

"I want to thank you for meeting me here," he said as we strolled up the well-groomed fairway.

"My pleasure, Father. After all, we go back a ways."

"We're old friends, Eddie. Call me Tommy," he said, looking around at his surroundings. "My brother would have been proud of this course."

"What do you hear from Richie these days?"

He shook his head. We both, I assumed, believed that Richie was dead.

"I loved him, Tommy, but we both know that he had enemies."

"Who doesn't? Even God has his enemies."

"So what brings you to Boston?"

"Actually, Eddie, I was hoping to hit you up for some cash." He laughed. "Actually, I was hoping you'd make a charitable donation to the Church."

"That can be arranged."

"I can't believe we're playing golf on what was once our old stomping grounds. How times change, huh?"

Back when we were kids we used to come here on hot summer days to cool off and test our mettle. Leaping into the onyx quarry waters was a rite of passage. Half of South Boston would come here to drink and beat the oppressive slum heat. There was lots of beer and it gave us the impetus to jump these dangerous cliffs. As we stood staring down the granite faces, gathering up the courage to jump, we knew that just below the waterline existed a debris-filled Atlantis: telephone poles, household appliances, and car antennas waiting to impale our young bodies. Swingles was the scariest of the quarries. If you jumped any one of them you were immediately treated with respect. Only the boldest and bravest of us had the balls to jump. Father Tommy once jumped Heavens when he was sixteen and swore never to do it again. I watched one day as his brother Richie performed a suicidal swan dive off of Purps, a hundred and ten foot jump with a tree to clear. One time we were all hanging out when this kid we knew sailed off of Rampa. We waited and waited for him to surface, but he never did, and after an hour of trying to find him we all scurried back to the neighborhood with word of his death. I had terrible nightmares for months afterwards and quickly developed a paralyzing fear of heights. I swore never to jump the Swingles quarries. And I kept my word.

Richie's influence was crucial in getting this golf course built. He was connected; he knew how to charm and influence people. We negotiated the lease for this pit in the mid-nineties when no one else wanted the liability. I owned a successful contracting and trucking business that also acted as a front for his criminal activity. Because of my expertise in the field, we were able to land a lucrative contract with the city of Boston to remove all the Big Dig fill. We then turned around and negotiated a contract with the county to fill in the Quincy Quarries with the very same fill. We would eventually move twelve million cubic yards into that death pit, preventing many more kids from dying in these quarries. On paper it was a beautiful solution to two major problems: where to put all the fill, and where to get enough dirt to fill the fifty-four quarries. Our third proposal was the icing on the cake, and that was to build a luxury golf course over the Quincy Quarries. What was once the devil's dumping ground was designed to cater to the discriminating golfer willing to pay a premium for such accommodations.

Father Tommy took out a seven iron and leaned on it. After fifteen years in Arizona he was barely recognizable to me. He was and always would be the reserved, older brother of my best friend.

It was no wonder his brother got mixed up in criminal activity. Richie was a sociopath, though a charming one at that. Not one to abide by other's rules, he lived by his own. He could be loyal and kind one minute, and ruthless the next. He'd give you the shirt off his back or just as easily use it to wrap around your neck. He'd call me on occasion, in the middle of the night, and ask for my help. He'd pick me up at the house, the victim stuffed in the trunk of his car. We'd cruise past the Mr. Tux store marking the entrance to the quarries. It would take us some time to lug the body up the path, and only by glint of flashlight could we navigate the various trails. Once we arrived atop the designated cliff, he would hold one end of the corpse and I the other. The corpse would be weighted down. Then we'd toss the poor stiff in, waiting long enough to hear the echo of splash far below. For years we ditched bodies in almost every quarry up here: Tit, Blue Rock, Goldfish, Rampa, to name just a few. I considered myself a businessman, but you just didn't say no to Richie when he asked for a favor.

Tommy had a nice lie. He took a few gingerly practice swings before looking back and winking. The man looked like hell. Arizona's sun and the Irish flu had taken a toll on him, judging from the varicose veins on his nose. It had taken me a few seconds to even recognize him when I met him at the putting green this morning. He pumped my hand warmly, dressed casually for our round of golf. He had the same baby-blue eyes as Richie, and the same sparkle in them too. It wasn't even noon and he already had a gin and tonic in hand. But he was a priest and I'd been brought up to respect priests, a vestige of my Catholic upbringing.

"Why did they move you out of Boston?"

"There's a severe shortage of priests, if you haven't noticed," he said, looking up from his stance. "You can take the priest out of Boston, Eddie, but you can't take Boston out of the priest."

"It's not like we don't have shortages here." I was well aware of the shortage. The wife and I rarely missed the Saturday mass at St. John the Baptist. Our current priest-in-residence hailed from Venezuela and spoke with a thick accent.

"What can I tell you, pal," he said, arms extended, resembling his brother. "I just work here."

We holed out. At the twelfth tee Tommy hit a nasty rug-burner that skidded about thirty feet. "Goddamnit," he muttered. I followed with a nasty slice that sailed out of bounds. We agreed to use mulligans and our second shots fared much better. We gathered our carts and pressed on.

"Hope God don't keep score," I joked, holding up the card.

"If so, then I'm in the wrong profession." He lit a cigarette.

I was content for once. At the age of fifty-five I had been gradually settling into a more comfortable phase in life, and much of that was on account of Richie's absence. As part owner of this golf course, I had a legitimate income and my partners were respectable citizens. My kids graduated from college and were all doing well. I'd been trying to look to the future and put my criminal past in the rearview. So it was a complete surprise when Tommy called after fifteen years, requesting that we meet for drinks.

Two nice chips and we were looking at pars. After putting out, we stood staring up at a particular ledge that we had once jumped as kids. The architect for this course had purposely left the graffiti untouched on the granite faces, as if to juxtapose the low brow with the high, the gritty past with the genteel present. It was a unique golf course; I knew of none other like it. This particular bluff had been a thirty-foot drop with a dangerous crag below that required a running start.

"Believe we were dumb enough to jump? Such fools we were back then." He was cleaning the head of his iron with a towel.

"God protects only fools and drunks."

"Make no mistake, Eddie, we were such fools back in them days." Tommy placed his iron over his shoulder blades, cigarette in mouth, and swiveled his hips. "How many kids you think died up here?"

I shrugged. I didn't care to know.

"Remember that day I jumped Heavens? That was about a seventy-foot drop, and I was shitting in my trunks. Promised God I'd become a priest if I made it out of that quarry alive."

"You certainly kept your word."

"I never judged you for not jumping, Eddie, especially after we watched that kid die trying. Richie could be a cruel bastard, the way he mocked you for that."

I nodded, the memory sending a chill down my spine. The mere mention of my cowardice seemed like a backhanded compliment. Failing to jump the Swingles was one of my few regrets in life.

"God was watching out for me that day." He shook his head wistfully. "That could have been me who died in that piss pot."

"I don't like admitting it, Tommy, but I had a terrible fear of heights."

"Should have put your life in God's hands like I did. Richie would have been a lot easier on you had you jumped." He teed up on the thirteenth. "He did take a sadistic pleasure in busting your chops."

"What do you think ever happened to him?"

"Don't be naïve, Eddie. A guy like that doesn't just disappear into thin air. We both know that he was murdered."

"How can you be so sure?"

"Chalk it up to divine intervention."

His answer caught me by surprise. I only wanted to change the subject. That I balked at that hundred-foot cliff was one of the worst days in my life. I became the laughingstock of the neighborhood that summer and got into fistfights every day. It would have been better if I jumped and died had I known what humiliations awaited me. But after watching that kid die I'd become paralyzed with fear. Even the twenty and thirty foot jumps induced panic attacks that lasted well into the night. I even fainted once on a class trip to the top of the Pru.

The Boston skyline was beginning to appear. To our right was the blue-green ocean. The lush grass contrasted nicely against the graffiti-scrawled quarry, marrying an ugly past to a more genteel present. The tip of the Bunker Hill monument could be seen, which ironically was cut from these very quarries.

Father Doyle hit a wicked slice that got caught up in the wind and drifted out of bounds, and so I encouraged him to hit another. After his second shot landed in bounds, I played a nice draw that landed on the edge of the green.

The smell of methane gas wafted up to us, a result of the twelve million cubic yards of fill occupying the fifty-four quarries. The smell is similar to a bad fart. Underfoot was Boston's historic past, and this never ceased to amaze me, that we were not physically in Boston and yet were standing atop Boston soil. And deep below that were the remains of those who would forever be entombed in this middle ground.

"It's good of you to make a donation to the Church, Eddie. Those poor Indians have gotten screwed over."

"Glad I can do it, now that I've made a few."

"You've done real good for yourself, Eddie." He gazed around at his lush surroundings. "If only Richie were here to enjoy the fruits of his labor."

"It was me who did most of the heavy lifting," I said, half in jest.

"Of course you did, Eddie. I wasn't implying otherwise. But we both know that without Richie all this would have never come about." He flicked his cigarette butt onto the sod.

"Bet Richie's looking down on us as we speak."

"Or up." Tommy put his forefingers up over his head like horns and laughed.

The direction of this conversation was beginning to concern me. Was his comment a reference to his brother's reserved spot in Hell? Or an acknowledgment that he was buried in the quarries beneath us?

"He was a good kid at heart, Eddie, but it was the environment we grew up in. You knew what it was like. We were dirt poor. And my old man was a mean drunk."

"Your father did have a nasty temper."

"Unfortunately, Richie inherited that temper. I could always find our old man drinking down at the L Street Tavern, when he wasn't screwing whores or getting into bar fights."

"Other then golf, Tommy, how did you turn out so well?"

"Who said I did?" He shot me a grin.

"You take more mulligans than a South Boston funeral director."

We laughed, but I was becoming wary of this conversation.

"In your opinion, Eddie, where do you think Richie ended up?"

I ignored his question and concentrated on my shot. Using my nine iron, I punched one over the green. After kicking his ball out of some tall grass, Tommy chipped up to within ten feet of the flag.

"We playing soccer or golf?"

"Relax, Eddie. It's only a game."

It took him two putts to hole out. I three-putted, my nerves getting the best of me. At the fourteenth tee the Boston skyline came into full view. I could see Tommy marveling at the panoramic vista. Above us a Peregrine hawk circled overhead. The fourteenth hole was a dog leg right and so I advised Tommy to aim between the Hancock and Prudential buildings in order to set up a nice approach shot. Tommy pulled out his two iron and examined the shaft.

"You know what they say about the two iron, Eddie?"

"Even God can't hit one."

"Unless he's Tiger Woods." Tommy took a few practice swings through the manicured grass. Then he looked at me. "You may not believe this, Eddie, but Richie was a man of faith."

I wanted to laugh, knowing the true nature of his brother. I once had the misfortune of watching him torture a guy for three hours with pliers and a handsaw before finally putting him out of his misery.

"I heard his confession every week."

"A couple of Hail Marys and all his sins were forgiven?"

"Hey, I don't make the rules."

"He confessed to you all his crimes?"

"Especially the ones you two committed in these quarries." He measured his ball on the tee. "I suggest you consider doing the same, Eddie, if you have any hope of eternal salvation."

I shuddered to think what Tommy knew.

"What do you say, Eddie. We don't need to do it in the confessional booth like in the old days. That's a relic of the past. The rules have changed; you can even have roast beef on Fridays now."

He wiggled his hips and then poked a beautiful tee shot between the two iconic skyscrapers. Numb, I watched on. I'd only expected a renewal of our friendship, a few drinks and a pleasant round of golf.

"Maybe God can't hit a two iron," he said, turning to me with newfound confidence, "but this old Southie boy still can."

Using a three iron, I drew my tee shot in nicely.

"Nice poke, Eddie." We commenced pulling our carts. "So what's it going to be?"

"I never claimed to be an angel, Tommy."

"It's Father Doyle, now that we're conducting the Lord's business," he replied, making the sign of the cross. "A quarter mil would do a lot of good for those poor Indian kids."

"A quarter mil?" I laughed. He couldn't be serious. "This a shakedown?"

"The natives are restless, Eddie. And it's for a good cause."

"Supposing I did confess to you. It's your word against mine."

"Oh no, Eddie, you have me all wrong. Canon law vows me to secrecy. Think of this as having attorney/client privilege, only with God."

We stopped mid-fairway and stared at each other. Then I uttered the phrase I hadn't recited in a very long time. "Father forgive me for I have sinned." And confessed to helping Richie dump bodies up here.

A year before they filled in these quarries, a group of citizens filed a motion with the court to stay the process. They sued to have the quarries dredged so that they could rebury loved ones they believed to have been interred here. A judge agreed to delay the process for one year, and in short order the bodies began piling up. We filed lawsuits and appeals, but it was futile. I watched on nervously as they pulled out the dead. Some were the corpses I helped Richie dispose of. Most were jumpers. The remainder were victims of foul play: prostitutes, kids gone missing, wives and girlfriends. Not every missing person was found. Some were too far down to recover. The dredging process was both labor-intensive and lethal. Underwater rockslides posed a constant threat to the divers. The *Globe* quoted them as saying that it was some of the worst conditions they'd ever encountered. During the dredging, the D.A. formed a grand jury and Richie was indicted for the murder of three of his close associates. They came to me with an offer of immunity if I testified against him, but I told them to stick it; I confessed ignorance to Richie's crimes. It was around that time that Richie went on the lam.

The view of the Boston skyline was now in full view. The Big Dig lay dormant beneath the hustle and bustle. Underneath the city's bowels was the poorly constructed tunnel, the entrails of which Father Tommy and I now stood upon. Our Irish forebears cut the granite that framed many of the area's buildings and monuments. This soil we stood upon was not just any old dirt. This was our native city transplanted atop our summer haunt, a place where we came to relax on hot summer days and seek out cheap thrills. Now it was a place of leisure, and a monument to those who were buried beneath it.

Tommy took his two iron out of the bag.

"Twice in one day, Tommy? You're tempting the golf gods."

"And by gods, I pray you're referring to The Holy Trinity." He addressed his ball and then struck it. It arced beautifully and then rolled onto the green.

I debated on what club to hit.

"Contrary to what you might think, I do not stand in judgment of you," he said as I readied to hit the ball. "He who has not sinned cast the first stone, right?" He waited until I swung through. "But I have this sinking feeling that you're not telling me the truth, Eddie, and I really need you to do this if we're to save your soul."

My ball landed in the sand bunker. Angry, I scolded myself, pounding the club head onto the grass.

"Look, I have no idea where Richie is."

"I think you do."

"What do you want from me?" I pointed the iron at him as if it were a shotgun.

"Relax, Eddie. All I ask for is a full confession. Then I can cash your check in good conscience."

"If it wasn't for Richie I'd have never gotten mixed up in his business in the first place."

"Don't blame Richie for your sins," Tommy said, shaking his head in disgust. "Did he force you to jump off these quarries?"

"You're a real piece of work, Tommy."

"Christ lives inside you. He is on his knees begging for your forgiveness."

"For a quarter mil, He better live inside me!"

"It's not like I don't know everything anyways," he said. "Richie told me what you guys did."

"This is bullshit. I didn't agree to meet you here in order to do penance."

"I can't say it for you, Eddie. The words of contrition must come from your own mouth. After all, Christ died for your sins." He gazed imploringly at me. "Richie confessed his sins to me, as well as the sins he was planning to commit in the future."

"Huh?" I was dumbfounded by the implication.

"I knew my brother better than anyone. He couldn't change who he was."

"You mean to tell me that you knew your brother was planning to kill, and yet you did nothing, and absolved him anyway?"

"Oh, Eddie, don't be so holier than thou. It's God who decides to forgive, not I. These are the rules we agreed upon when we entered our faith."

"Christ, you're as coldhearted as your brother." My hands were shaking. I could barely hold the club. I swung, kicking up sand. The ball skittered over the green and into some rough.

"Let's face it, Eddie, Richie's our cross to bear." He pointed to his ball, which was about four feet from the hole. "Look at that putt I have for bird. That a gimme?"

"Let your conscience be your guide, Father Doyle."

"Mark me down for a bird then," he said, scooping the ball up with his putter.

I chipped on and made my bogey. The idea of finishing this round made me sick. I'd just as soon cut him a check for two grand and split. He stood looking up at the granite outcropping with the graffiti scrawled over it. It brought me back to that day when I failed to jump in front of all the other kids.

"Richie was supposed to meet you here shortly before the quarries were to be filled."

"How did you know that?"

"As I said, he told me everything."

I teed up on fifteen and hit my ball down the center of the fairway. Clutching my club, I sidled up next to him in a threatening manner. No one could push me around. I could smell the gin on his breath. The ping in my hand now felt like a weapon.

"What are you implying?"

"Implying, Eddie?" He stepped back as if insulted. "We're just two good friends catching up on old times."

I recalled that fateful day when Richie ordered me to meet him here. He'd been on the lam for three months after the indictment was handed up. He directed me to bring him fifty grand in cash and told me to meet him at Heavens. I was paranoid, convinced that Richie believed I was going to testify against him. The business was in my name; his stake had always been silent, cemented with a handshake. If he wanted money then I was obligated to give it to him, and this was made abundantly clear when we started out. Because of that I decided on a premeditated strike.

"He was going to kill me," I said. "The D.A. wanted me to testify against him, but I refused to cooperate. Of course Richie didn't know that."

"Eddie, Eddie, Eddie," he said, shaking his head as we continued our walk. "All my brother wanted was the money that was due him. I would have known if he was planning to kill you. You had a moral obligation to him."

Suddenly I felt a searing pain shoot through my knee. I collapsed to the ground in agony. When I looked up, Father Tommy was holding the two iron in his hands like a baseball bat.

"It seems God can hit a two iron after all, Eddie. Just so happens he's better at hitting knees than golf balls."

"I'm sorry, Tommy," I croaked. "I was afraid for my life."

"Thatta boy. Get it all off your chest, you piece of shit!"

He swung the club again and this time teed off on my other knee. I could feel the joint explode into shrapnel. I looked around the golf course for help, tears in my eyes. But we were the only ones out here. It was such an exclusive course it did not get heavy play. Behind Tommy's head I could see one of the Swingles crags. Would it be the last thing I'd ever see? His face was now twisted into something hideous. The resemblance between him and his dead brother was striking, especially considering that Tommy had always been the quiet, reserved one.

Blinded by the sun and the intense pain exploding through my knees, I glanced up and saw that he was pulling up his golf shirt. My vision was blurry from the pain; tears formed in my eyes. When his shirt was pulled up around his neck, I realized that the devil was staring down at me.

"Richie!"

"Took you long enough, Eddie."

The faded green tattoo covered the entire front of his torso. A tattoo of Jesus nailed to the cross, the two criminals hanging on his left and right. He'd gotten it in the seventies at a tattoo parlor on Dot Avenue, and he'd always been proud of it. He had numerous tattoos on his neck and arms, which he must have covered up with makeup.

"I trusted you, Eddie. You were my best friend. All I needed was some cash to live on. I wasn't going to kill you."

"I'm sorry."

"I loved you more than I loved my own brother."

It was then that I realized I had killed the wrong Doyle.

"Why'd you send Tommy to meet me?"

Richie took a few practice swings with the two iron and then looked down the fairway as if calculating the distance.

"I heard that you had met with the D.A., but I didn't think you'd rat me out after all we'd been through. Still, I couldn't take the chance. Everything was in your name. I needed you alive to get my money. Tommy was weak. He'd do anything I asked."

"I'll give you whatever you want, Richie," I groaned.

"Know why they sent him away, Eddie? Because my brother was a child molester." He laughed. "Now who's the bad guy?"

"I'm sorry, Richie."

"Sorry! Just fill out the damn check, Eddie, and make it for a half a mil." He pulled the checkbook out of my pocket and tossed it onto my chest.

I clutched the pen, grimacing.

"Make it out to the Catholic Church, in the name of Father Thomas Doyle. I'm going through a mid-life career change. You'd be surprised how good the Church takes care of its perverts."

"You've been impersonating your brother all this time?"

"In name only, partner. Thank god for the strong family resemblance."

"I can't picture you, of all people, saying mass, Richie."

"Are you kidding? They don't want me anywhere near a church. I live the life, Eddie. Come and go as I please. Collect a little stipend for my troubles, too."

I passed him the check. He folded it up without looking at it and then slipped it into his pocket. He walked around to my head. I could feel him dragging me by the shoulders. We arrived at the edge of the fairway. There was a bluff to the left of this hole that was the last vestige of Heavens. Below, about forty feet, was a hazard filled with cold spring water and a slew of errant golf balls.

"Tommy was a coward like you, Eddie. He never jumped Heavens," he said, positioning me at the edge.

"But I saw him jump it."

"No, you saw him falling. I pushed his sorry ass off."

"You should have pushed me instead."

"What do you think I'm going to do now?" Holding my ankles, he dangled me off the bluff. "Sink or swim, pal. Because you're about to enter Heavens."

Suddenly I felt myself falling. It felt oddly liberating to be free. All I could think about were the corpses that Richie and I had years ago disposed of up here. Now I would be one of them. I asked for God's forgiveness as I hit the water. It rushed with cold glee into my mouth and nose and ears. I slipped down, down, down into that deep, dark pool. I felt sorry for my family. All the dirt in town could not overcome the fact that this was still the devil's dumping ground, and I was surely to be its final victim.

Bottled Up

Stephen D. Rogers

My husband would kill me if he ever learned I was sitting in my cruiser with a bottle cradled between my thighs.

Why did I need a bottle of hot water? So I could prepare formula.

Why would I ever need to mix formula while working a detail? Because our babysitter broke up with her boyfriend and suddenly showed up with Jason, saying she needed to go home immediately, as if she'd accomplish more at one in the morning than she would at two.

Not my fault my husband was out of town when it happened.

At least Jason slept through the transfer.

No victim; no crime.

A late-night construction detail? Perfect road conditions? Holly's the only vehicle I've seen in the last two hours? Piece of cake. Jason probably found the jackhammer vibrations soothing.

Besides, what were the odds he'd remember this by the time he learned to talk?

A car blew by me doing at least ninety. Crested the Bourne Bridge and disappeared onto the Cape. No way the driver could miss my activated lightbar. That left liquor-blind or panicked flight.

I called in my pursuit, conscious that Bourne PD would respond.

A bluebird flew out of the state police barracks, indicating that yet another reporting agency was getting into the act.

Maybe if the feds got involved, Jason's presence in my cruiser could be leaked to the international media, just in case my husband missed the item reported nationally.

The state trooper hugged the rotary to head down 6A.

I followed.

Would the driver race along the canal until options opened up at the intersection with 28, or turn right into the development?

After switching frequencies, I asked, "This is Standish thirty-three. Anybody have a visual on the Grand Prix?"

Nobody did.

I turned right and slowed, calling in my position and requesting backup. There were only two ways out of the development, separated by less than three hundred yards. If the driver had come in here, he could be contained.

Unfortunately, there might be fifty homes strung along the loop. If he realized his situation, he could head straight for one of the darkened houses, grab a hostage.

I wish I'd seen the license plate. That anybody had.

Slowly cruising the development, I flicked my searchlight to clear shadowed driveways.

Was the driver a local? Someone new to the area might not realize he wasn't going anywhere until the road started to curve. That's where he'd ditch the car.

Jason stirred. Gave a little cough. The rear-facing car seat should have been in the back, but I certainly wasn't putting him behind the plastic shield.

Nobody had a visual on the Grand Prix. If he hadn't beaten us to 28, he was trapped inside this development.

My backup was in place.

"Roger that."

Clear.

Next driveway. Clear.

The curve to the left became more pronounced. Was this where the driver started to panic? Started to examine options? Gathered wits or guts or bullets?

Clear.

There was no question we were headed back to 6A.

A Grand Prix sat in the next driveway. I stopped and called in the plate before approaching, pressed for time, haunted by the idea of hostages.

No sign of the driver. The hood was still warm.

Shined my flashlight around the property.

Nobody hiding in the shrubs.

Front door of the house was closed, locked. Windows along the front intact.

I returned to my vehicle. Jason. His tiny little nose.

Dispatch: "Vehicle was reported stolen two hours ago. Logan Airport, long-term parking. No description of the suspect."

I swiveled the searchlight to canvass the area.

"Standish thirty-three to Standish twenty-nine. Anything?"

"Negative."

Jason stirred and I placed a hand on him until he settled again.

Dispatch reported calling the house and speaking to the owner.

"Number one ten?" The bedroom must be at the back, since I hadn't seen a light.

"Affirmative. No Grand Prix in the drive when they went to bed. They're staying in their room. Two adults, no kids, a German shepherd sleeping downstairs."

The dog that didn't bark. "Have you called neighbors?"

"We're on it."

"Any—" Jason chose this moment to wake. Screaming.

"What was that?"

"Disregard." And forget you ever heard it.

I scooped the powdered formula into the bottle of warm water, shook, and tipped the concoction into his waiting mouth, all while scanning for the missing driver.

If he cut through the woods, away from 6A, he'd head straight into the military reservation. What kind of security were they running, and did any of them report to the feds?

There he was, near the right-rear corner of the house. I propped up the bottle with Jason's blanket. Was the driver armed and dangerous?

The dog began barking.

Updating Dispatch, I added, "Thirty-three pursuing on foot."

I swung the door closed and drew my gun as I sprinted to the left.

Would he run or breach the residence?

The back of the house was clear. I braced my gun hand on my flashlight. Windows. Door. I spun in a slow circle.

Couldn't hear a thing over the dog.

Approached the corner where I'd sighted him.

He was sprinting toward my cruiser.

Toward my son.

"Freeze. Police."

Before the second word was out of my mouth, I was running.

He had twenty feet on me but I had motivation.

An activated lightbar grew visible through the trees.

I holstered my gun without slowing, dropped the flashlight.

Ten feet.

He'd reached my cruiser. The door. He grabbed the handle and yanked.

Jason let out a shriek.

The man froze.

I flew through the air. Cut him down at the knees. Twisted him under me as I pulled out the cuffs and immobilized him.

Backup arrived.

Jason was wailing now.

While an officer brought the suspect to his feet, I rescued my son from the cruiser.

Patted his back until he burped.

Kissed his little nose.

Wondered if we were going to survive the coming explosion.

The Tally

Judith Green

Inside the school bus: bliss. Let out at midday, last day of school! Margie and her best friend, Peggy Button, sat squashed companionably into the last seat, heads together, listening to a combination of static and The Beatles on Peggy's new transistor radio. Suddenly Margie shrieked and slid sideways as the bus lurched out around a log truck sitting on the side of the narrow road. She righted herself, smoothing her dress over her thighs, and glanced back out of the small rear window.

The log truck was loaded with birch bolts—cut just longer than she was tall and stacked cross-wise—headed for Mr. Simpson's dowel mill. There was no one in the truck's cab, but Margie spotted a blue pickup truck pulled right off into the woods alongside it. Two men crouched behind a heap of bolts in the pickup's bed. One man poked up his head to stare at the retreating school bus, until the other grabbed him by the shoulder and jerked him down.

"Look, Peggy, wasn't that your father?" Margie asked. "It was his pickup, anyway, 'cause it had that one green fender."

Peggy leaned over to look out the window, but the bus was rounding a curve, and both trucks had slid behind tree branches heavy with early-summer green. "I don't see anything. Besides, he wouldn't have his pickup way out here. He'd be in a log truck."

"It was your father's pickup."

Peggy shrugged. "Hey, you know what? We're fourth graders now!"

Margie sighed. "Well, can I hold the radio?"

□   □   □

"Today on the bus I saw Peggy's father, up by Back Pond." Margie was working her way around the kitchen table, laying out paper napkins. Her mother stood at the stove, mashing potatoes while red hot dogs sizzled in a frying pan. A dish of canned string beans, reheated to a dispirited gray, sat on the counter. "Peggy didn't see him, but it was her father."

"Uh-huh," Mama grunted. "Get a wiggle on, will you?"

Margie plucked five forks from the dish drainer by the sink. "He was playing hide-and-seek with another man."

Mama poured salt into the palm of her hand and dumped it into the potatoes. "Randal Button playing hide-and-seek? What on earth do you mean?"

"Mr. Button's pickup was in the woods behind a log truck, and it was full of those special birch bolts. They were peeking at us over the load."

"You mean the log truck was full of the bolts."

"Yes, but the pickup was full, too."

Margie felt herself go prickly under her mother's blue-eyed gaze. "Hm," Mama said.

"Hey!" came a shout from outside. "Anyone home?"

Margie ran to the door. Out in the yard, the slanting evening light poured over her uncle's shiny new Dodge truck and outlined his lanky frame as he walked, grinning, toward the doorstep. "Uncle Clark!" she called. "I haven't seen you in forever!"

"Gotcha!" And her uncle swung her squealing with joy, into the air, then tucked her under his arm and carried her into the kitchen.

At the stove, Mama glowed with pleasure. "Uncle Clark had to grow up and fall in love sometime," she teased. "But since Mary's let him escape this evening, I'll just throw in a few more hot dogs. Margie, set another place—"

Clark whirled Margie across the floor to the dish shelf. "Here you go, Mathilda."

"Margie," she said, as she grabbed for a plate.

"Whatever you say, Mathilda."

The screen door whacked open and Margie's brothers thundered toward the sink to splash themselves clean. Their father was just suddenly there, drying his hands on a towel.

"So, Clark," Mama began as she brought the bowl of potatoes to the table. "How're—things?" In answer, Clark blushed to the roots of his dark hair.

"You don't hurry up and pop the question," Mama said softly, "you're going to lose her."

"You think I don't worry about that every blessed day?" Clark asked. "But what can I do until Old Man Simpson makes my fore-man's position permanent? He was grumbling today that maybe he'd give the job to Jerry Millett—the bastard said it just loud enough so he knew I'd hear it."

"Language," Mama chided.

"Sorry, Sis. But I run around that mill like a crazy man! You know Simpson won't ever let us order any new parts, so we got everything jury-rigged, held together with spit and string. Someone's gonna get hurt!"

"You do have a choice, Clark. Dad's not getting any younger. He'd give his eyeteeth to have you help him run the farm."

Clark's shoulders slumped. "You know I'll always be there for him, and help with the planting and haying and all. But Mary wants to live in town. And that means serious money." He looked at Mama, his blue eyes hound-dog sad. "C'mon, Sis. You're right there in the office. You see Simpson every day. Can't you put in a good word—"

The clanging of the telephone cut him off. No one moved as one long ring was followed by a shorter one, then another long one. Theirs was the longest ring on the party line: Margie always felt she'd die of suspense.

"I'll get it!" Ted blurted.

"Let me!" Billy whined.

But Mama rose and walked to the wall and lifted the receiver. "Hello? Oh, hi, Gloria. That's okay, we're almost finished. Mm? Tomorrow would be perfect! Mr. Simpson's asked me to put in some overtime, so I'm sure Margie would love to come over."

Margie whooped. This summer was starting out super!

"What?" Mama was asking. "Oh, he wants to go over the tallies for the loads the log trucks brought in for the last month. Just some accounting. So I'll drop her off about nine? See you then."

The receiver clicked back into its holder. "Well," Mama said, "I hope Hazel McAllister is satisfied."

Daddy raised an eyebrow. "She listening in again?"

"Ayuh. I heard her pick up her phone. So she got an earful of Peggy Button wanting Margie to come over. Plenty of good gossip in the social life of a couple of eight-year-olds!"

Mama sat down at the table. "Anyway, Clark, that reminds me. Margie said she saw one of Mr. Simpson's log trucks today pulled off by the side of the road up by Back Pond—full up, just sitting there—and Randal Button crouched down behind his pickup. What did you call it, honey? Like he was playing hide-and-seek."

"Huh," Clark said.

Mama looked at him speculatively. "What do you suppose Randal was up to?"

"I don't know anything about it," Clark said, and dug his fork into his mashed potatoes so hard that the tines scraped against the plate.

□   □   □

The two girls had abandoned their Barbie dolls in the midst of a romantic Hawaiian vacation on the front steps of Peggy's porch, and now Peggy was pushing Margie in the tire swing that hung from the ancient maple tree. Peggy had got a little mean: she wound Margie up until the rope was twisted all the way to the branch, then let her go. Margie twirled, screaming, until her hands could barely grasp the warm, slick rubber.

"Girls, that's enough!" Peggy's father called from the driveway, where he'd been doing something mysterious under the hood of his pickup. "Go find something else to do."

Margie slithered out of the tire and stood, wobbly as a colt, just as a big black car slid into the driveway, long and sleek and gleaming.

The car's glossy sides were perfect: no rust marred its under-edges, no comfortable dents pocked its fenders. The insides had the lush glow of red leather. The car hummed throatily as the door cracked open and a man in thick, horn-rimmed glasses got out.

He was tall, bent forward as if his head had already begun to travel before his feet got the message. He wore a dark suit coat and a necktie—on a Saturday? Perhaps he was coming from a funeral.

"Button." The man's voice was low, like talking about someone in the hospital, but even so Margie and Peggy stood to attention.

Peggy's father seemed to wilt where he stood in his own drive-way, one hand on the tailgate of his battered pickup. He did not look at the other man. Margie heard the screen door swing open and pat shut as Peggy's mother came out onto the porch.

"Button, as of today your services are no longer needed," the man said. "I won't pay someone to steal from me." And with that, he turned and walked unhurriedly back to his car. The door thunked shut, and the car slid away, leaving a sort of shimmering hole in the air where it had sat under the spreading branches of the maple.

Peggy's father didn't move. He just stood there, clutching the tailgate of his truck. But Peggy's mother's eyes sparked with fury.

"That bastard! Letting you go? Just like that? That—"

"Gloria," Peggy's father said.

Peggy's mother glanced down at the girls as if seeing them for the first time. "Peggy, get in the house. Margie, is your mother ever coming to get you?"

"She—I—" Margie realized that Peggy had scooped up her own Barbie and disappeared.

And now another car came crunching over the gravel toward them. The man coming back? No—it was Mama's battered old Plymouth. Margie dashed to the car, wrenched open the door, and leapt in.

"Celeste! I hope you're satisfied!" Peggy's mother's screeched.

Mama stood up out of the car on the far side. "I didn't do anything." Mama's voice was careful. Prim.

"Oh, of course not!" Peggy's mother shot back. "You were in the office all day with Mr. Simpson, and now he comes all the way out here his very self to fire Randal! I suppose that's just a coincidence?"

"He wanted to look at the load tallies," Mama said. "I couldn't exactly refuse."

"And you arranged the tallies just right, didn't you, so he'd be sure to see—"

"Gloria, I didn't—"

"I thought we were friends!" And the screen door slammed.

All this time, Peggy's father had not moved. Now he let go of the truck and shuffled toward the house. Margie saw him pause to stare down at her Barbie doll still lying on the bottom step of the porch.

"Mama—" Margie began.

"Not now!" Mama rammed the car into reverse. She was breathing in short, angry huffs.

"But—"

"Not now!"

Margie kicked at the dashboard with one foot, then the other: bang-bang! Bang-bang!

"Margie, stop it. You'll scratch the paint."

As they approached the stop sign at the end of Peggy's road, Mama reached an arm across to steady Margie in the front seat. Margie flinched away. Stupid old car. Uncle Clark's new truck had seatbelts.

□ □ □

In the pew beside Mama, Margie wiggled her toes in her new sandals, while the minister rolled at last to the end of the sermon and started talking about the summer pageant.

"Remember that our theme this year," he said, "is Noah's Ark. We still need help with painting animal cutouts for the children to carry. And here's our big surprise: the Men's Fellowship has kindly offered to build the bow of an ark onto the front of the church!"

Margie gazed up at him, at his fingers grasping the edge of the pulpit like a row of uncooked sausages. She hoped she got to be a zebra.

After the service, she tagged after her mother to the sign-up table in the vestry. "I'm afraid I can't help much with painting the animals," Mama said, "so put me down for the dinner after the pageant."

"Oh, right," said Mrs. Ketcham. "You're busy during the week."

"What I hear," said Mrs. Laliberte, "she's mighty busy on Saturdays, too!"

"Randal Button out of work, just like that, and him with a family to feed." Old Mrs. McAllister hobbled toward them, her ankles sagging over the tops of her black shoes as if her legs were melting.

"And Jeff Hodges, too."

"And Matt Baker," added Mrs. Laliberte. "And Miriam's got a

baby due!"

"If Mr. Simpson's laying off," Mrs. Gordon asked, "where in God's name is anyone going to find work around here?"

"Hist!" Mrs. Ketcham cut her eyes toward the aisle of the church. "Here he comes!"

It was the tall man from the big black car in Peggy's driveway. His mouth was a straight slit, as if someone had cut it into his face with a pocketknife, but his eyes jumped from person to person, in constant motion. At his side was a sweet-faced lady in a flowered shirt-waist dress, her big black pocketbook hung over her arm.

"Good morning, Brenda," Mrs. Simpson said. She wore stockings and high-heeled shoes, even in the summer heat, and she smelled good, like lily-of-the-valley. "I'd be happy to help with the pageant in any way I can." Her voice was pleasant but strong. A teacher voice.

"That would be wonderful," Mrs. Ketcham said. "I'll put you on the list."

"And I can—" Mama began.

"I've already got you down," Mrs. Ketcham snapped. "Now, Millie, you'll help with the children? And Patsy—let me see—"

As if she'd been cut loose from her mooring, Mama drifted away from the table toward the open front door. Margie followed her. Outside, the Simpsons were climbing into the big black car, which was parked on the grass in the best spot, just beside the front walk.

□   □   □

Margie leaned against the kitchen counter, clutching her Magic 8-Ball. "Will Uncle Clark get married to Mary?" she intoned. At last the answer swam up from the murky depths: Maybe.

Big deal. It wasn't any fun unless Peggy was there, fighting to be first to see. Margie set the 8-Ball aside and turned back to the slices of Wonder bread she had laid out along the counter.

She dipped a knife into the Jiffy jar and slowly spread a glob of peanut butter on each slice, then added strawberry jam and another slice of the gleaming white bread. She transferred the sandwiches to four plates and the plates to the table, set out a coffee mug and a jar of pickles, put the kettle on to boil, and poured glasses of milk from the jar in the fridge. Done.

She wished it took longer to make lunch.

Ted and Billy barreled into the kitchen, released from stacking firewood, and grabbed for their PB-and-Js as if they might get away. Daddy came more slowly, squelching along in the high rubber boots he wore in the milking parlor.

On the stove, the kettle's whistle rose to a screech, and Daddy turned off the gas. But then he just stood, eyeing the jar of instant coffee on the counter as if he didn't know what it was for.

"What's wrong, Pop?" Ted asked. "We got a sick cow, or sumpin'?"

"Huh? Oh. I was just thinking about how much of yesterday's milk went to the pigs this morning. Bunch of folks never picked up their orders. The Milletts, Raylene Brown, the Pringles, Everett Pike. Everett's bought a gallon of milk every Monday and Thursday for the last ten years."

"Maybe he's on vacation," Billy offered.

Daddy shook his head. "You couldn't pay Everett to take a vacation. No, I guess they've just changed their minds about who to buy their milk from." He unscrewed the coffee jar lid now. But he didn't reach for the kettle.

"Your mother just won't see what's happening to this family," he said, and walked away, leaving the sandwiches still side-by-side on his plate.

□   □   □

It was Saturday. Laundry lay heaped on the floor, and Mama had just rolled the washing machine over to the kitchen sink when the telephone rang. Their ring.

"Oh, Clark! You did it!" Mama cried. "And what did she say?"

Margie dashed over and pressed her ear against the other side of the receiver in time to hear her uncle announce, "She said yes, of course. Who'd pass up a chance to marry me?"

"Oh, well," Mama chuckled. Then she froze as the tiniest click sounded in the receiver.

"We haven't set a wedding date yet," Uncle Clark rambled on, "but—I haven't had a chance to tell you about our plans—"

"Wait, Clark. Tell me this evening, at the pageant. Right now we've got company." The way she spat out the last word, Margie knew Mrs. McAllister was listening in.

But when she'd said goodbye, Mama didn't go back to the laundry. She just stood by the window, gazing out into the dooryard. Then she suddenly scooped up her pocketbook from the table and headed for the door. In an instant she had climbed into the car. The engine roared to life.

"Mama! I want to come too!" Margie dashed after her. "There's nothing to do here."

Mama's head drooped until it touched the steering wheel. She waited while Margie clambered in.

They drove out onto the main road and turned left, toward town. But as they came down the long hill and went right past the post office, past the store, past the gas station, Margie knew where they were going: down to the river. To the dowel mill.

They bumped across the empty, rutted yard and stopped in front of the small, green-painted building that held the office. For a long moment, Mama sat gripping the steering wheel. Then she climbed out of the car, unlocked the office door, and disappeared inside.

Margery waited.

Mountains of birch bolts loomed along the edges of the yard. Through the open side of the saw mill shed, Margie could see the big metal teeth of the saw.

Margie slipped out of the car and slunk toward the office. Inside, Mama sat at her desk, paper slips spread out in front of her as if she were playing a game of solitaire.

Margie ghosted over to stand at her mother's elbow. They were tallies from the log trucks, she knew, for the loads of bolts. Written up by woodsmen uncomfortable with the whole concept of writing, the paper slips were wrinkled, grubby with dirt and chain saw oil, the pencil strokes raw and uneven.

Mama's fingertips paced across the bottoms of the slips. Here, on some, the paper was cleaner, as if tidied with an eraser, and the pencil lines were smoother. Someone had used a pencil sharpened with a pencil sharpener, not a jackknife.

Mama stood up so suddenly that Margie leapt back out of her way. She strode across the tiny room to a file cabinet, yanked open a drawer, and pulled out a file folder. She laid the open folder next to the slips on the desk. Her eyes roved from the papers in the file to the tallies, back to the paper, back to the tallies.

A tear slid down her cheek. She wiped it away with the heel of her hand.

A crunch of gravel outside, the deep hum of a car motor. Mama whisked the paper slips into her desk drawer, then grabbed the file and dashed toward the cabinet.

The office door snapped open, and Mr. Simpson stood silhouetted in the doorway. Mama froze before the open drawer.

Mr. Simpson eyed the file in her hand. He cleared his throat in a thick, phlegmy harrumph. "Well, Celeste. Did you find what you were looking for?"

Margie could hear her own heart thudding in her ears as Mama looked at him, looked away. Automatically her hands replaced the file folder in its slot, pushed the drawer shut, smoothed the front of her skirt. She picked up her pocketbook and took Margie by the hand. "We were just leaving."

She marched Margie toward the door. Mr. Simpson stepped aside, but his glare followed them all the way to the car.

☐ ☐ ☐

"Well, hello there," Mrs. Simpson said brightly. "You're Celeste's little girl, aren't you?"

"Yes'm," Margie whispered. She watched Mrs. Simpson's creamy, tapered fingers as they smoothed another napkin and added it to the pile on a tray. Those hands never weeded a garden, she thought. Or even washed dishes. Why was Mrs. Simpson suddenly at the church, helping out? Folding the napkins was Margie's job.

Mrs. McAllister was at the sink, helping Mrs. Laliberte wrestle a pot of macaroni into a sieve, while Mrs. Ketcham chopped purple cabbages for the cole slaw. Mama stood at the counter, as alone as if she were in another room, splitting shortcake biscuits and laying them out on plates.

"That means Clark Laidlaw is your uncle." Mrs. Simpson gave Margie a quizzical look behind the double sheen of glasses. "I understand he's getting married?"

"Yes'm," Margie said again, and glared over at Mrs. McAllister. What else had the old bag told everybody?

Mama was finished with the biscuits. "Let's go now, honey," she said. She sounded tired. "I've got things to do before the program this evening."

Margie followed her mother up the stairs and into the church, where the animal cutouts were stacked in readiness on the back pews. Margie hadn't got to be a zebra. They'd lined the children up by height, and she'd got stuck in with the baby second graders. She was a pig.

She wandered out the open front door of the church onto the wide front steps, inside the framework of the ark. From the inside, the ark didn't look like much: scaffolding, with planks laid across for the men who were working high overhead nailing on the last of the burlap gunny sacks that served as the ark's siding. But from the outside it looked like the colored pictures in her Bible: the huge prow rising up, and the broad gangplank laid up to a big square door-way in the side. It was pretty neat.

Later today, the children would line up two by two on the lawn and march along after Alan Whittemore, dressed as Noah. The min-ister would read about the forty days and forty nights and the dove—one of the Kindergarteners—returning with the olive branch.

"Hey! Mathilda!" called a voice over her head.

She looked up, shading her eyes against the bright patch of sky above the dark sides of the ark. "Uncle Clark? How'd you get way up there?"

"Ladder, silly. You think me and Randal, here, can fly?"

The man beside him on the plank glanced down. It was Peggy's father. He looked at her sourly, then grasped the next burlap sack and dug in his nail apron.

"Oh, honey," Mama said, coming out onto the steps, "you shouldn't be out here while the men are working."

"I was just—"

A loud whack reverberated in the broad wooden step. With a shriek, Mama yanked Margie back through the doorway into the church.

"Sorry," yelled a voice from above. "Hammer got away from me."

The hammer lay inches from where Mama had been standing. It had hit so hard that it had cracked the step.

"You asshole!" shouted Uncle Clark. "You threw that hammer!" And the scaffolding rattled as Clark turned and swung a fist at the other man.

"Naw—it just slipped! Jeezum, Clark, cool down! Jeezum!" Mr. Button leapt for the ladder, which bounced and clattered against the planking as he scuttled downwards. He hit the ground and dove for the open doorway of the ark. In the next instant, his heavy work boots pounded down the gangplank.

The ladder rattled again, and here came Uncle Clark, his face purple with anger. But Mama was ready for him: as his feet hit the lawn, she grasped him by the back of his shirt and clung tight. Margie threw her arms around her uncle's waist, burying her face against his side.

Clark pulled against them. "Let me go, dammit!" But gradually the tension slid out of his body, and he slumped to sit on the church steps, his head in his hands. "He could have killed you, Celeste."

"I think Randal's aim is better than that," Mama said. "He meant to scare the daylights out of me. And he did."

Clark looked at her now, his eyes bleak. "You can't go on living in this town like this."

"Oh, yes, I can," Mama said. "Give them time, they'll find something else to talk about."

Clark shook his head. "I dunno."

"I didn't do anything, you know," Mama said. "Mr. Simpson already knew his trucks were short. All he had to do was call around to the other mills—the spool mill in Brownfield, that furniture place in Lovell—and ask who was bringing in birch bolts from around here. By the time he had me get out the tallies—"

"Still, you shouldn't have—" Clark's words trailed off. "Well, it's obvious I'll never be foreman. You being my sister and all, none of the guys will take orders from me."

Mama laid her hand on Margie's shoulder as if to steady herself. "When you called this morning, Clark, you said you had something to tell me."

Clark turned his face away, staring at the burlap, which stirred in the afternoon breeze. "I've enlisted," he said. "I report to Fort Leonard Wood next week."

"No! Clark—"

"Mary's coming with me. We'll get married down there."

"But— They'll send you to Viet Nam!"

"Uh huh," Clark agreed dully. "But when I get back, assuming I'm still in one piece, Mary and I can live the good life in New York or somewhere."

"But what about Dad?"

Clark sighed. "I'm wicked sorry about the farm. But I'm not like you." He pointed at the hammer, which still lay tipped into the crack it had made. "I can't live like this."

He stood up and planted a kiss on the top of Margie's head. "See you, Mathilda." Then he stepped through the opening in the hull of the ark and was gone.

Margie plopped down onto the step, hugging herself, while hot tears slid down her cheeks and into the corners of her mouth. Mama stood a moment staring down at the hammer. Then she plucked it off the step and paced across the patch of shadowy grass to the doorway of the ark as if she meant to go out and return the tool to its owner. "Clark!" she bellowed.

In answer, a truck door thunked shut. She stalked out, down the gangplank.

Now footsteps sounded on the staircase inside the church, a gabble of voices: the ladies had finished laying out the dinner. "Thank you so much for all your help with the napkins." Mrs. McAllister's voice was buttery.

"Oh, you're quite welcome," Mrs. Simpson said as they all came out onto the front steps. "But I've got to go. My husband'll be here any moment."

Mrs. Laliberte leaned down. "Margie! Sweetheart! Why are you crying?" Then she straightened up. "What on earth is that sound?"

Outside, there was a rhythmic, metallic sound, steady, unhurried: bang! and then bang! and then bang!

"Celeste! No!" It was Uncle Clark's voice.

Mrs. Ketcham scooted down the steps and across the lawn to the ark's doorway. "Oh, my God!" She gasped.

Mrs. McAllister shuffled after her, but Margie leapt up and dashed past her to peek out through the opening.

Out in the bright sunshine, Mama was working her way across the hood of Uncle Clark's new red truck— bang! and then bang! and then bang!—with Mr. Button's hammer.

"Celeste!" came Uncle Clark's anguished wail. The truck's engine roared as he tried to back away, but another car was just pulling up behind him. In desperation he jumped out and grabbed her by the arm. "What are you doing?"

Mama spun around to face him, her eyes blazing. "Did you think I wouldn't know? Did you think I wouldn't recognize your handwriting on those tallies? What kind of cut did they give you, Clark? You help those men with their thieving, and then leave me to take the blame!"

"Celeste—"

"Well, well. The truth comes out at last."

At the voice, both their heads snapped around to face the big black car with the red-leather seats which had pulled up behind Uncle Clark's truck, its engine grumbling. Mr. Simpson stood in the V of the open door, regarding Mama over the gleaming black roof.

"Lionel!" Mrs. Simpson tripped across the grass to the car, her open-toed shoes slapping. "Lionel, she's gone crazy! She's ruining that truck! Make her stop!"

Mr. Simpson's knife-slash of a mouth curved into a slim smile. "Oh, I don't think I'll stop her, dear. Celeste has just proved very useful."

With that, Mama wrenched out of Uncle Clark's grasp and swung the hammer—bang! and then bang! and then bang!—continuing across the side and down the bed of the pickup, while her brother stood watching her, ashen-faced. With a little shriek, Mrs.

Simpson slid into the black car and slammed the door.

And Mama hit the tailgate of the truck—bang! Then she turned and stepped over to the big, black car, and bang! and then bang! She swung Mr. Button's hammer against the shiny, black fender, and across the passenger door below Mrs. Simpson's pale, howling face at the window, and on down the length of the car—bang! and then bang! and then bang!—over and over and over.

Little Things

Steve Liskow

They were only on the third hole, but Brian's dad kept paying attention to Sam and her dumb daughter, Amy, instead of him. He only got to see Dad every other weekend, so he didn't want to share him with anyone.

Amy held her putter like she wanted to climb it. The green rubber grip stretched above her blue eyes when she addressed the ball, yellow like her pigtails. The tip of her tongue peeked out of the corner of her mouth and her eyes got skinny. She stepped back like she was going to run up to the ball to hit it, but she almost missed and it dribbled halfway up the hill then back down, almost to her feet. At least she didn't knock it into the geraniums so they had to go back and get another.

"Nice try, Amy," Dad said. Humidity spilled over the course like syrup and the bug zappers snarled blue sparks. Brian knew he had to hit the ball clear over the ditch or it would fall into the water and he'd have to add two strokes. He wouldn't break his record that way. He put his red ball on the mat and watched Amy hug Sam's denim legs. She sucked her thumb and wore all pink. Girl colors. Well, she was only six, two years younger than he was. Sam's fingers curled in the little girl's hair.

"Come, on, Brian, get a hole in one."

Brian aimed his putter at the third nail hole from the top of the ramp. If he hit it right, it would bounce off the wall, over the water, and down the chute toward the hole. Dad taught him to pay attention to little things like that. He kept his head still and eased the club back, shorter than Amy's so he could handle it better. Sure enough, it thumped off the wall, sailed over the water, and rolled down the chute. He held his breath when it slid past the hole and stopped only inches away.

"Outstanding," Dad said.

"Beautiful," Sam agreed. She smiled at him every chance she got, but her eyes looked afraid of him. Brian wasn't sure Amy could even talk.

"Can I go knock it in?" he asked.

"Don't bother," Dad said. "That's a gimme."

"What's that?" Amy could talk after all.

"It's so close that if you put the club in the hole, the ball's closer than the grip. I know Brian can make that putt, so I'm giving it to him. That's a gimme."

Brian scurried to pick up his ball and when he turned, Sam was lining up her shot. She tried to copy his, but hit too far to the right and barely made it over the water.

"I guess I'm going to have to take lessons from you, Brian." When she brushed her blond hair back, he saw two silver studs in her ear. She and Dad smiled at each other, then his shot rolled down the chute and bounced off the back wall. Brian held his breath while the ball trickled toward the hole, slow, slower, even slower, then fell in.

"Wow, Dad!" When he looked up after retrieving the ball, Dad and Sam were kissing. Amy's face looked like it made her stomach squish, too.

On the fifth hole, the one with the tunnel, Amy stubbed that long putter on the Astroturf and the ball rolled about two feet. Her lip got real big and Dad tried to muss up her hair like he did Brian's, but she shrank back against Sam's leg so fast she almost knocked her over.

"It's all right, honey," the lady said.

People clumped up behind them 'cause Amy was so slow. Brian wondered if she and Sam had ever played miniature golf before. He cleared his throat like Dad. "You want to try my club? It's shorter so it won't get in your way."

Amy took it and hit the ball through the tunnel on one swing. They heard it rattle around in the pipe, then plonk off the board at the other end.

"Good shot, Amy," Dad said.

Sam patted the little girl on her butter-blond head. "What do you say?"

"Thank you." Amy looked at Brian's feet while she handed the club back to him. His own shot bounced off the wall too hard and ended up in the corner where he had to stand with one foot on the green rug and the other on the sidewalk.

Amy took his club again and stood over her ball, her tiny pink hand gripping the rubber with her thumbs on top. No wonder she had trouble.

"Not that way," Brian said. He didn't think he said it mean, but Amy's face fell in on itself like water going down the bathtub drain. Sam pulled her close.

"He's not Daddy," she said softly. "He didn't mean anything, did you, Brian?"

"Uh-uh," he said. "I'm sorry." The bug zapper made them all jump.

Dad putted, then sat on the bench and watched Sam bend down to put her ball on the mat, blue like her big eyes. She wore jeans and a dark blue tank top that made her white arms look long as a base-ball bat. Mom always wore skirts and shoes with heels. Mom had dark hair, too. Sam swung her putter through the ball smoothly and it slid around the corner, stopping two steps from the hole.

"Beautiful." Dad stepped up behind Sam and put his arms

around her to help her aim her next shot. He was almost hugging her and Brian forced himself not to make barfing sounds.

Amy popped up next to him. "He doesn't hug Mommy hard."

"What do you mean?"

"He doesn't grab her so her arms turn blue like Daddy did when he was mad."

"Really?" Brian had to bounce his next shot off the corner, but he wasn't sure which way would work better.

"Uh-huh," Amy said. "She used to wear sunglasses after he got mad, too. Even in the house."

"Sunglasses?" Brian wasn't really listening, but he knew he should be polite. Amy was only a little kid; she didn't know she talked too much.

"Yeah, big ones. Elevators. Like your daddy's."

Dad's aviators hung from the front of his shirt. Lots of cops wore them, he said. So perps didn't see your eyes. A little thing, but little things added up.

"Is your mom a cop?" Brian asked.

"Uh-uh. My Daddy is, though. Was."

Brian's shot bounced the wrong way and put him behind the hill. Now he had to hit through the really skinny path to get close. If he was lucky, he could still get a four.

Sam sat close to Dad on a bench while he added up everyone's score for the first nine. Brian took Amy's long club back to the ticket place and changed it for a short one like his. He hoped she'd notice that he got her one with a pink grip that matched her clothes.

More people were coming in, whole bunches of kids his age, or teenagers out on a date on a summer Saturday evening. Old bald men in faded shorts above chicken legs and women with blue hair and screaming grandchildren, too little to be there. Brian reminded himself that he was with Dad, and nothing could spoil that, even having to share him.

When he got back, Dad was checking his cell phone for messages. He was off duty, but he had to make sure nothing was shaking. Things shook a lot, which was why Brian lived with Mom now except on every other weekend.

Amy sat in her mother's lap. "Does your phone take pitchers?" she asked.

"Nope," Dad said. "I can't play songs on it, either. Just your basic phone and text messaging."

Sam hugged Amy tighter, but she squirmed free and took the putter Brian offered her.

"Thank you, Brine."

"You're on a roll, Bri," Dad said. "You had a 37 on the first nine. If you can do that on the back, you'll have a 74."

Sam's ponytail blazed in the setting sun. "That's really good. I'll bet it would be a record, wouldn't it?"

Brian nodded. "Yeah, the best I've ever done before is 76. I could do two whole shots better. I'm gonna do it, too."

"I'll make a bet with you, Bri," Dad said. "If you break your record, we'll all have ice cream." The Cone-E Island Ice Cream Bar lay just across the parking lot, next to the driving range.

"Cool." Brian knew they'd have ice cream anyway because Dad was trying to make friends with Amy. He could tell that Dad and Sam liked each other by the way her hand slid into his while they waited for the group ahead of them. Amy was still a little scared of Dad, though. Well, this was the first time they'd met, and she didn't even come up to his pockets.

The windmill on the twelfth hole always gave Brian trouble. If you didn't time it right, one of the blades smacked your ball down the side chute instead of letting it go through the middle pipe. If that happened, you had to go around two more corners to reach the hole.

"What's that say?" Amy pointed to the big red letters next to the windmill. The mosquitoes were coming out now that the golf course people turned on the lights. The water hazards glowed greenish yellow and the windmill's blades twinkled with red. Little white lights blinked in the flowerbeds.

" 'Please do not touch windmill blades,' " Brian read.

"I can't read writing yet. I'm only going into second grade next fall."

"Oh, right." Brian watched Sam lean against Dad. If he thought real hard, he could remember when Dad and Mom looked at each other that way.

"My daddy read to me sometimes," Amy said. "He used to tickle me, too. Does your daddy do that?"

"I'm not ticklish," Brian told her. "Maybe it's only girls." He tried to remember if Mom was ticklish. Maybe he'd try tickling her when Dad took him back tomorrow night.

"I never told Mommy about it," Amy said. "Daddy said it was our little secret."

Brian's ball dodged past the windmill blades and disappeared through the tunnel.

"Good shot, Brian." Sam's butterscotch voice flowed over his shoulder. "Go ahead, Aims. Brian just showed you how to do it."

Amy got ready, but her feet pointed too far left so she'd miss the pipe even if the windmill blades didn't get in the way.

"Can I help you?" Brian asked. He laid his putter on the ground so it pointed at the tunnel. "Put your toes even with the club. Okay. Now when the windmill blade's in your way, hit the ball."

"When the blade's in the way?"

"Yeah. It'll move by the time the ball gets there."

Amy's ball disappeared down the pipe and her face glowed brighter than the lights in the geraniums.

"Wow, Aims. Great shot," Sam said.

"My daddy's phone took pitchers," Amy told Brian. "If your daddy's did too, we could get a pitcher of that shot."

Brian watched Sam's putt bounce down the chute on the left and Dad's go to the right. Amy followed her mother, so he went with Dad.

"It looks like you and Amy are hitting it off," Dad said.

"She's okay," Brian said. He didn't add, "for a girl," but they both knew it.

"You found her a putter with a pink grip, didn't you?"

Brian slapped a mosquito off the back of his neck. "You and Sam like each other, don't you?"

Dad watched the blond lady ruffle her even blonder daughter's hair. "Yeah. But we're still getting to know each other." Dad had tried to know other ladies since Mom left, but Sam was only the second one Brian had met. When the other lady looked at Brian, she sounded like she was trying to push a fat laugh through a skinny straw.

Brian's next putt rolled all around the hole twice, then disappeared. A two. If he kept this up, he'd break his record for sure. He could almost taste his chocolate cone. Amy clapped her little pink hands while he took his ball out of the cup. She stood right with her thumbs down this time, and her own putt stopped inches away from the hole.

"Is that a jimmy?" she asked. Her hips swung and her eyes looked at Dad the way Sam's did.

"Gimme," Brian said. "Sure." Dad cleared his throat and stared at the bug zapper.

The next hole had water, so they had to wait for the people ahead of them to fish their balls out with the big metal scoop. Dad sank to the bench and Sam's face lit up when he whispered in her ear.

"Did your mommy go away?" Amy asked.

"Uh, she left my dad, yeah."

"Is she in heaven?"

Brian's golf ball felt slippery and he almost dropped it into the flowers. "No, she's in Wethersfield."

"Where's that?"

"Maybe half an hour from here."

"She didn't eat her gun, I guess." Amy bounced her ball on the sidewalk, thock, thock, thock. "Like my daddy. I was at my gramma's that night."

Cold danced across Brian's shoulder blades. Amy didn't seem to understand what eating your gun meant, a little thing, like Daddy just went out to the car and he'll be back in a few minutes.

"Mommy went grocery shopping for dinner, and when she came back, she found him in the garage."

The people ahead of them finally moved to the next hole and Dad motioned to Brian to go ahead. His mind was on Amy now, and he scuffed his shot into the water.

"Darn."

Sam dumped her ball into the water, too. So did Dad. Amy's ball sailed over the moat and bounced into the good corner where she had an easy shot. Dad plucked all three balls out of the moat and they all hit again. Brian's ball slid up next to Amy's.

Up near the hole, Sam leaned back into Dad's chest. They were both smiling.

"Is he tickling Mommy?" Amy asked. "I guess not, she looks like she likes it."

Brian's next shot slid off to the right and into another corner. With the penalty for the water, he already had four and a tough shot left. The chocolate cone seemed to move farther away.

"They were trying to talk things out," Amy said. "That's why I was at Gramma's."

"Talk things out?"

"Mommy used his phone and they yelled at each other real loud."

Four teenagers were coming up the hole across from them, their voices like hammers. One of them was smoking a cigarette and the sharp smell pricked Brian's nose. When they got close, Amy shrank into her mom's leg again.

"Nobody's going to hurt you, Aims." Sam's blue eyes seemed to snap like the bug zappers. Dad stepped over near the boys and gave them The Cop Look. They quieted down and the kid with the cigarette ground it out and dropped it into the trash.

Brian's next putt rolled past the hole, but only stopped a few inches away.

"That's a gimme," Amy told him, and Sam's eyes softened again. A six, and only two holes to go. One of them was easy, but the last hole was really hard, with the ramp only about two golf balls wide. If you missed, you fell into a maze that would take at least two more shots to get through.

"Mommy wore her sunglasses for a day or two after Daddy went away," Amy said. "But she doesn't wear them in the house anymore."

Brian tried to fix his eyes on the spot a foot ahead of the tee, the place he wanted to roll the ball over to keep it on the right line. Dad taught him how to do that, one of those little things to pay attention to. But he missed the spot by a whisker and watched the ball roll off the edge and into the maze.

"It's okay, Brian," Dad said. "I think you can get a six here and still break your record." Brian thought he was just saying that to make him feel better.

Amy stuck her tongue out again when she lined up her shot, but her ball fell off the bridge and bounced off the wall to end up among jagged shark teeth, a really hard shot. Dad hit his shot straight over the bridge, but Sam's ball bounced next to Brian's.

"What's the best way through here, Brian?" she asked. Up close, she smelled like lemons and Cutter insect spray. Mom smelled like real perfume.

"Um, I think that way," he said. "Does Amy like chocolate?"

"Actually, she's more a strawberry kind of girl." Well, sure, she wore everything pink. "I'll bet you like chocolate, though, don't you."

"Yeah. It's my favorite."

"Well, make this shot so I know how to follow you, and I'll bet Don'll be getting us all cones when you break your record."

He'd forgotten Dad had any other name until Sam said it, but there it was. He was really "Donald." Mom was "Laura." Cone-E Island's lights shimmered across the parking lot. Brian lined up his shot and hit it between the teeth and out to the corner. A little harder and it would have bounced right next to the hole for another gimme. Sam clapped.

"Why don't you hit it in so I don't knock you into a bad spot again."

The 19th hole was a steep cone so most balls bounced away from the opening. Dad started adding up the scores while Amy and Sam missed, then showed the card to Brian, his thumb next to the bottom of the column. Seventy-three.

Brian didn't even feel his club swing through the ball. They watched it roll up the slope and disappear: a bell clanged and red, white, blue, and green lights flashed to tell everyone that Brian had won a free game.

After he got his pass and they turned in their putters, Dad and Sam held hands across the blacktop and Amy skipped next to her mother. Sure enough, she ordered a double-dip strawberry cone. Sam grabbed a bunch of napkins along with two plastic spoons so she and Dad could share a banana split. Brian felt chocolate coat his tongue and lapped fast so the ice cream didn't melt on his hand.

Just as they reached the table, Amy's ice cream tipped onto her top and splatted on the tile floor.

"Oops," Dad said. "Good thing we've got extra napkins." He

bent over Amy, but the little girl's face turned white.

"No!" she shrieked. Everyone else in line stopped talking. Dad turned red and stepped back.

"Let me," Sam said quietly. Tears big as dimes rolled down Amy's cheeks as Sam hugged her. Dad went back up to the counter for another cone and Brian felt like his hands and feet were too big. Sam gently cleaned the ice cream off Amy's pink T-shirt, the colors matching so closely you could hardly see the stain anyway, but it was probably cold.

"It's okay, Aims," Sam said. "Don didn't mean to scare you; he was just trying to help."

Amy bit her lip, but her tears slowed down and she hid her face in her mother's tank top. Sam's eyes searched the bright shirts around the cash register and found Dad turning from the counter with another strawberry cone. Brian found the free game pass in his pocket. He wanted Amy to have it, even if it was only a little thing.

When Sam spoke again, her voice was like melting ice cream, warm on the top but icy cold in the center.

"Daddy's dead, remember?"

Brian put his pass on the table. When Amy saw it, her arms loosened from around her mother's neck and pink slowly flowed back into her cheeks. Once Brian knew she was going to be all right, he bit off the tip of his cone so he could suck the ice cream through the bottom.

How could you forget that your daddy was dead?

Bob's Superette

Woody Hanstein

I sat in the back of the darkened plane and nursed my last beer. It was 2:00 A.M. Seattle time, and going by the map in back of the airline magazine we were probably somewhere over Michigan. Toward the front of the plane a couple of passengers still had their overhead lights on, but otherwise the only sign of life was the dull throb of the aircraft's engines. A redheaded stewardess with more than a passing resemblance to my first wife bent the rules and sold me four cans of Budweiser before they shut the galley up for the night, but those beers on top of the bourbon I'd drunk back at the airport bar only made me feel worse about going back home to Crenshaw to watch a handful of people bury a man like Harry Turner.

When I first left Maine for boot camp in Great Lakes I used to think about Crenshaw all the time. I imagine it'd be the same for any eighteen-year-old kid growing up in a town that small—at least that's what I told myself to fight off the homesickness that it took me a long time to shake. I left the navy after four years and spent the next twenty working Corps of Engineers dredging ships, first up and down the Mississippi and then out on Puget Sound. As those years went by I had other things on my plate, and eventually it got so I hardly thought about home at all. When I did, though, it was often about Harry Turner and how Bart Kendall terrorized me the summer I turned fourteen.

My days with the army corps ended a couple of years ago after a disagreement with the chief engineer on my last ship turned physical. I was still living in the northwest though, doing sheet metal work now at a Boeing plant outside of Tacoma. When I was back in Crenshaw five years ago and saw Harry Turner last, he looked frailer and older than I could believe, but it was still a shock when my sister's letter came and I learned that he was dead. She's not a big writer, so all that was inside the envelope was Harry's obituary cut from the county's weekly newspaper and, in the space above it, the words she'd written in red ink, Thought you should know.

For as long as I could remember, the obituaries in that paper always started with a short headline at the top that boiled down the person's life into just three or four words. It was usually something like She Loved Gardening or He Taught Math or the one about Mr. Knobloch, the disabled old man who lived next door to us—He Collected License Plates. From as soon as I first learned to read, those headlines fascinated me, and they made me wonder, as young as I was, just how my own life would look when it was over and someone had to pick three or four words to stick on top of it.

When Harry Turner's obituary spilled onto the kitchen table the day before, the headline above it said He Ran Bob's Superette for 30 Years. Next to the obituary was a black-and-white photo of a handsome, dark-haired young man in a military uniform. Harry Turner was quite a bit older than that when he first came to Crenshaw and reopened Bob's Superette, but in that photo there was no mistaking his narrow face and shy, down-turned eyes. His obituary said Harry was seventy-nine years old when he died and that he was injured fighting in Korea, and after that he managed a restaurant outside of Boston before he came up to Crenshaw and bought Bob's Superette.

As I finished off my last beer I looked out the window and studied the dark earth below us. The blackness was broken up only by tiny pockets of street lights marking widely scattered towns, all of them surely bigger than Crenshaw. Alone in the plane, my fond memories of Harry Turner and of my home town were crowded out by thoughts of Bart Kendall and how bad things might have been that summer he got out of prison.

□ □ □

I had nightmares about Bart Kendall even after he was finally convicted and old Judge Harlan sentenced him to serve ten years down in Thomaston. I was just eight years old at the time, and it was my mother's idea I attend Kendall's sentencing hearing. Like a lot of her other ones, it was well intentioned but not very well thought out.

My mother's boyfriend at the time was a guy named Steve who fixed skidders for a living and put hot sauce on everything he ate. He drove my mother and me to court for the sentencing hearing in the yellow Dodge Charger he waxed every Sunday and treated better than any of us. Steve skipped out on the actual courtroom part, claiming an important errand, so he wasn't there to see Judge Harlan call Bart Kendall the scum of the earth and tell him how if ten years wasn't the most he could give on an aggravated assault charge that he'd be glad to double that and make it twenty.

I sat through the whole thing trying to keep from wetting my pants and wishing I was anywhere else but there. Near the end of the old judge's lecture Bart Kendall turned around and looked at me and then smiled in a way that was scarier than any threat he could have possibly made. It was that smile, more than anything else, which infected my dreams for the next couple years.

Steve picked us up at the courthouse when the hearing was over. He was an hour late and smelled like whiskey. "Well, I guess that shuts the book on your legal career, Sport," he said. Steve lived with us for a year, and that whole time he never called me Arthur, not even once. With him it was always Sport or Chief or the one I hated most because the ocean was two hours away and it made no sense at all—Captain.

I didn't answer Steve's question, but if I never set foot in another courtroom again it would have suited me fine. A month before the sentencing hearing, I was subpoenaed to Kendall's trial where, before a jury made up mostly of white-haired old ladies, a pretty blond prosecutor had me tell how, the summer before, I saw Kendall and a smaller man I didn't know arguing as they fixed a flat tire on the old county road, which ran in front of our trailer up in Crenshaw.

It was the two men arguing that woke me on one of those stifling summer nights so close it makes falling asleep seem like an impossibility. Then, under a full moon, I watched Kendall rear back and kick the jack out from underneath the truck's front bumper. It said Chevy in white letters on the dark pickup's tailgate, which is what I still remember seeing as the truck came down with a bang on top of the little man who had crawled half-underneath it. Then the smaller one began to scream.

I didn't know at the time that the man's back was broken, but I ran to the front of the trailer where Steve was in the mud room pulling on his boots and my mother was already on the phone calling Barney Collins, the part-time deputy who lived down the road and couldn't be full-time because he only had one good eye. I stayed inside and watched Steve jack the truck off the little man, whose screaming turned quieter, more like a moan but just as disturbing.

Before Barney Collins got there, Steve came back inside and told me not to say it was Bart Kendall who kicked out the jack. Bart Kendall's not somebody to fuck with, Steve said, but everybody in town knew that. I had once seen him fire a load of birdshot at Ronnie Johnson's dog just for barking, and that spring he had done something bad to my friend Howie's sister, who was sixteen years old and the prettiest girl in town. Nobody ever said exactly what it was, but soon afterwards she moved down to North Carolina to live with her father, who Howie said she didn't even like.

After the ambulance took the little man away, a regular deputy with red hair and a tattoo of a kangaroo on his arm talked to all of us alone. When it was my turn, I told him exactly what I saw and how I knew it was Bart Kendall. I even let him come back to my room when he asked so he could see how bright the moon was on the roadway. I'd like to believe I told the deputy the truth to help out the man who'd been hurt or at least to pay Kendall back for whatever it was he did to Howie's sister, Gina, but really I told him what I saw because I was eight years old and Steve had told me not to.

The reaction in Crenshaw to Bart Kendall's conviction was more one of shock than of relief, because for as long as people could remember he had gotten away with almost anything. After he got sent to Thomaston, my friend Howie's uncle who was a game warden told me how proud he was of what I'd done. He told me how Kendall had once been charged for drunk driving that killed a local school teacher, but the case got dropped before trial after one witness disappeared and the second one's house burned to the ground. Howie's uncle said that Bart Kendall wasn't all that big or strong or smart but that he had no fear at all and was so violent he even scared some of the local deputies from wanting to go near him.

I was the toast of Crenshaw for a few days after Bart Kendall went to prison, but that wore off soon and my life got back to normal. Steve left my mom that next summer, which was an improvement for all of us, and I fished and rode my bike and did most other things boys do growing up in a town that small.

Some of those things centered around Bob's Superette, which was the only store in town. It was the place where Howie and I went to drink soda pop and look at comic books and buy ice cream sandwiches on hot summer days and watch hunters bring in deer to be tagged every November.

Bob's Superette meant a lot to almost everyone in Crenshaw. It was our grocery and our coffee shop and our sporting goods store, all rolled into one. It had a meat counter and homemade donuts that got fried fresh every morning and a supply of dairy products and canned goods. Bob's sold fishing lures and hunting licenses and flannel shirts and newspapers and motor oil and fan belts and, for the tourists that took Route 33 north to Thompson Lake and up into Canada, bug dope and camera film and souvenir T-shirts with corny slogans.

Bob's was decorated with a half-dozen different calendars hanging on the walls and usually a handful of people drinking twenty-five-cent coffee from Styrofoam cups and debating something from last night's selectmen's meeting or else complaining about why the roads don't get plowed like they used to. On the front counter by the register there was a big, brine-filled jar of pickled eggs sitting next to one filled with chunks of sausage and beside them a stack of weekly newspapers that contained little more than those obituaries that fascinated me and some week-old news and probate notices and ads for wood lots and pickup trucks that still ran good.

They put a lottery ticket machine in next to the pickled eggs the summer I turned ten, and, the year after that, a new cooler in the back that went up to the ceiling and was filled with nothing but beer. Otherwise, though, the only thing that changed in that store were the calendars. More days than not, my mother would send me down to Bob's on my bike for something. For a dozen eggs or a stick of butter, or if my sister or I did something special in school like win a spelling bee or make the wrestling team, for one of the homemade fruit pies two sisters baked up the road in Polk's Mills.

There was an actual Bob at the start, my mother told me, but he died long before I was born, so his daughter Gladys took over the store. She was short and pudgy with a face like an uncooked dinner roll, but she was nice as could be. She would trust you if you were a nickel short for candy and would let us read through the comics and sports magazines without buying them so long as our hands were clean and we didn't crease them up.

I was still in the sixth grade when Gladys started slipping. At first she began to give you quarters with your change instead of pennies and then she started looking for dog food in the dairy case, and then, near the very end before she closed the store for good and went into a nursing home over in Skowhegan, she would just blurt out, no matter what the temperature, My golly it's warm in here and then start undressing right there behind the counter.

I don't remember anyone using the word Alzheimer's back in 1977, but I could tell whatever she had was getting worse. It was still startling though when I got sent down to Bob's for baked beans one fall day and there was a sign taped to the front door that said Closed Until Further Notice.

The store was closed for a few months, and as you could probably imagine, it made living in Crenshaw seem a whole lot different. Then, one early winter afternoon when we rode the school bus back from Farmington, there was a panel truck with Mass plates backed up to the front door of Bob's Superette. A week after that, the store opened for business, and most everything was just as it had been except that it was Harry Turner there behind the counter instead of Gladys.

Winter settled in, but nobody in town learned very much about Harry Turner as those weeks went by. He lived alone above the store the same way Gladys had, but in those first few months nobody had ever even seen him outside of it. That the store was open again was the important thing and that the donuts were still crispy and that when January came a fresh batch of calendars replaced the old ones. Harry was always helpful and would smile politely at the jokes customers told, but he was a tight-lipped man who volunteered nothing about himself no matter how much people poked and prodded.

It was the very end of the summer I turned thirteen when Harry Turner offered me a job. The woman who worked weekends was no longer free on Sundays, and he asked me if I'd be interested in taking her place once the school year started. I was flattered to be asked but curious too. So curious, in fact, that I somehow found the nerve to ask him why he'd asked me instead of one of the other kids in town who spent as much time in Bob's Superette as I did. He looked at me for a long time through the thick lens of the black, military-issue eyeglasses he always wore. "I just think you'll take to it," was all he said, and then he went back to stamping prices on cans of corned beef hash.

I got my mother's approval that night when she got home from the shoe shop and began my first job the following weekend. I stocked shelves and weighed meat and checked out customers on the thirty-year-old cash register. I worked every Sunday that whole school year, and gradually I think I maybe got to know Harry Turner better than anyone else in Crenshaw. He lived all alone and even though he had other employees, because I was so young I think he maybe felt more comfortable talking to me. I found out his wife had died a few years earlier during what was supposed to be a routine heart operation and that she never could have children. One day he told me how he ended up buying Bob's Superette because he needed a change from the city after his wife had passed and because she had liked the store so much whenever they'd stopped on their way to visit her parents up in Canada.

Harry had a mild, peaceful manner, and even though we really never spoke much about anything important, I somehow felt more comfortable being with him than anyone else I had ever known. He taught me how to cut meat and to balance the store's books and to speak enough French so I could take care of the Canadian tourists when they came south in the fall to watch the leaves change. When the following summer arrived he increased my hours and raised my pay and I was fourteen years old and not sure how life could get any better.

Then Bart Kendall came back to Crenshaw. It was on a bright July day that I will never forget. I was mopping the floor behind the meat counter and Harry was ringing up a customer when the door slammed open so hard it knocked the warning bell off its bracket and sent it skidding across the brown linoleum floor. Kendall walked inside and strolled the store's few aisles until he saw me. He had on dirty jeans and a blue work shirt with the sleeves cut off so his new jailhouse biceps could be better admired in all their bulging, tattooed glory.

He obviously knew the question racing through my brain because all he said were the two words "good behavior." Then he shook his head and smiled like he had the last time we were in court. I froze where I was and could feel my heart pump.

"You'll be seeing me again," Kendall said before walking over to the pastry case and selecting a couple of donuts. He poured a cup of coffee and immediately drank down what looked like half of it even though it was kept near scalding hot. Then he headed out the door, shouting over his shoulder for Harry to put everything on his tab, which was a pointless thing to say because he didn't have one. Harry tried to call Kendall back inside, but he just walked over to a rusty pickup with a bad muffler that he started up and headed north on Route 33.

I tried to warn Harry about Bart Kendall, but he just shook his head and said, almost too quiet to hear, "Stealing is stealing." Then he called the sheriff's office to report what Kendall had done.

A half-hour later Arnie Schmidt showed up and did his best to convince Harry that going after Bart Kendall was a losing proposition. But Harry wouldn't back down. Arnie Schmidt said he'd write it up and send it to the D.A.'s office, but that a guy promising to run a tab wasn't the same as one who was stealing and that Harry shouldn't hold his breath waiting for charges to be brought. I found out later that Arnie Schmidt had been scared off a case by Kendall

once before after Kendall ruined the engines in nearly all the equipment Schmidt's father's used in his excavation business, but of
course neither Harry nor I knew any of that then.

For the next week we saw Bart Kendall every morning at nine
o'clock sharp. Despite Harry asking him to leave every time, he'd
get some food and guzzle his cup of steaming coffee and spill things
on purpose and then make sure to say something about his tab before
leaving in his broken-down old truck. Harry never looked particularly upset about the encounters, but he'd call the sheriff's office
after each one and leave a message for Arnie Schmidt, and then
Kendall would be back again the next day, just as punctual and dis-
ruptive as the day before.

Worse for me by far was that Kendall started coming by our
trailer. At first he would just drive by, real slow in his loud truck, and
from the first time he did I doubt I slept two hours straight. A few
days into it all, my sister found her four rabbits all dead in the hutch
she kept out back and the next day my bicycle disappeared and after
that it was our mailbox. All of those things had to be Bart Kendall's
doing, but it was no real surprise when Arnie Schmidt told my mother we needed more proof before the law could get involved.

Then I got hurt. It was the night our living room window got
shot out. I was on the couch watching the Red Sox and sitting right
in the path of the curtain of shattered glass. When the boom of the
gunshot died away and my ears resumed working, I heard the rough
sound of Kendall's truck about the same time I realized I was bleeding.

My mother took me down to the ER in Farmington where they
sewed up the cuts on my forehead and on both my arms and where
I met with a woman detective from the state police. After the hospital, we all spent the night down at my aunt Julia's house, because
none of us wanted to go home.

Early the next morning, against her wishes and those of my aunt, my mother drove me back up to Crenshaw so I wouldn't miss work. Harry was there before me like always, and when he saw me he turned off the burner under the donut fryer and took off his apron and asked me if it was Bart Kendall. When I told him yes he didn't say anything else. He just shook his head from side to side for a time, and then very softly told me I had a floor to mop.

Maybe what happened a little before nine o'clock would have caught my attention if I had been older. Harry had come in from the storage shed out back, and he made a new pot of coffee. Then he told me to count up the beer in the cooler even though he'd had me do it just before we closed the evening before. I was back by the cooler when the door slammed open, and I turned to see Bart Kendall come in and pour his coffee and chug half of it and then take his donuts and bump a magazine rack to the ground on his way out the door.

As soon as Kendall left, Harry took the brand new pot of coffee over to the sink where he poured it out. Then he washed the empty pot for what seemed like a long time. I was so glad Kendall was gone for the day I didn't give any of it much thought until Arnie Schmidt came by just before I got done at four. He looked like he'd just won something, and he asked Harry if he'd heard about Bart Kendall.

Harry said, "How do you mean? Are you finally going to do your job and charge him?"

"No," Arnie said. "He's dead."

"How?"

"Heart attack, looks like. Some woodcutters found him in his truck out past Varnell Pond."

"How about that," Harry said, and then he thanked Arnie for coming by.

I had been restocking the candy display when Arnie had walked in, and when he left I put my carton of Hershey bars on the counter and sat down on the floor. I'd seen in movies before when people said they were so happy they could cry, but I'd never understood it until that moment when it dawned on me that I wouldn't die that summer. Then I realized, despite my embarrassment, that tears were running down my cheeks and there was nothing I could do to stop them.

Harry walked over and reached down to pat me on the shoulder, but his expression was the same as always. "Why don't you run on home, Arthur," he said. "You've had a long day."

I took him up on his offer, but as I headed out the door suddenly things fell into place. I snuck out back and waited until a family with a van full of kids showed up and I knew Harry would have his hands full. I took the spare key from the nail hidden beside one of the storage shed's rafters and opened the little room. I didn't have to look long, because there in the trash can by the workbench was an empty yellow box of rat poison.

I locked the shed up tight and went home and slept the whole night through. In the morning, while Harry was banking, I checked the shed again, but the empty yellow box was gone. Whether they even did an autopsy on Bart Kendall's body was something I never knew, but he certainly wasn't missed.

I finished that summer with Harry and kept working at Bob's Superette all through high school even though I could have made twice the money banging nails with my mother's new boyfriend. During those years Harry and I never spoke a word about Bart Kendall or his sudden demise. Throughout all that time, as deep as our bond was, we never really got close in any way that people would notice. Harry did come to my high school graduation in a suit I didn't know he owned, and when I left to join the navy he gave me a wristwatch that I still wear to this day. Besides that though, he was mostly just my boss.

My plane will land in Boston soon where the sun will just be coming up. I'll rent a car and drive up to Crenshaw, but there's really nothing there for me now. My mother's living with my sister over in New Hampshire, and our old trailer was scrapped years ago. The last I heard, Howie was on an oil rig somewhere in the gulf coast, which leaves that old store as the only thing remaining that claims any piece of me.

I could get a better breakfast a hundred different places on the four-hour drive north, but I think I'll hold off and have a couple donuts at Bob's Superette. Too many years have gone by for them to taste like they did when Harry would pass me one fresh out of the fryer on a cold winter morning, but I still think that's what I'd like to have.

Verdict

Glenda Baker

Not guilty!" the foreman announced.

Tracy gave her lawyer a hug. "Thank you so much!"

"I knew you'd be acquitted of killing your husband," the Boston attorney said. "All I did was prove that a hypnotist can't make you do anything you don't want to do."

"Oh," Tracy said, "but I did want to."

Contributors' Notes

Glenda Baker is a lifelong New Englander living in Hudson, MA. She is the former owner/editor-in-chief of *New England Writers Network (NEWN) Magazine* and is a member of the International Women's Writing Guild and SINC NE. She is the author of *Because It Works* and *Summer Storm and Other Stories*. In 2007 her longer short story "Just Try Again" appeared in *Still Waters*.

Norma Burrows was born and raised in New England. She currently lives in the seacoast area of New Hampshire with her family. Her stories have appeared in previous Level Best Books anthologies *Seasmoke* and *Deadfall*. She is a member of Sisters in Crime.

John R. Clark is the entire staff at the Hartland, ME, Public Library. In addition to writing in the fantasy and mystery genres, he is a regular contributor to *Wolf Moon Journal* and the *Sebasticook Valley Weekly* newspaper. When not writing, he gardens and wins things. http://sennebec.livejournal.com/

Nancy Brewka Clark has published poetry, drama and fiction in numerous collections including *Beloved on the Earth* (Holy Cow! Press), *Visiting Frost: Poems Inspired by the Life and Work of Robert Frost* (University of Iowa Press), *Regrets Only: Contemporary Poets on the Theme of Regret* (Little Pear Press), *Glass Works* (Pudding House Press), and the Audition Arsenal series

(Smith and Kraus), as well as *The North American Review, Orchard Press Mysteries, Tattoo Highway,* and *Meeting House Magazine.*

Judith Copek is a retired IT nerd. When she isn't cooking up stories, poems, essays, and novels, she's in the kitchen trying new recipes, or in the garden tending to "ingredients." Her novel *The Shadow Warriors* is available in a trade paperback. A founding member of the New England Crime Bake, Judith also belongs to Sisters in Crime and Mystery Writers of America.

Frank Cook is the author of several nonfiction business books and is completing two novels. His story, "The Greatest Criminal Mind Ever," is his second published work of fiction, both appearing in Level Best Books anthologies. He is married to Pat Remick, an Al Blanchard award-winning author and 2010 president of Sisters in Crime New England. They live in Portsmouth, NH.

Kate Flora is the author of eleven books, including her Thea Kozak series, her Joe Burgess police procedural series, and an Edgar-nominated true crime, *Finding Amy.* She is writing a new true crime and revising a suspense novel. Flora's stories have appeared in the Level Best anthologies, in *Sisters on the Case,* an anthology edited by Sara Paretsky, and in *Per Se,* an anthology of fiction. She teaches writing for Grub Street in Boston.

Nancy Gardner has published short stories in the *New England Writers Network (NEWN) Magazine* and *Mouth Full of Bullets* e-zine. She is currently working on a mystery novel, a cozy set in today's Salem, MA, during Halloween season. Before turning to full-time mystery writing, she wrote articles for education and business journals.

Judith Green is a sixth-generation resident of a village in Maine's western mountains, with the fifth, seventh, and eighth generations living nearby, where she was director of adult education for her eleven-town school district. She has twenty-five high-interest, low-level books for adult new readers in print, and is currently working on a novel starring her Maine high-school English teacher and sleuth.

Woody Hanstein has been a trial lawyer for nearly thirty years. He also teaches at the University of Maine in Farmington and coaches that college's rugby team. He is the author of five published mysteries, all set in the foothills of western Maine.

Steve Liskow has appeared in two previous Level Best Books anthologies and has twice won Honorable Mention for the Al Blanchard award. He has acted, directed, or designed for over ninety plays in Connecticut, where he leads a playwriting workshop. He is currently working on a play, a PI series, and a mainstream novel.

Ruth M. McCarty is a partner and editor in Level Best Books. Her short mysteries have appeared in several anthologies. She has received honorable mentions in *Alfred Hitchcock Mystery Magazine* and *New England Writers Network* (*NEWN*) *Magazine* for her flash fiction and won the 2009 Derringer for Best Flash Story for "No Flowers for Stacey," published in *Deadfall*.

Alan McWhirter has been a criminal defense trial attorney and a volunteer soccer coach, referee, and administrator at local, state, and national levels for over thirty years. He is a member of the Connecticut Soccer Hall of Fame. Also an avid genealogist and model train enthusiast, he lives with his wife, Barbara, in Cheshire, CT.

Susan Oleksiw is the author of the Mellingham series featuring Chief of Police Joe Silva. The most recent title is *A Murderous Innocence*. The first in a new series featuring Indo-American photographer Anita Ray is *Under the Eye of Kali*, due in May 2010. She is the author of *A Reader's Guide to the Classic British Mystery* and co-editor of *The Oxford Companion to Crime and Mystery Writing*. Her short fiction has appeared in numerous publications including *AHMM*. She is a co-founder of Level Best Books.

Vincent H. O'Neil is the Malice Award-winning author of the Frank Cole murder mystery series, which includes *Murder in Exile, Reduced Circumstances*, and *Exile Trust*. Born and raised in Massachusetts, he has lived all over the world but currently resides in Cranston, RI.

Stephen D. Rogers has published over five hundred stories and poems in more than two hundred publications. His website, www.stephendrogers.com, includes a list of new and upcoming titles as well as other timely information.

Hank Phillippi Ryan, award-winning investigative reporter, is on the air at Boston's NBC affiliate, where she's broken big stories for the past twenty-two years. Her work has resulted in new laws, people sent to prison, homes removed from foreclosure, and millions of dollars in refunds and restitution. Along with her twenty-six EMMYs, Hank has won dozens of journalism honors. Her first mystery novels, *Prime Time* (winner of the Agatha Award) and *Face Time* (Book Sense Notable Book), were best sellers. *Air Time* and *Drive Time* follow in 2009 and 2010. Her website is http://www.hankphillippiryan.com.

Hollis Seamon is the author of *Body Work: Stories* and *Flesh: A Suzanne LaFleshe Mystery*, described by *Library Journal* as

"Powerful prose, a great story and an engaging mystery debut."
Seamon's stories have appeared in many literary journals, including
*Bellevue Literary Review, Greensboro Review, Fiction
International, Calyx,* and *Chicago Review.* She teaches at the
College of Saint Rose, Albany, NY.

J. E. Seymour lives in a small town in seacoast New Hampshire
and has had short stories published in two Level Best Books
anthologies, *Windchill* and *Deadfall,* in *Thriller UK* magazine, and
in numerous e-zines. http://home.earthlink.net/~j.e.seymour

Joseph Souza grew up near the Quincy quarries and worked in
Southie during Whitey Bulger's criminal reign. He has a degree in
criminology from Northeastern University and once worked in the
Organized Crime division of the DEA. In 2004 he was awarded the
Andre Dubus award in short fiction from USM. He lives in Portland,
ME, with his wife and two children.

Mike Wiecek lives outside Boston, at home with the kids. He has
traveled widely in Asia and worked many different jobs, mostly in
finance. His stories have won a Shamus and two Derringers; he was
a finalist for the PWA's Best First PI Novel. His novel *Exit Strategy*
was short-listed for the ITW Thriller Award. www.mwiecek.com.

Nancy Means Wright is the author of fourteen books, including
five mystery novels from St. Martin's Press and an historical novel,
Midnight Fires (Perseverance Press). She was an Agatha Award
winner and Agatha Finalist for her two kids' mysteries
(Hilliard/Harris). She has published short stories in *American
Literary Review,* Level Best Books anthologies, and *Ellery Queen
Mystery Magazine* (forthcoming). She lives in Cornwall, VT.

Quarry
Crime Stories by New England Writers

edited by
Kate Flora, Ruth McCarty
& Susan Oleksiw

Please send me _____ copies @ $15 per copy _____

postage & handling ($2 per book) _____

Total $_____

Please make your check payable to Level Best Books.

If you wish to pay by credit card, you may order through our
website at www.levelbestbooks.com.

Send book(s) to:

Name _____

Address _____

City/Town _____